Fire in the Foothills

PHYLLIS BOHONIS

3rd Season
Publications
www.3rdseason.ca

Fire in the Foothills
© 2013 Phyllis Bohonis

This is a work of fiction. Any resemblance to actual persons, events, locales or organizations is purely coincidental. All rights reserved.

No part of this book may be reproduced or transmitted in any form or by any means, electronic or mechanical, including photocopying, recording, electronic transmission, or by any storage and retrieval system, without written permission from the author.

Interior design by Crowe Creations
Text set in Times New Roman

Cover artwork and design © 2013 Anish Parmar

3rd Season Publications
ISBN: 978-0-9920616-0-9

CreateSpace
ISBN-13: 978-1490965406
ISBN-10: 1490965408

*To Ray, Mick, Sharon and Lynda
who never allowed me to waver on my journey.*

These Things Are Love

To know and understand the souls
Of lovers dancing in the night;
To touch a shoulder, brush a hand,
See dark eyes fill up with light;
To hear soft laughter when there's none;
To share a joke that's not been told;
To kiss warm lips without regret,
Never feel the winter's cold;
To open a heart whose hinges creak;
To smile at Death and laugh at Hell;
These things are Love, I understand
    — But I don't understand it well.

© 2007 Sherrill C. Wark
Mostly of Love & the Perils Thereof: The Sequel

1

"You've certainly caught Steve's eye." Liz leaned close so she could be heard above the bar noise.

"Steve? Steve who?" Tory turned to the woman next to her.

"The old guy at the bar, staring at you in the mirror."

"Old guy? Where? How old?"

"Probably isn't much older than us," said Liz. "Sixty maybe, but he has an ornery streak broad as his back. Never a pleasant word for anyone. Seems to hold his whiskey, though. Lord knows he drinks enough of it. But still manages to drive his pickup home. Matter of fact, his cattle ranch is just past your aunt's place. He only comes into town for supplies every week or so. And to wet his whistle. First time I've ever seen him show an interest in a woman. Maybe it's because you're new in town and he hasn't had a chance to cut you down to size yet."

"Well, it doesn't matter why he's staring, he'll probably never lay eyes on me again. I don't think I'll let it keep me awake tonight."

Tory's attempt at keeping her tone light might have satisfied Liz but the man's staring was making her more than a little uncomfortable. His gaze never moved from her even when she looked directly at him.

After a few more songs and another glass of beer, and pushing away one of the doctors from the hospital, who had come along with Liz and the gang, Tory decided she could leave without hurting anyone's feelings. Her aunt had suffered a debilitating stroke a few weeks earlier and Tory's companions were on staff at the Weston, Alberta, hospital.

Tory talked to her daughter and grandchildren back in Ontario a couple of times a week and had found herself missing friends and activities in Peterborough. So when Liz Coates, the head nurse, had suggested she join them for a Friday evening out, she had hesitated only briefly before accepting. However, a fan of Country and Western music she was not, and the conversations were either about the hospital, the price of beef, or how the hot, dry summer had affected the feed crops. Tory appreciated their honest attempts at friendliness—except for Dr. Needham, the one she and Liz had dubbed "Dr. Needy"—but it soon became apparent she had little in common with them.

Over the years, she had visited her Aunt Lottie a few times in Weston, but mostly the older woman had come east. After Tory's grandparents, Lottie's parents, died and the farm ceased to operate, Lottie, who had never married, sold off most of the property but had kept the house and the quarter section it was situated on. The old woman loved to garden and had managed to keep the farmhouse looking like something from the pages of a country *House and Gardens*. Tory knew she would feel guilty ordering a For Sale sign to be placed by the driveway.

While driving the ten miles from town to the farm after leaving the bar, thoughts of her aunt were running through her head. As her only niece, Tory had been given power of attorney and had immediately flown to Alberta from Ontario and moved into Lottie's farmhouse after the stroke. At 87, Lottie's chances for survival were about even. Tory had been prepared to wait a couple of months and if her aunt's condition hadn't improved, she would sell the property and have her aunt transferred to a hospital in Ontario.

The night was overcast and the only light was from her headlights.

The distance between her car and a vehicle behind was slowly closing. When there were no more than a few yards separating them and the driver started flashing his headlights, she felt the first twinges of apprehension. She was still several miles from her aunt's house and individual farms were spaced quite far apart. Her anxiety increased when the driver used his horn. The height of the headlights told her it was a four-wheel-drive of some kind. Hoping it was some young farm-hand who might have consumed too much beer, she moved over to give the truck a wide berth. However, the driver continued to lean on his horn even as he came alongside. When she glanced over, she saw the same piercing eyes that had been reflected in the mirror above the bar.

What should she do now? There were no houses in sight and by his hand motions he seemed determined she should stop. Tory didn't like this so decided to keep going, at least until she came to the next driveway. It seemed he had other ideas, however, because he sped up and passed her. A short distance ahead, he slowed, angled his truck across the road and came to a stop. She was more angry than frightened now, so after flinging her door open, she stormed toward him. Too late, she realized she was standing, vulnerable, in the middle of an unlit country road.

"What the hell do you think you're doing?" She might as well go down swinging.

"Didn't anyone ever teach you that yer safer stayin' in your car with the windows closed?"

"I have friends following along any minute now so I think you should just climb back into your truck and carry on about your own business."

"When your friends catch up to you, get 'em to change that back tire. It'll be flatter than a pancake before you reach home. Must be a slow leak." His mouth twisted into a sarcastic smirk. "Sorry I bothered you." He spun around and started back toward his truck.

Realizing she either had to face the embarrassment of being caught in a lie, or wait on this lonely road with a flat tire until another stranger came along, she opted for the stranger at hand. "I'm sorry. I didn't know what you wanted."

He turned, those cold gray eyes brushing over her in the beam of her headlights. The man she knew only as "Steve" nodded once, turned and proceeded to climb into the driver's seat of his truck.

"Wait!" It seemed he had taken her at her word that help really was on its way. "Will you help me?"

"Your friends all got broken arms?"

Angry for having been caught in this humiliating situation, she replied, "There are no friends coming."

He remained with one foot inside the truck and one foot on the running board for a very long moment, then climbed inside and closed the door. Her panic was short-lived. He straightened his vehicle and the backup lights blinked on. He maneuvered it behind hers so that his lights illuminated her whole vehicle. Then without another word, he climbed out, opened her door and popped the lid of her trunk. She watched helplessly while he found her jack and opened the cavity that housed the spare tire. More correctly, he found the cavity that *should* have housed the spare tire.

"You always drive around dark roads at night without making sure your vehicle has all its parts?"

"This isn't my vehicle. Or I would have known the spare was missing."

"By the looks of these tires, you should have four spares in here. There should be a law against old women driving when they don't look after their cars."

"You've got a lot of nerve. Who do you think you're calling an old woman? You... you... you old coot!"

He threw the jack into the trunk and closed it. She was staring at the flat tire and didn't notice the way he was watching her. He reached inside the car and pulled the keys from the ignition. After locking her car, he walked back to his truck. "Get in."

She stayed where she was.

"Suit yourself." He shut his door behind him, put his truck in gear and started to pull out around her.

Mouth open, she watched him drive away. A couple hundred feet down the road, his brake lights came on and then his backup lights once again. When the passenger door opened for her, she jumped in but rode in silence looking straight ahead. Without any direction from her, he turned into her aunt's driveway, drove around back and stopped by the kitchen door. He waited until she had entered the house and had turned the kitchen light on, then he drove away.

Tory quickly threw the latch across the door and made a mental note to get some sturdier deadbolt locks the next time she was poking around the hardware store. The bright blue and chrome clock on the wall above the table ticked loudly for several minutes before she whispered to the empty room, "He knows where I live."

The whole sequence of events had been rather strange: he had left the bar a short while before her, and yet he was behind her coming home. And wasn't it a coincidence that not only did she have a flat tire on a desolate stretch of road but that her spare tire was missing also?

While quite happy to be safely inside, she needed to talk to someone, to hear a familiar voice. It was too late to call her daughter so she dialed the number of the hospital to hear the reassuring voice of a nurse confirming that her aunt was resting comfortably. Feeling better, she watched the late news, and it was only after she was lying in bed, replaying the evening in her mind, that she suddenly sat straight up: *If the hospital calls in the middle of the night, I have no way of getting to Aunt Lottie.*

2

SHE SLEPT FITFULLY ALL NIGHT, finally falling into a sound sleep just before dawn. Fresh out of the shower after she woke around 10:00, Tory heard someone knocking on the back door.

"Sorry to wake you, Mrs. Hardisty. I'm returning your aunt's car."

A round-faced young man was standing on the back porch handing her the keys. Only then did she realize she had forgotten to retrieve them from that ornery old cowboy who had removed them from the ignition.

"How did you know they were mine?"

"All of us at the garage know Miss MacArthur's car, even if Mr. Turner hadn't told us where to deliver it."

"Deliver it?" She looked out into the driveway and sure enough there sat the Ford Escort proudly sporting a new tire.

"What do you do, patrol the roads at night looking for cars to tow?"

"No, ma'am. Mr. Turner told us where to find it and he was even waiting with the keys when we arrived."

"Mr. Turner?"

"Yes, ma'am. He phoned first thing this morning and told us to pick it up and get the tire changed fast. He said you would need it to get into town this morning."

Tory opened her mouth to reprimand him about fixing a car without permission but thought better of it. "How much do I owe you for this and can I write you a check?"

"That's OK, Mrs. Hardisty. Mike, my boss, said for you just to come in to the shop when it's convenient and settle up."

Thinking that her aunt had probably taught most of the residents in this small town, Tory realized they would recognize the vehicle and provide Tory the same friendly courtesy that her aunt would have received. She thanked the young fellow, gave him a generous tip and wondered too late whether she should have offered him coffee. He had probably noticed the chocolate cake she had baked. The one thing that didn't sit right with her was the nerve of that Steve person taking it upon himself to get her car fixed without so much as a would-you-like. The nerve. Granted, she appreciated that the car was repaired and ready before she even needed it, but it took a lot of gall to order service done on a vehicle that didn't belong to you. It really steamed her that she would have to say thank you to a man who had scared her half to death the night before and then had been so rude. Goosebumps rose on her arms just thinking about him.

After downing a breakfast of cold cereal, she carried her coffee and the *Calgary Herald* outside to the deck. What a beautiful fall morning it was.

Her thoughts strayed to what disastrous results might have occurred through her foolishness in stopping on a deserted road in the dead of night when forced off the road by a complete stranger. She might not have been here to enjoy this fresh clean scent coming off an autumn breeze. The goosebumps returned when she pictured the old cowboy glaring at her in the bar mirror. Shaking it off, she concentrated on her coffee and on the view of the purple-hued mountains in the distance.

After finishing her second cup, she decided to head into town to pay for the tire. She would also see about those deadbolt locks at the hardware store. She hoped that today, the staff at the hospital would have goods news concerning her aunt.

The little town of Weston was nestled in the foothills of the Rockies. With the mountains always in the background, the scenery was a kaleidoscope of constantly changing colors and angles as the sun crept across the sky. When she arrived at the garage, it was just as she had thought. Her aunt had been Mike Anderson's teacher in grammar school some forty-two years before. Now he was the proud owner of Mike's Auto.

"You didn't have to rush in to pay. Miss MacArthur's been getting her car fixed at this garage for as long as I've owned it. I had no doubt you'd come and pay next time you were in town, just like your aunt."

"Thank you, Mike. Can you tell me why Aunt Lottie's spare tire was missing?"

He scratched his head and appeared surprised to hear this. "As far as my memory serves, she's never had a flat tire and never needed to use it. I'll replace it for you, but I'll have to order it from Calgary. I don't keep those donut-sized ones in stock. In the meantime, I'd advise you to replace the other back tire soon, as well. It's getting pretty smooth and the tires should match anyway."

After answering his questions about the state of her aunt's health, she left for the hardware store.

Tory was happy to find the locks she wanted for the front and back doors—she didn't want to go another night without them. She also purchased an electric drill to install them. Shopping done, she headed to the hospital where she was disappointed to learn there had been no improvement in her aunt's condition since she had asked the previous evening. Every day she hoped to hear that Lottie had blinked, smiled, or squeezed the doctor's finger. She knew she was prolonging the agony of settling her aunt's affairs and arranging to have the elderly woman transferred to her own home town. For some reason, she wasn't ready yet to throw in the towel, thought she owed it to her mother, as well as to her aunt, to give her just a little more time.

After washing the lined, kind, old face, and the gnarled fingers and running a brush through the fine white hair, she decided to go to the cafeteria for soup. There, she ran into Liz and told her about the events of the previous evening and how Steve Turner had taken it upon himself to have her aunt's car towed into town for a new tire.

Laughing, Liz said, "That sounds exactly like something Steve would do. He thinks we're all as useless as lace on a bowling ball and he lets every one of us know any chance he gets."

"Really."

"Rumor has it his wife left him years ago. Took their son with her. Everyone figures that's why he's such a cranky, bitter man. We all stay well clear of him. He seems to make a living off his ranch and never leaves it for any length of time."

Back in her aunt's room, she settled in to read aloud. It was a romantic book set in the days of the French Huguenots in Quebec. Her eyes were moist when she put the book down an hour or so later and kissed Lottie's cheek. "I hope you're enjoying the story, Auntie." She had brought a radio from home and now turned the volume up slightly, anticipating that her aunt could hear the music and keep abreast of the news.

Tory stretched and rolled her shoulders to loosen them then adjusted the Venetian blinds to block some of the late afternoon sun from shining into her aunt's eyes. She would leave earlier today to allow herself time to install the door locks before nightfall.

Deadbolts on both doors now, she felt comfortable enough to prepare a supper of ham slices, salad and biscuits, and to watch the evening news.

Before she knew it, she woke with a start near the end of the first quarter of the Stampeders' football game. *Must have needed the sleep,* she thought while closing the window blinds.

Headlights? When she leaned closer to the glass, it was too dark to ascertain the make or color of the vehicle, but it was a truck which moved forward slowly then continued up the road out of sight. *Glad I got those bolts on the door.* Quickly pulling all the blinds down, she wondered whether someone had been watching her sleep in the chair. *Don't do that to yourself! It was probably someone leaving flyers in the newspaper box.*

For the next four days there were no further unsettling incidents so she soon set those once-rattling events aside. The beautiful weather continued—a real Indian summer. Tory utilized the enjoyable weather by cleaning her aunt's outside windows, ordered a load of wood for the living room's large fireplace and was just then trying to figure out where to stack it when something made the back of her neck prickle. She looked up to see Steve Turner leaning against the railing of the deck, watching her.

"What the—?"

"Why didn't you have the guy you bought it from stack it for you?"

"He gave me a price for cut and delivered. He never offered to stack it."

"Just like a woman not to ask."

"I'm not crippled. I can stack it myself."

"Suppose you didn't think about who was going to split it for you either."

"I'm sure I can do that too."

"Suit yourself."

Halfway to his truck, he stopped. "You ever chopped wood before?"

"How hard can it be?"

"You're a city woman, ain't ya?"

"I don't think that's any of your business."

"Don't suppose you ever used an axe?"

"Well... Not exactly."

"Sounds like a no to me."

Slinging a "stubborn useless women" comment over his shoulder, he went into the shed and returned with a wheelbarrow. Mumbling too low for her to hear, he started throwing the pieces of wood into it. Mouth open and thinking up all kinds of smart aleck retorts, Tory watched him. Before any smart retorts got beyond her lips, however, he had already filled the barrow. After wheeling it to a platform near the far end of the deck, he started piling the short logs into neat rows.

"I don't need anyone hanging over me while I work, you know. Haven't you got some women's stuff to do in the house?"

Flabbergasted, Tory turned several shades before spinning on her heel and storming into the house muttering under her breath. "Who the hell does he think he is? He just takes it upon himself to butt into my affairs. Who asked him to have Aunt Lottie's car towed into town? And who in hell asked him to come and stack my logs? Who? Why that skinny little runt has some nerve!"

At the table, she forced herself to breathe deeply in an attempt to calm down. *How am I supposed to go to the hospital this morning? I'm not about to just drive away and leave him here stacking wood. Although it would serve him right.* Her work gloves came off with angry tugs then she slapped them onto a shelf in the closet. Boots and jacket were thrown on the floor. She poured herself a glass of water and glared out the window.

Watching him, she realized he was not as skinny as he had first appeared. Sinewy would more aptly describe him. When he removed his cowboy hat to wipe his forehead with the sleeve of his plaid, flannel shirt, his white, poker-straight hair framed a weathered, permanently tanned face. *Probably from working outdoors daily, year after year.* She watched as steel-gray eyes that had a determined, almost mean, look to them, surveyed the woodpile. She knew she was right to be afraid of him. He was not a man with a happy disposition. She would be very glad to see the back of him... after the wood was split and stacked.

When he looked toward the window, she quickly pretended to be adjusting the curtains—he had said he didn't like to be watched over. He shook his head then filled the wheelbarrow again.

She busied herself with upstairs chores and on her return to the kitchen, she heard the back door closing. *What the hell? What's he been doing in the house?* Determined to find out, she opened the door just in time to hear his truck start. Before she had gotten around the corner of the house, he was already turning at the foot of the driveway. With a glance in her direction, he took off up the road toward his ranch.

Tory didn't like the idea of his coming inside uninvited but when she saw the water glass on the counter, she decided to give him the benefit of the doubt regardless of the insistent goosebumps—and besides, all the wood had been neatly stacked on a raised platform. Her goosebumps turned to red-faced embarrassment when, dressed and ready to leave for the hospital, she saw the neatly stacked kindling and an armful of logs on the hearth by the fireplace. *What a strange man.*

Over the next ten days her aunt's condition remained unchanged and after talking it over with her daughter and son-in-law, Tory knew, however difficult it would be for both her and her aunt, it was time.

The weather turned cold almost overnight so with thoughts of possible early snow, she would get her aunt's house cleared out quickly. Much to her distaste, the attic had to be tackled; she didn't even want to think about all that old junk down in the basement but that task was necessary, too. Family heirlooms would have to be shipped east.

Sunday night, Tory fell asleep quickly under the homemade quilt but at 2:30 AM, the ringing of the phone startled her awake. As she feared, it was the hospital and the news was not good. Aunt Lottie had suffered another stroke and Tory was advised to come right away. She dressed quickly and went down to the car and almost burst into tears when she saw it sitting at an angle, the tire on the driver's side flat. She attempted a laugh as she said aloud, "but only on the bottom."

She called the hospital to advise them of her situation and was assured by a nurse that someone would be there shortly.

Tory's elation at seeing a truck turn into her driveway within fifteen minutes quickly turned to dismay when she saw whose truck was inching its way toward the house. Who would have called him to her house? She went out the front door, thinking she would have to bite her tongue if she wanted to see her aunt this night.

"Don't listen too well, do you, girl? Coulda swore I told you to get a new tire on that wheel."

Bite your tongue, Tory. You need his help right now.

"Get in. No sense hanging around only to find out again there ain't no spare—or if there is, that it's flat too."

Bite your tongue, Tory. She got in.

"Damn women. Never listen. Useless. Shouldn't be allowed to drive."

Bite your tongue... oh, hell. "Either you shut up, or stop the truck and let me out right here."

The tires skidded on the gravel as the truck came to a stop. "The way I see it, you got few choices, missus. You can either ride in with me, you can walk, or you can wait for the next bus coming by."

Near tears, Tory looked him square in the eye. "Tomorrow you can call me whatever stupid names you want, but tonight my only concern is my aunt. I don't know if she'll still be alive when I get to the hospital, so I'm in no mood for listening to a scrawny old cowboy take out his goddamn woman anger on me right now. So put a lid on it and just drive!"

"Lucky for you you're related to Miss Lottie, else I'd let you out right here." His mouth hardened into a straight line once again and Tory turned to stare stonily out her window.

He dropped her off at the front door of the hospital and she ran inside without a word. When she reached her aunt's room, the bed was empty and her stomach tightened. Back at the nurses' station, staff told her they'd taken Miss MacArthur to the intensive care unit. The "unit" proved to be nothing more than a room across from the nurses' station at the emergency entrance. Still alive, she was attached to monitors and a nurse and doctor were with her, but the prognosis was not good.

"If she wasn't such a healthy woman," said the attending doctor, "she wouldn't have made it this far." The doctor placed a hand on Tory's shoulder. "We'll have to take it hour by hour, but I have to be honest, I'm not optimistic about her making it till morning."

Tory sank into a chair beside the bed and took her aunt's hand, stroked it, held it to her cheek, prayed that Lottie would either pull out of it with some quality of life remaining, or be released to share the happiness that surely must be awaiting her in heaven. Not knowing how long she had been sitting weeping and holding that frail hand before a nurse came in to check her vitals, Tory wiped her aunt's hand, wet from her tears, with the sheet. Waiting in the hall, she knew she'd never felt so alone before, or so helpless. There was no one to offer a shoulder or a kind word.

"She gonna make it?"

"What?"

It was Steve Turner, approaching from the waiting area. "Miss Lottie. Is she gonna make it?"

"I don't think so." She turned to watch the ministrations of the nursing staff inside the room. Her aunt looked so small, so frail. "You were right. I am a totally useless woman. Here I am, healthy as a horse and there's absolutely nothing I can do for her. She doesn't deserve to die like this. She should have gone out with dignity, not shriveling up and withering away, day-by-god-awful-day."

The tears came and there was no way she could stop them. This poor woman was putting up a valiant struggle, and for what? To be moved to another hospital, far away from her beloved mountains? A red and blue handkerchief was placed in her hand. As she took it, she turned into the shoulder of the man next to her and sobbed loudly. She could feel a hand patting her on her back like a baby being burped. She heard the nurse say she could go back in again, but she continued to look at her aunt through the glass. The man beside her continued to alternately pat then rub her back. Finally he asked if she wanted some coffee. When she nodded, he left and returned a few minutes later with two foam cups containing a hot brown liquid that vaguely resembled coffee.

Steve stayed with her, not really offering anything in the way of conversation, until dawn arrived with a promise of snow. He offered to see about getting her tire fixed and having her car delivered to the hospital. She thanked him with the enthusiasm of someone who has been up all night sitting with a dying relative.

Later, the same young fellow who had delivered her car the first time came quietly down the hall. She saw him give the car keys to the nurse at the desk. She stood, thanked him, tried to give him a tip but he refused.

"Wouldn't be right, ma'am. I hope Miss MacArthur's gonna be OK. You look like you need to get some rest yourself, ma'am." He hurried down the hall toward the front entrance.

She followed his suggestion and fell asleep quite readily on a cot down the hall.

Several hours later, feeling somewhat refreshed, she returned to the emergency area where Steve Turner stood leaning against the glass of Lottie's room looking intently into the room. He turned when she got close to him, his eyes more blue than gray, and somehow, in the hospital light, not so menacing.

"The boy returned my car, thank you."

"How's Miss Lottie? Any change?"

"No. She's in a coma. They don't expect her to come out of it."

"Can't they do something?"

"It's a waiting game now."

"You have breakfast?"

"Not hungry."

"Then I'll go. Got animals to look after. This snowfall could get pretty heavy before it's over." He started to walk away.

"Mr. Turner?"

He stopped and turned.

"Thank you. For everything."

His eyes met hers. The blue faded to gray once again and she could almost hear the invisible shield slam shut.

He nodded and left.

3

AS THE SNOW CONTINUED TO fall, Lottie MacArthur remained what the medical staff referred to as "stable." By late afternoon, Dr. Humphrey suggested to Tory that she go home before it got too dark and too stormy to drive. "There's nothing more you can do here and if anything changes, we'll call you."

"There's nothing for me to do at home either except wait for the phone to ring."

"Go home. Get some rest," Dr. Humphrey insisted. "Doctor's orders."

Tory capitulated and went in search of her car in the parking lot only to find it covered with eight inches of snow. With her coat sleeve, she brushed the snow away from around the door and slid the key in the ignition. It started. "Good little car." Tory whispered as she patted the dash and turned the defrost on full.

She knelt on the seat to look for a snowbrush in the back seat and found... nothing. She popped the trunk and searched there in vain, as well, so with gloveless hands and jacket sleeves, she got to work. By the time she finished the passenger side, the driver's side was covered again. *This will take forever,* she decided, and pulled out of the parking lot hoping the the remaining snow would fly off as she drove. Both front and rear defrosters kept the windshield and back window clear enough, but she had to lower the side windows at every intersection. The roads were slick and she risked sliding to a stop and not being able to get traction to move again—she offered thanks that she now had two new tires on the rear to help keep her from sliding off the road. Once outside of town and on the winding, hilly side-road to her aunt's place, she knew she would have to keep moving. She kept to the center of the road, almost plowing through the axle-deep snow, all the while hoping she would not meet another vehicle. But three miles from her driveway, as she came out of a long curve, she met a truck and had just enough time to turn her wheel to avoid a head-on collision. She over-thought the skid and ended up in snow deep enough to block movement of her door. She shouldered it, but it didn't want to cooperate. Then at her window were two steely gray eyes shooting bullets.

"Of all the stupid, idiotic... goddamn it... Women! Who knows what they're thinking? Don't know enough to stay off the road. Shouldn't be allowed to drive!" After wrenching her door open, a hand reached in to pull her into the almost-knee-deep snow. He slammed her door shut and dragged her to his truck.

"Get in!"

Normally a more-than-competent driver, Tory was beyond embarrassed by now. All this business of attempting to get back and forth to town in her aunt's car was making her look like a menace on wheels. *Correction, a "stupid, idiotic" menace on wheels.*

Not another word was said as he found a place to turn around and with the help of his four-wheel drive, made it to her place without incident. She got out without thanking him and made her way to the house. In her anger, she didn't notice that the driveway had been plowed but when she let herself in through the kitchen door, she was surprised to find the house warm and cozy. *I didn't turn the thermostat back up when I was called out last night! What's going on?* In the living room, her amazement was complete, but the sight of the fireplace going made her uncomfortable again. Who had access to her aunt's house? And who was coming in and out when she was not around? Maybe someone was still inside. That thought made her stomach knot. But then she heard footsteps on the deck, a rap on the kitchen door, a knob turning and Steve Turner had let himself in.

"Was it you who came into my house while I wasn't here? And if so, how did you get in here?"

"I have a key."

"You have a what?

"A key."

"Who gave you the right to come waltzing into this house uninvited?"

He looked at her with ice cold fury for several very long seconds, then turned and walked out without a word. For a fraction of a moment she thought she detected something else. What was it? Hurt? *Oh, no. Now I've made an enemy of this frightening, strange man who has a key to the house. Well, his key wouldn't work against dead bolts.* She moved quickly to the kitchen to slide the bolt in place. *Wait. This will only work when I'm here. The bolts wouldn't keep him out when I'm not.*

The living room door was secure and only after she had gone through the rest of the house, checking every room, did she feel completely certain that she was alone.

With the kettle on and a pot of strong tea in her future, she relaxed somewhat but knew her chills were not due to the storm. The weather forecaster on the radio informed her that the snow would continue until at least noon the next day. "Well, Aunt Lottie, hang in there. Hopefully I'll be able to get my car out before you need me again. There's no way I want to be in the company of your very strange neighbor again."

Remembering how he had behaved at the hospital, she wondered how he could act almost normal one minute and completely deranged the next.

How did he know I needed a ride to the hospital anyway? Would someone there have called him? Maybe someone knew he was probably the closest neighbor and didn't realize how weird he is. And why, oh why in the world, would he have a key to this house?

She forced herself to stop worrying and instead concentrate on the ramifications of her aunt's possible turn for the even worse. Tory herself must remain in her own limbo of wait-and-see for the present. She would call her daughter and update her on Aunt Lottie's current condition and subsequent change of plans...

There was no dial tone.

Clicking the receiver made no improvement. This was unfortunate, the hospital wouldn't be able to reach her. What could she do? She had no vehicle and no phone. No means of communication. She was even unable to call the garage to come dig her car out. And sure as hell, Mr. Personality wouldn't be helping her again anytime soon thanks to her own rudeness toward him. She had no choice but to wait for the plows and the telephone crews to show up on their own. For the first time since her arrival at her aunt's, she wished she owned a cell phone.

She would microwave one of the homemade TV dinners in the freezer and hope that the Monday night football game would take her mind off everything, including the wind that seemed to be picking up outside. Dr. Humphrey had been right to make her go home when he did. She stoked the fire and when she reached for another log, she noticed that the supply of firewood had been replenished and more kindling had been cut.

Had her unpleasant neighbor possibly wandered in and out of this house while her aunt was living here? Was that why he had a key? He must have helped Aunt Lottie with some of the chores. Was that why he had made sure she had enough firewood to last through the storm? Had he been the only person to look after her aunt when she had no family close by? Had her aunt been frightened by him, too? Enough that she let him come and go rather than cross him? Then she remembered that three times he had come to her assistance when the car had let her down. *OK then, if he isn't a bad guy, why is he so overbearing and mean?*

At that moment the lights brightened momentarily—then went out. *So much for watching football to take my mind off things. At least there's enough light from the fire to find the candles.* She set them on end tables but didn't light them, deciding instead that if she couldn't do anything else, she might as well try to sleep. She grabbed the afghan from the back of the sofa and stretched out.

She awoke to the sound of snow crystals hitting the windows. It was dark but Tory confirmed by her watch that it was morning. The storm clouds were heavy with unfallen snow and made it seem earlier than it actually was. She placed wood inside the cook stove in the kitchen and put a kettle of water on to boil for tea. It wouldn't be her morning coffee, but it would have to do. The battery radio on top of the fridge offered nothing but static. Cold cereal, half a banana and a little cream—there was only about a quarter of a cup left so she would have to ration it—would be her breakfast. The toilet was going to be another problem but one that melted snow would solve. She had nothing to do but read once it was light enough.

Around mid-morning she caught a sound above the wind. Moving to the front window and hearing nothing more, she attributed it to an overly stimulated imagination. *No, there it is again. It's a motor. The plows must be out.* But several minutes passed and she saw nothing. *Ah,* she realized. *It's coming from out back. What the hell?*

Then footsteps on the back deck, a pounding on her back door and a snowmobile beside the deck. She quickly unlocked the door, curious to see who had arrived and why. Her first thoughts were of the police with news of her aunt. The person removed hood and goggles to reveal Steve Turner.

"What are you doing here?"

"I know I'm not welcome here, but I wanted to make sure you were OK, what with the power being out and all."

She was dumbfounded. "You came out in this just to make sure I'm OK? You could have gotten stuck somewhere and nobody would even have known. And you have the gall to say that women are brainless? Are you an idiot too? And must you insist on thinking I'm completely helpless? How stupid can one *man* be?"

"Well that, too. But mostly to let you know I got patched through to the hospital on my wireless radio. There's no change in Miss Lottie's condition. She's still stable. At least as stable as she's gonna be, I'm told. I thought you might be worrying."

Tory didn't know whether to hit him or hug him, so she just continued to stare at him with her mouth open. Who was this man anyway? Looking at him in his parka, with goggles hanging around his neck and a balaclava covering most of his face, he looked like something out of a murder mystery movie. Those bullet eyes bearing down on her didn't help.

"I figured you're probably one of those women who's a real bitch without her morning coffee. Guess you answered that question for me." While he was speaking his hand went inside his parka and he pulled out a big metal thermos.

Now she did move. She reached across and in one motion she pulled the mask off his face and asked, "Who the hell are you anyway?"

"Steve Turner."

"I know your name, but who are you? What are you?"

"Your neighbor."

"You son of a bitch. You enjoy frightening unsuspecting women. I'll bet you get off on it! Do you go around scaring little kids, too?"

"If you're gonna be rude I'll take the coffee and go." He turned away.

"You just try it." She grabbed a mug from the cupboard and started loosening the lid of the thermos. The fragrant aroma of the coffee was almost enough to make her kiss Steve's ugly face. She savored the taste of the first mouthful.

Steve smiled openly.

When she noticed him grinning at her, she laughed. "And to think I was actually afraid of you."

"You still should be. I'm not to be trusted. I have a very short fuse and an uncontrollable temper. Some people even say I have a screw loose."

"I'll worry about it after I drink this coffee."

"You gonna make me stand in this doorway all day?"

"I'll let you know after I drink this."

"Talk about people with loose screws." He removed his parka and snow boots, then his snow pants. "A man doesn't even get asked if he wants to warm up a bit before going back out into the snow."

"How far is it from your place to here?"

"Just under six miles."

"Idiot."

He stepped past her into the living room where he sprawled on the floor, feet toward the fire, the holes in his socks showing a mis-matched set underneath.

"Sorry," said Tory. "Want some of this coffee? It's still nice and hot."

"Prefer tea. If you got any."

"Just made a pot. What do you take in it?"

"Cream and sugar."

"Why are you so anti-social?"

"I'm not. I just don't like women."

"You're gay?"

"Nope. Just don't care for them"

"Why are you being nice to me then?"

"You're Miss Lottie's kin."

"But she's a woman."

"She's a human being, and just about the kindest one I ever met. There ain't anything I wouldn't do for her—even looking out for her fool relatives."

"Now I'm a fool on top of everything else? What's the difference between a fool and an idiot. I'm sure you have mental categories in there somewhere?"

Tea finished, he rose from the floor. His cup went into the sink and he started dressing for the trip back. "If I hear any news from the hospital, I'll let you know."

"You don't mean that you'll drive all the way over here on that machine again do you?"

"Ma'am. I've been riding around on snowmobiles in the wintertime for so many years I can't even count them. They're cheap on gas and can take you where even a truck can't go. A man would be a fool to go by truck if he can get there by snowmobile. All you gotta do is dress for the weather and use some common sense."

With that, Steve was out the door leaving Tory shaking her head. *That man is getting stranger and stranger. Well, at least I know he won't harm me. After all, I'm related to Aunt Lottie.*

The wind continued to blow though not as fiercely as it had during the night, and the snow had let up. Tory knew the plows would be out soon enough but it wasn't until close to dusk that she heard the plow on its way up the road toward Steve's place. *Good,* she thought, *I'll wait for it to come back and ask the driver to call for a tow truck.* She was shoveling the snow off her front steps when she heard him return so made her way down the driveway. As he passed he thumb-pointed behind him at Steve's truck.

Steve stopped and yelled for her to get dressed to go. Her her aunt was barely hanging on.

While she got ready, Steve banked the fireplace and secured the screen, then went back outside to open a narrow path for her.

Knowing that the man was fond of her aunt made it easier. Tory knew he probably wanted to be there for Aunt Lottie, too.

At the hospital, she was almost afraid to look through the glass to her aunt's bed. She hesitated outside the room, then, shoulders back, she pushed in. Her aunt had shriveled to the size of a 9-year-old, and was curled in the fetal position. Tory fought back tears as she pulled up a chair to the side of the bed. She held Lottie's hand to her cheek.

"Oh, Auntie. If you're ready to say goodbye, it's OK. You've earned your rest."

Tory was sure she felt a very gentle pressure from those gnarled fingers just as Steve's face appeared at the glass window. She motioned for him to come in but he hesitated. She waved him in again and smiled when he came to her aunt's bedside.

"Aunt Lottie, Steve is here. Steve Turner. He wants to shake your hand and say goodbye, too. He's taking good care of me at your house, so don't you worry."

Then she slid the frail little hand into his bony, calloused one and moved aside.

Steve cleared his throat and seemed momentarily at a loss for words. "Miss Lottie, there's a lot of snow fell out there overnight. I don't suppose you're going to have to worry none about that where you're going. You won't have to worry at all." Then leaning in closer, he whispered so softly Tory could barely hear him, "If you see little Jimmy, give him a hug from me, will ya?" Again hesitation then, "I'm going to miss your homemade bread and all." His voice broke. "You take care." He held her hand to his cheek briefly, then left the room.

Tory had just taken her aunt's hand in her own again when the monitor flat-lined bringing in Dr. Humphrey and a nurse who told Tory to wait outside. Tory squeezed Lottie's hand and moved out of the way.

Steve's eyes were moist as he stared into the room, so Tory put her arm through his and leaned against his shoulder until Dr. Humphrey came out of the room.

"She put up quite a fight but her body was just too tired."

Steve steadied Tory with a hand under her elbow and walked her back into Lottie's room.

When Tory had said her final farewell to Lottie, Steve suggested he take her home. Tory found herself complying with his suggestion.

On the drive home, Steve asked. "Do you think she knew we were there?"

"Of course she did. She waited till we got there." Tory's eyes brimmed with tears. She knew any further attempts at conversation would have her blubbering and Steve could add "baby" to his "idiot" and "fool" categories.

To her surprise, Steve took his free hand and laid it on top of hers. Without saying a word, he had spoken volumes.

"May I ask a favor?" To his nod, she added, "Would you help me with the funeral arrangements?"

"Of course."

The power had been restored during their absence, so she was able to heat up a pot of soup she'd made from the vegetables that had started to wilt in the fridge. She asked Steve if he'd like to share a bowl with her.

"You put peas in it?"

"What if I did?"

"Hate peas. I won't eat anything that's got those damn little green things in it."

"Well, since the soup has no peas, I'll assume you are graciously accepting my invitation?"

He said nothing more but went about stoking the fire and reloading the woodbox while he waited to be called to the table.

She had also found some bread in the freezer and after slicing it with an electric knife she warmed it in the microwave. Butter and sliced brisket from the soup were added to the table. When she had the bowls and their steaming contents in place she called Steve to sit down.

Her soup was a hit. She knew by the expression on Steve's face when he swallowed the first spoonful, although he never said a word. He did however ask if she had made the bread. When she said she had found it in the freezer, he replied that he would've recognized the taste of Miss Lottie's bread anywhere. After several attempts to make conversation by asking about Steve's farm and family and receiving little more than one-word answers, she gave up. Obviously, he was not a talker and she was not about to draw him out. After finishing a second bowl of soup, he took his empty dish to the sink, refused coffee and pulled his jacket off the hook.

"Don't forget to lock the door behind me," he grinned. "You got a dangerous neighbor just down the road." And with that and a wink, he left.

4

THE SUN WAS WARM AND there was not a cloud in the sky the morning of the funeral but puddles were everywhere from the melting snow so it seemed more like a morning in early March than mid-October. Tory had spent the evening before in the viewing room at the funeral parlor accepting condolences from many of Aunt Lottie's former friends, students and business acquaintances. With the help of the coach, Tory had chosen six current and past members from the high school curling club, which her aunt had supported financially for years, to be pallbearers. Assuming that most people would be working on Friday morning and that most had paid their respects the evening before, she was not prepared for the crowd that overflowed the church. She hoped the Ladies Auxiliary had prepared for this and wondered if the church basement would be big enough to hold everyone for the post-service lunch.

When the casket was carried up the steps into the church, she searched the crowd for Steve Turner. She not only knew that her aunt would have liked him to be treated as family, she needed him herself for support. Searching the crowd, Tory spotted him near the back of the church and asked the usher to fetch him. Steve turned when his arm was tapped, listened for a moment, shook his head in refusal, but then looked up at Tory, and acquiesced. She slid her arm through his and they proceeded up the aisle to take their seats in the front pew. More than once during the service she felt Steve's hand on hers and saw that his eyes were watery.

Everyone said it was a beautiful service with Lottie's favorite hymns and the angels smiling down in the rays of sunshine through the stained glass windows. Surprisingly, the food seemed to multiply like "fishes and loaves of bread" so Tory was pleased that everyone had had enough to eat. Lottie's ashes would be buried in her parents' plot on the south side of town.

Back at the farmhouse, Tory went from room to room, starting to do something then leaving it only to start and leave something else. When she heard a vehicle in the driveway, she found herself hoping it would be Steve. She needed to share her loneliness with someone who might be feeling the same emptiness. When she heard the now familiar footsteps on the deck, she found herself smiling and opened the door before he even knocked.

As he stepped through the door, he seemed confused by her pleasure at seeing him and removed his hat—something he hadn't done before but when Tory hugged him, he stiffened.

"I was just thinking how much I needed a friend right now."

He gave her one of his rare smiles, and she thought for an instant that he was almost pleasant looking. "Who says we're friends?"

"We have a common interest, Steve. It's very obvious how well you took care of my aunt. I'm sure you spoiled her rotten."

He seemed to hesitate and the humor disappeared from his eyes. "Miss Lottie and I have history. She did more for me than I could ever do for her. I was always afraid she'd be gone before I had the chance to ever pay off half what I owed her."

"I would like to hear about your friendship with her—if you feel like talking about it."

"I don't much care for women. Lottie's the only one I could trust since... well... for a long, long time. Some memories are better left buried so those I don't want to talk about." The steely eyes darkened like a thunderstorm for a moment and then he seemed to shake the clouds and smiled again. "I guess you got some of your aunt in you, even if you ain't the best driver around."

Tory had to laugh in spite of herself. "That's probably the nicest thing you're ever going say to me and since I'm proud to have some of my aunt in me, I'll take that as a compliment and thank you for it." She motioned for him to go into the living room by the fire. "I'll put the pot on and make you a cup of tea."

"Two fingers of rye with one finger of water would be better."

Tory prepared two glasses.

He wrapped his work-roughened hand around the crystal glass and sat there watching the fire for a while before taking a sip. Then he spoke, his voice catching emotion. "I came by because I wanted to thank you for honoring me with a family place at Miss Lottie's funeral today."

"I've only known you a few short weeks, but I think you were more family to Lottie than I ever was. I wrote to her on a somewhat regular basis. Phoned several times a year. I always hated that she was alone over the holidays, so I often invited her east for Christmas but she wouldn't come. Assured me she had lots of good friends and was never alone. I'm ashamed that it's been so many years since I visited, but with my own family... I'm sure you understand. Children, grandchildren."

Steve nodded.

"I wish I'd taken the time to find out just what kind of good friends my aunt actually had. I might have felt better about her being here, so far away from us." She laid a hand on his where it rested on the arm of the chair. "I'm glad I got to know you. I think under that rough, tough exterior there lies a heart of pure gold."

"Don't be so silly. Isn't it just like a woman to—"

"Don't worry, your secret is safe with me."

"Oh. While I think of it, Mrs. Hardisty, I'd best return the key. With her gone and you putting the house up for sale and all… Nobody'll be wanting folks wandering around with keys to the place." He reached into his pocket. The key was old and worn and belonged between his gnarled thumb and forefinger.

"Please keep it. I'd feel much better knowing you're keeping an eye on the place. And another thing, unless you start calling me Tory, I'm going to feel obligated to call you Mr. Turner. I sure as hell would hate to have to do that."

"Yes, ma'am. Tory. Ma'am."

She watched him back down the drive. He was a strange one all right. Certainly not one of the most available bachelors around town. In fact, a couple of the nurses at the hospital were surprised that she had drawn him out as much as she had.

Tory spent the weekend going through her aunt's possessions and on Monday morning, her appointment for the reading of the will was mercifully brief. The will was a basic one, leaving almost all her possessions to Victoria "Tory" Hardisty with a small bequest to the high school curling club and another to the United Church. Tory was surprised and pleased to learn that her aunt had owned several life insurance policies, one of which was rather large and in which Steve Turner was named beneficiary. She wondered if he'd been aware of this. Lottie had invested her money well over the years and Tory discovered that besides the farm and the insurance policies, her aunt had built quite a nest egg. When the dust settled, Tory would be more than comfortable in her own old age. Her aunt's safety deposit box contained investment papers, stock certificates and a few pieces of jewelry that had been her grandmother's. Lottie's property would officially be put up for sale and that would be that. Tory headed home with memories of happy times in her mind and a certain sadness in her heart.

On reaching the farmhouse, instead of turning into her own driveway, she kept going toward the Turner ranch. She had never gone beyond her aunt's house as the road led into the mountains and eventually became a dead end. She was surprised to see that Steve had quite a large acreage and the buildings were kept in very good repair. A number of cattle were enclosed within a corral close to the barn. The familiar blue pick-up truck was parked near the house. She pulled in behind it.

Several unanswered knocks on the kitchen door told her that Steve was not inside so she wandered toward the barn. The recent snow had all but disappeared except for where it had been plowed into banks. Just when she was about to enter the barn, a rider on horseback came over the hill behind the house. As he rode closer, she recognized the cowboy hat Steve always wore and the white hair at his neck catching a glint of the sun's rays. He picked up the gait and brought the horse to a stop right in front of her. She patted the nose of the horse as she greeted Steve.

"Sorry. I was out checking for strays. Been here long?"

Tory followed him into the barn and watched while he removed the saddle and bridle from the horse and rubbed him down.

"You got time for tea? Coffee?"

"I don't understand why Lottie would do that."

Tory didn't know which was greater, his surprise or his concern that Lottie had left him this sizeable life insurance.

"It rightfully should be yours. You're kin."

"I've been well taken care of in her will, don't you worry about me. She always had a reason for everything she did so leaving you this money had a valid one behind it."

"Darn women. I never can figure them out. I thought Lottie was different."

"Well, it's yours whether you want it or not. You might as well accept it and get the benefit of the interest while you decide what you want to do with it. I must get back to the farmhouse. The real estate agent is coming by tomorrow so I need to make sure the house looks its best."

The phone was ringing as she came in the door and she was pleasantly surprised to hear Liz's voice on the other end of the line. "A couple of us are going to the movies tonight and we hoped you might come with us."

"Thanks, Liz, but I'm not up to a movie. I've been going through my aunt's things, was at the lawyers about the will today. I'm feeling kind of melancholy."

"That's all the more reason to come out and lose yourself in a love story. I figured you would be knee deep in memories and maybe needing a change of scenery."

After several minutes of bantering back and forth, Tory decided that perhaps Liz was right. Maybe an evening out would do her some good. She'd have more than ample time to sort through the rest of Lottie's belongings.

The movie was enjoyable even though bereft of any real story line. It was a simple "chick flick" as her daughter called them, but it had lightened her mood so she let them talk her into going to The Roadhouse again where they had gone the last time. She made a mental note to check all of her tires before she left the parking lot.

The music was loud C&W again, but there were not many drinking inside. A few dancers two-stepped their way around the dance floor as the women made their way to a corner table, as far from the loudspeakers as possible. She ordered a light draft and settled in while her companions rehashed the movie and filled her in on the latest hospital gossip. The nachos they'd ordered arrived and when Tory stood to take her jacket off, she felt an arm slide around her waist. She turned to see the ruddy face of Dr. Needy who reeked of beer and who was prodding her onto the dance floor. He was dangerously unsteady on his feet as she removed his arm from around her body.

"Thanks, but I don't care to dance."

"Don't be like that, doll. Jus' wan' a little dance with ya, nothing else." He slid his arm back around her.

"Please take your hands off me. I told you, I don't care to dance."

"Hey, c'mon. How do ya know until you try it? I'm pretty good you know." By this time he was leaning on her, puckering up to kiss her cheek.

His arm wrenched away from her waist as a male voice said "The lady told you she don't wanna dance."

"It ain't any of your business, you old drunk."

He might have said more but Steve had already spun him around and was aiming him toward the door.

"Let these ladies alone in peace and quiet. I catch you near her again, I'll go out to the parking lot with you next time. Now git."

Steve did not approach Tory and her friends' table but instead went to a bar stool.

"Boy oh boy, Tory, you certainly mellowed old Steve," said Liz. "He never would've done anything like that before. He would've said we deserved it for being out here in a bar. In a man's world. Our place is in the home, you know."

"He never gave me time to thank him." Tory spoke her thoughts out loud. "I don't know if it would embarrass him if I went over and thanked him. I should."

"You might get a grunt out of him. He doesn't talk to women. I was surprised you had him sitting with you at the funeral. But then I remembered he was your aunt's neighbor.

"He was really good to her."

"Lottie was so well respected by everybody I'm not surprised if he made an exception for her."

Tory stood up and walked to the bar. As she got closer she could see his reflection in the mirror and realized he was watching her walk toward him. She sat on the stool next to him and put her hand on his arm. "Steve, thank you for helping me shake off that man. I really appreciated you coming to my defense."

"Women shouldn't be out at night without an escort."

Hurt, she tugged on his arm until he looked at her. "Are you saying I invited trouble?"

"When women come into a bar unescorted, some men think they're fair game."

"I can't believe you think that."

"I didn't say it's right, it's just the way it is. Some men see a pretty woman without a man and right away they think she's sitting there, just waiting to be picked up."

That he had called her pretty didn't go unnoticed. She smiled and squeezed his arm. "That's a very old fashioned notion, but I appreciate your help and I promise to keep my bar hopping to a minimum."

He looked at her in the mirror.

"I certainly don't want you getting any black eyes or losing any teeth on my account," she added.

He finally smiled and turned around on the bar stool to watch her walk away.

"Give me a call if you come across anything in her papers that might show when or if recent repairs were done," Sally the real estate agent had told her the next morning, but try as she might, she couldn't find anything in her aunt's files that might help. She would have to call Steve.

"A new furnace was put in four years ago and the septic was replaced just two years ago. I'll check with the contractors and see if they have a copy of the contracts. The municipality should have a certificate for the septic. It woulda had to pass inspection."

"Thanks, Steve. I appreciate that. By the way, I'm cooking roast beef for supper. Can you come?"

When he showed up at her back door later that day, she was in a really down mood.

He awkwardly asked, "You got something bothering you. Want to spit it out?"

She burst into tears and immediately felt ashamed of herself. "This house has been in the family for so long, I feel like I'm selling a part of my heritage. It's hard for me to picture strangers living in it. I only remember my grandparents and aunt living under this roof."

She wiped away her tears with the back of her hand; then Steve was handing her his handkerchief and pulling her to his shoulder.

"I bought my farm twenty-seven years ago. Lottie's the only neighbor I've ever known. It'll be hard for me to have strangers here, too, not to stop and see if anything's needed, not to be called when the furnace goes out in the middle of winter. Lottie always had a warm loaf of bread for me, or an apple pie or chocolate cake. She never judged me when I drank too much or spent the night in jail because I couldn't drive home."

Tory allowed herself the comfort of his arms for a while longer then, pulling away slightly, she looked directly into his eyes, at the moisture there, and said "It's true, isn't it? Your bark is much louder than your bite."

He surprised her by winking. "You promised my secret would be safe."

"It is. It is. Let's get supper on the table before it gets cold, OK?" Reluctantly she moved away from his embrace.

"Why are you in such a hurry to sell the house if you feel such ties to it?"

"I can't live in two places."

"Just live here."

"I have a condo in Peterborough. That's where my home is."

"Baah! Home is where your heart is, I was always told. Does your condo call to you the way this place does?"

"Well, no… There's nothing here for me. My family, my friends… They're all back east. What would I do here?"

"What do you do back east?"

"Play cards with my friends, go out for lunch, go to the Peterborough Petes' hockey games. I do volunteer work at the hospital. I fill in at work for a friend when she needs me."

"Why don't you just try it for one winter and see what happens?"

"Steve, I've already had a too-early taste of your winters and I'm not sure I like them."

"Suit yourself. I just hate to see you make a rash decision when you're still upset over Lottie's death. Maybe by spring you'll still feel the same and the house might sell better then anyway. If you sell now, you might always wish you hadn't."

What difference would another few months make? She could take her time going through her aunt's things, maybe slip up to Edmonton to visit a couple of her ex-husband's nephews, or go to Calgary to see cousins of her mother's that she hadn't talked to in years. She really did feel comfortable in this house. *Who knows? Maybe I would enjoy that feeling of being connected to my mother, my aunt and my grandparents.* Once the house was sold she could never again stand in her mother's bedroom and picture her sitting at the window as a young girl. She could never again sit in front of the fireplace at the exact spot where her stocking had hung on the mantel when they visited her grandparents at Christmas. It would be wonderful to see the apple trees in bloom again in the spring and once more see her aunt's tulips in all their glorious color.

She would have to make another trip east to bring some winter clothes and to make arrangements for the care of her condominium for the winter months.

"I'll think about it," she said. "But if I do try it, it will be for only one winter."

"Good," said Steve, a smile tugging at his lips.

The next morning, as she picked up the phone to cancel the appointment with the realtor, she shook her head and couldn't help but laugh out loud. *Tory, girl, what are you doing?* Never one to act on impulse, Tory was going against her sensible nature. *Oh well, what's the point in being retired if you can't do what you want, when you want?* She continued to dial. That done, she called her daughter to inform her of the decision to winter in Alberta. *Becky thinks I've lost my mind. Well maybe I have.*

Then later that morning, when she went into town to see the banker, she was surprised that he already knew of her decision. "You forgot, didn't you. It's a small town. Yesterday, Sally Knight was pretty pleased at the prospect of having the listing for Miss MacArthur's property and now today, she's all disappointed about losing a commission but delighted that you decided to keep the house for a while. So are most of the townsfolk."

"Why in the world would it make a difference to them?"

"We're proud of our history, Mrs. Hardisty. There's been a MacArthur living in that old farmhouse for as long as anyone can remember. Now there still will be."

"I'll only be staying the winter."

"We'll see, Mrs. Hardisty. We'll see."

5

TORY CAME OUT OF CUT & Curl to see that snow clouds had started to move in again. *Might be a good idea to stock up on groceries,* she thought. *And while I'm at it, get extras, stock up the freezer with baking. Who knows? Maybe I can talk the gang into coming out for an old-fashioned Christmas.* She could picture Maggie's and Josh's Christmas stockings hanging on the mantel in the old farmhouse.

Overnight the snow came. Not as much as last time, but enough to keep a body home until the plows came out. Steve phoned in the morning to make sure everything was running smoothly and to let her know he'd be over to clear the driveway later. How her aunt must have relied on these phone calls! Within minutes after the plow passed by, Steve, his own blade on the front of his truck, came along, plowed out her driveway and left. *He must have several driveways to do,* she thought.

She spent the afternoon baking. Life in Peterborough had always been too full to allow whole days at home to just bake bread, cookies and cake—or knit, or sew. *Speaking of which,* she thought, *I just might pull Aunt Lottie's sewing machine out. Try my hand at Christmas crafts. I used to be pretty good at making those.* If they turned out, she could donate them to the Ladies Auxiliary, or perhaps to a church bazaar, or even to the hospital to cheer things up for both staff and patients.

It was getting dark and she was taking the last loaves of bread out of the oven when she heard a vehicle pull in and Steve's footsteps on the back deck. He walked right in without waiting for her to open the door for him, a dark cloud of anger floating with him.

"The whole town knew I got a new neighbor before I did!"

"Oh, really."

"Least you coulda done was let me know you decided to stay on."

"I told you I'd think about it. What does it matter whether I stay or leave, anyway? You not liking women and all." She looked at him sideways to see if he'd caught her teasing. He hadn't.

"You being Lottie's niece, I thought we were friends. Kind of. Then I go into town and find out that I'm the only one doesn't know you decided not to sell the house."

"If it's any comfort, by the time I got into town yesterday, the whole town knew about it before I even told the lawyer. Must have been Sally."

"Sally's always had a big mouth."

"I thought you'd stop in for tea when you finished my driveway. I would have told you then."

Silence.

"Come on. Let me make it up to you with a loaf of homemade bread." She waved the last loaf from the oven under his nose.

"Give me the keys to the car. I gotta move it to clean the snow better."

"I can do that in the morning. I enjoy having something to do outside. I won't be going anywhere tonight."

"Fine. I'll be on my way then."

"Steve, don't be angry with me. I didn't realize how much not knowing about my decision would upset you. But now that you're here, how about having a bowl of soup with me? We need to discuss some matters."

"What kind of soup?"

"Tomato and cabbage."

"Are there peas in it?"

"Did I say tomato, cabbage and peas?"

He shot her a look, nodded, removed his parka, then his boots, washed up in the mud room then sat at the table.

Tory watched with pleasure as he broke a slice of bread, spread butter on it then slide it into his mouth. He said nothing and she could tell he was trying hard not to grin at her.

"Grandmother taught both Mom and Aunt Lottie how to make bread. I was shown the same way and my daughter knows how to do it as well."

"I'll make you a deal. I'll take that loaf of bread you offered if you promise to make more during the winter, and I'll try to get over my mad. And I'll have another bowl of soup and best put two pieces of that chocolate cake on my plate while you're at it."

"That sounds fair," said Tory. "May I ask a favor?"

"More than likely, but it still depends."

"I need to go back east for a bit to deal with some things. Was hoping I could get a ride to the airport in Calgary. No definite arrangements made yet, I wanted to talk to you first. If you're not able, I'll take the bus."

"I go in about once a month to the city. Don't much like it, but I can get away anytime you want. I'll keep an eye on the place while you're gone too." He dug out his key and held it up.

Steve didn't come around again until it was time to take her to the airport and while they drove, he kept looking her over. Even now, as they walked through the concourse, he was staring.

"Is something torn?"

"No."

"Am I wearing my breakfast?"

"No."

"Damn it, Steve. What are you staring at me for?"

"Guess a man can't even look at woman, even when she's all dressed up."

"Aw, Steve. How sweet. Are you saying I look nice?"

"Wouldn't be looking at you otherwise."

Knowing how hard that must have been for him to say, she smiled and took his arm as they entered the Seattle Coffee House.

"We have lots of time," said Steve as they ordered a sandwich and coffee. "When do I come pick you up?"

"I haven't booked a return yet."

His look of concern made Tory smile.

"You are coming back, though." It was a statement rather than a question.

"Of course. There's no financial advantage to booking round trips anymore so I decided not to commit myself until I know what's waiting for me at home. I've been away for quite a long time. And I'll be away for even longer—it's not like I'm taking off on a weekend holiday trip, you know. I want to go to Burlington. See the family. Maybe a week. Maybe two. I don't know yet."

Tory wasn't sure if he was angry or relieved but either way, she was touched that he'd wanted reassurance of her return. *Is he taking a liking to me?* she wondered. *Surely not. Must be my cooking he's taken a shine to.*

Tory was further surprised when Steve followed her right up to security and waited there while she went through. "Goodbye, Steve. Thanks again for the drive. Much appreciated."

"Yeah, well, you make damn sure you let me know when you're coming back. I'll come pick you up."

Two weeks later, she was back at the Calgary airport watching for Steve's signature cowboy hat. She had to admit it was kind of nice having someone to meet her this time. When she had first arrived in Calgary, she was alone and didn't have any idea what might be in store for her or for her aunt. And even when she'd arrived back home, no one was there to meet her at the Toronto airport; the limo had taken her straight to her door in Peterborough. Once there, she walked into an empty apartment.

He spotted her first and took her arm from behind. She felt the welcome squeeze on her arm. Tory was surprised at his appearance. He was always very clean and well groomed, but somehow he looked different, almost—good looking. She laughed to herself thinking how she'd always pictured him in her mind as "not ugly, but not good looking either." She thanked him for coming for her and told him she was glad he drove a truck because she'd brought a lot of things with her, enough to last her through the winter.

"Typical woman. All a man needs is a change of underwear and his razor."

It was almost 9:00 PM when they had everything unloaded and into the farmhouse. "It's good to be home," she said quietly.

"I thought Peterborough was your home."

"Oh. Did I say that out loud? It's just that when I got off the plane in Toronto there was no one to meet me and when I arrived in Peterborough, it was to an empty apartment. When I got off the plane today, I had a friend waiting for me. It felt good. And now, to arrive back at this beautiful farmhouse with all its memories…" she smiled. "I'm beginning to wonder if you aren't a really wise, old man."

"Old man is it?"

"I'm sorry. You've referred to me as an old woman. I took a liberty."

"Old man Rutledge over at the gas station is an old man. Not me. I still work harder in a day than any of the young bucks I hire on."

"I said I was sorry."

Silence.

Only after Steve had carried all her luggage upstairs, did she realize that the outside lights had been on and the furnace was humming. He must have been in earlier to prepare the house for her arrival. *He is bent on doing for me the same way he did for Aunt Lottie. This is going to take some getting used to, having somebody coming and going all the time.*

"All done," he said, returning to the kitchen.

"Tea? Coffee?"

"Well, if you're not too tired from your trip, I'd appreciate a cup of coffee. Mustn't wear you out, though. You being an old woman and all."

There was carrot cake in her freezer, which she found and put into the microwave to thaw. She enjoyed the sound of the coffee perking. She had purchased a metal coffee pot that could be used on the wood stove. No more relying on Hydro to enjoy a cup of coffee.

"I'm going to town in the morning if you want me to collect your mail. Just call 'em and tell 'em it's OK for me to be picking it up."

At the door, after two coffees and two helpings of carrot cake, Tory pecked his cheek and thanked him again for coming to the airport for her.

He said something so low she had a hard time hearing it but thought it was something about being neighborly and out the door he went. Tory saw very little of him over the next week or so and was surprised one morning when the phone rang and Steve was on the other end of it. "You said you liked hockey. Wanna go see a game tonight?"

"Sure. Who's playing?"

"Calgary and Vancouver."

"Calgary. You mean the Flames? We would go into Calgary? To the Saddledome you mean?"

"Well, they're not gonna come here."

Tory laughed.

"Something you might wanna do is… Well, I always throw something into a bag in case the weather changes. You never know what might come down out of the mountains in the wintertime."

"Oh. You mean…"

"Yes. We might have to stay over. I'll be there at three-thirty. Be ready."

"Shall I pack something to eat?"

"Plenty of time to eat there, it's not that far." The phone went dead.

A date? Is that what this is? A date? No. Not old Steve. He's just "being neighborly" like he always says. Should she be concerned if he started to drink at the hockey rink? It would be a very long ride back if he had consumed too much alcohol. Maybe she could insist that they stay overnight before they got there rather than risk an argument about him not being fit to drive later. *Oh dear, I'm getting myself all worked up for nothing probably. We haven't even left yet and I've already got him drunk and disorderly. Give him a chance, girl.*

He pulled into the driveway at 3:30 sharp. Her overnight bag she placed in the back seat, then climbed into the front. The late afternoon sky was bright and clear and there wasn't any indication of weather moving in. While they rode, she told Steve about her daughter, son-in-law and grandchildren coming for Christmas and asked if he had plans for the holidays.

He informed her he usually spent Christmas with a friend.

"I don't want you to change plans you already have, but I would be happy if you could share dinner with us."

"Do you cook a turkey?"

"I do. I always have a very traditional meal with stuffing, sweet potatoes, turnip, roast carrots, cranberry sauce and lots of gravy. Apple pie and pumpkin pie for dessert. I don't do plum pudding, though. Nobody likes it. I promise I'll leave the peas out of the pumpkin pie this time if you decide to come."

"I guess I could manage that," he said.

"Well if it's too much for you to handle, you can always come on Christmas Eve. That's more of a buffet and we do things the children will enjoy."

"Like what?" More inquisition.

"Singing carols, playing games, toasting marshmallows in the fireplace, Christmas stories…"

A barely discernible "I'll see."

He had only downed two beers during the game so she let him make the call about staying over or driving home and was strangely relieved when he opted for driving home. They should be there by 12:30, he informed her. When he turned off the freeway north of Airdrie, a fine powdered snow was falling and by the time they turned onto the narrow highway that would take them into Weston, it had turned into a heavy wet snow that was starting to blow hard. About forty miles from town, a pick-up going too fast came from behind and tried to pass. Steve moved over as far as he dared to the invisible edge of the road and the truck again pulled up beside them, passed, but immediately cut in front of them. Steve's truck fishtailed when it hit the soft shoulder, but the momentum of the spin took them into the ditch on the far side of the road.

Steve rocked the truck back and forth but even with four-wheel drive nothing happened. Because of the angle of the truck, he couldn't open his door so climbed over Tory so he could get out to assess the problem.

Soon he was shoveling snow and hollering at her to try rocking the truck. Not being familiar with the touchiness of the gas pedal, she pressed too heavily and ending up spinning the tires and spraying snow all over Steve who was pushing from the front end. A string of curses rose into the blowing snow.

From a tool box in the back seat he removed flares which he set out before returning to the driver's seat. "Flares are out. Gas tank's half full. Exhaust pipe's free of snow. We're OK to wait for the morning plow. I'm sorry about this, Tory. Wait. Let me get you a blanket." He rooted around in the back seat, found one and wrapped it around her then turned on the motor.

Except for a brief argument about one of the penalties during the game, they were largely silent until Tory fell asleep against Steve.

She roused once to ensure that Steve had part of the blanket, then drifted back to be gently wakened every now and again by Steve's arm movements as he turned the car and heater off and on throughout the night.

It was near dawn before the plow came by and when it did, Steve jumped out to wave it down.

"He'll throw a chain on us on his way back. Haul us out. You OK? Hope you didn't catch a cold or nothing like that."

"I'm pretty strong for an old woman. I don't usually catch things."

"Glad to hear that, for sure. When folks as old as you catch something, they end up with pneumonia." He laughed.

"You know something?" she said.

"What?"

"That's the first time I've ever heard you laugh. You should do it more often. It sounds nice."

6

November became December and the snow got deeper than Tory had ever experienced. She baked and sewed and donated most of the resulting crafts to the Ladies Auxiliary hospital store—socks and mitts went to the United Church; for a few hours once a week she volunteered at the library; and was planning, after Christmas, to ask Liz if any of her friends played cards. Steve continued to keep her driveway clear of snow and the firewood split and at hand, and she continued to invite him to at-least-weekly dinners.

It was toward the end of the first week of December that he offered to take her into Calgary for Christmas shopping. "And we could throw in another Flames game. Afterwards. It would be Flames and Flyers. What do you think? Feel up to it?" During this hesitant questioning, he appeared to find something of great interest in his stew. "We could stay overnight. Avoid repeating… the… disaster I put you through last time. And for which I'm still real sorry. You could shop the next day… I can certainly find something… I mean, I have some of my own business needs tending to."

"That's a wonderful idea," said Tory.

Steve's obvious relief—he stopped staring into his stew for one thing—at hearing a positive answer from her made her smile.

"Craft items I can't get here will be tops on my list. That will also solve a couple of problems on my gift list. But Steve. You amaze me. You want to take me shopping?"

"If I didn't I wouldn't ask. Women and their foolish questions."

"When then?"

"Friday night." With that, and without finishing his stew, he rose, thanked her, put on his jacket and boots and left.

The motor inn had a small piano bar and after the game, they had a drink together. Tory had one rye and ginger ale and headed off to bed leaving Steve alone, something she regretted the next morning.

She was awake at 7:00 and more than ready for breakfast by 8:30 so she went alone. By 9:30, she was fuming. *That skinny little runt,* she thought. *He's hung over and that means I'm going to be stuck in the motel watching bad TV all day!* A knock on her motel door stopped further thought.

She opened it. The "skinny little runt" stood there: showered, shaved, fresh-looking, smiling, ready.

"What are you laughing at?" he snapped. "I forget to do my pants up?" He looked down to make sure.

"I'm not laughing at you. I'm laughing at how ridiculous I am. Apologies?"

"You're ready. Humph. I'll go warm the truck. You get your stuff together." He glanced around the room and his eyes came to rest on her overnight bag waiting on the bed. "Well. Give that here. I'll take it with me." As he left, Tory heard him muttering. "First time a woman was ever ready on time. I'll be danged."

At the office she handed her credit card over to the clerk.

"Taken care of, ma'am," the clerk said with a sly grin and a top-to-bottom look-over of a surprised Tory. To her chagrin, he winked and added: "Your boyfriend already paid."

On the way to the shopping mall, Steve asked again what she had been laughing at when he'd arrived at her door.

"Want the truth?"

"What else would I want?"

"OK. I thought you'd slept in. Then when I saw you, I realized how absurd my suspicions were. You're always up at the crack of dawn no matter what."

"You thought I was hung over."

"Did not."

"Did too."

"OK. I did."

"Just like a woman. Anyways, we're here. Meet you at the food court, down there…" He pointed. "At 2:00. And don't be late."

"Or what?" Tory laughed. "You'll be all worried about me?"

"Exactly," he said.

Tory's smile slid away. "Oh."

"Good-looking gal like you might draw attention from the wrong sort. Wouldn't be the first time."

Tory was too dumbfounded to reply so she stepped down from the truck and headed into the mall, but she didn't hear the truck moving away behind her. *He's watching my butt as I walk away! That skinny little runt.* Her smile made an elderly gentleman touch what would have been the brim of his hat if he'd been wearing one.

"Ma'am."

Get that silly smile off your face, she told herself. *You have some serious shopping to do.* But somehow, the smile remained throughout the entire shopping event and Tory was certain that her happy mood was what made her purchase more than she'd intended.

She was fifteen minutes late getting to the food court and struggling with packages and bags. "Hi. I'm late. I know. Sorry. I lost track of the time."

"No. This is a good thing. You've renewed my non-faith in women. Here. Lemme give you a hand with those. Jeez, woman. Did you leave anything for anybody else?" He shook his head in disgust.

"Have you had lunch?"

"No. Figured we'd have tea—or coffee in your case—before we leave. Eat in a real restaurant on the way out. Unless you have more shopping to do?" A rare grin tugged at the corner of his mouth.

"Where are you parked. I have something else to do."

"I thought you were finished."

"Uh... I am. I just have to pick up the rest of my parcels..." Her voice drifted off and Steve had to lean forward to hear. "From the locker."

"Good God, woman. How many people have you got coming for Christmas?" His look was one of utter astonishment.

"They're not all Christmas presents, you know. I don't know when I'll get another chance to come to Calgary so thought I'd better take advantage of the opportunity."

"All you have to do is ask."

"Pardon me?"

"I'm not a mind reader. If you don't tell me you want to come to Calgary, how am I supposed to know?"

"I don't expect you to drop everything and take me to the city whenever the whim suits me."

"I come here pretty regular. If you want to come, speak up."

He could be a nice guy if he just wasn't so damn ornery, she thought. *It's as if being kind is a sign of weakness that he needs to mask with rudeness.*

As though reading her mind, he turned his face away from her.

They stopped for lunch at The Roadhouse Steve had told her made the best burgers in Alberta. After biting into hers, she agreed. "There's nothing in Ontario can even come close."

To her amazement, Steve ate two of them with a large side order of French fries.

Where does he put it all?

She had coffee, he had a beer.

Back on the road, he stated matter-of-factly "You know your hockey pretty good for a woman."

Tory smiled. "I'll accept that as a compliment even though it doesn't sound like one."

He made no comment.

They arrived home and unloaded Tory's purchases just as the sky was darkening. Steve shoved his cowboy hat back on his head and scratched his forehead as he looked at the enormous pile of bags on her dining room table. "How did you manage to find all this, pay for it, bag it and move on in a matter of just a couple of hours?"

"Have you forgotten? I'm a woman. It's inbred. It's in our genes."

He laughed. It was a full laugh that came all the way from his belly. She liked the sound of it. As he was going out the door she called out that a casserole from her freezer would be ready in a couple of hours if he wanted to come back.

"Thanks. That'll give me time to check on the livestock. See you later."

"Steve?"

He turned.

"I had a really good time."

He hesitated briefly then stepped out the door.

At 7:30 he was back with a bottle of wine he'd picked up for her in the city. "Townsfolk are mostly beer drinkers. Liquor store doesn't carry many brands. Least none of the good ones."

"For me? That's so sweet. Thank you."

"Never been accused of sweetness before."

"Maybe if you stopped biting people's heads off, they'd see what a nice guy you actually are."

His face turned hard. "No, I'm not nice and don't you go spreading rumors that I am."

She squeezed his arm. "I told you before, your secrets are safe with me. Now, I hope you like macaroni casserole and baked spareribs."

She had a feeling he partially meant what he had just said, that it was a warning of some kind. She couldn't control a slight shiver.

He again polished off two helpings before he put his knife and fork down on his plate. She poured him tea and watched his eyes light up when she put a big wedge of chocolate layer cake in front of him.

"I shouldn't tell you this," he said, "but I think your grandmother favored your mama over your aunt."

Tory was taken aback so laughed thoroughly at the thought. "How do you figure that?"

"She taught your mama to cook better than she taught Lottie."

"Is that supposed to be a compliment?"

Silence.

"I think it was. So just for that, you can have a second piece of cake."

He rubbed his stomach. "No room but I'd sure appreciate a piece to take home—for later."

Such a confusing man, she thought. *I must have imagined that masked warning.*

He rose from the table. "There's work to be done before bed. Thanks for supper. Thanks for the extra cake." At the door he put on his winter gear and turned the knob to leave.

Without thinking, Tory kissed his cheek and he lifted her chin with his gloved hand and looking her eye to eye, whispered, "You don't listen very well, missy," then turned and went out.

She was left standing in the kitchen, wondering what exactly he had meant. Surely at his age, he couldn't be a threat sexually—could he? She hadn't thought about that. She didn't think of him in a sexual way—at all. Was he reading something into their friendship that wasn't there? Perhaps she should listen better and heed his words.

7

"Hi, Liz. What's up?"

"Put your dancing shoes on, girl," came Liz's excited voice through the phone. "There's going to be a party."

"What are you talking about?"

"The hospital staff and auxiliary are having their Christmas party on Friday and you are invited."

"Liz, I don't work there. Why would I be invited?"

"Well…" Liz laughed. "Besides being Dr. Needy's favorite squeeze—"

"Don't even mention him!"

"I knew I'd get a rise out of you."

"And you did. Surely that's not why you're inviting me," pleaded Tory.

"You've donated more crafts to the tuck shop in a month than other town folk have in a year. The Auxiliary girls were upset that your name wasn't on the list. I promised to correct that."

"What can I bring? Besides a big sign with 'Keep Away Dr. Needy' written on it in four-letter words?"

"Why not a few stray men. You seem to have a... a certain magnetism about you."

"What?"

"Just kidding. We're always short of men. Probably what gives Dr Needy carte blanche to act like such a lech. Always more available females than men so we share the ones that do show up, except they're usually young enough to be our sons. And no, you don't need to bring anything else."

"Can I not help with food?"

"Nope, that's all taken care of. Just put on a party dress and be prepared to drink and dance the night away."

"If I do find a stray male...?"

"By all means, bring him along. Hey. You don't mean you're hiding one out at your place, do you?"

"You just never know. Thanks for the invitation. I'll be there."

Tory hurried to her closet to see what she owned that could pass for a party dress. On her second swipe through, she pulled out a long navy skirt and a pewter-colored crocheted top that looked pretty good together. With her pearl necklace and earrings she could consider herself dressed for a party. A hair cut was a must so an appointment would have to be made before Friday, and maybe a manicure. Looking at the clock once more, she decided it was late enough to have a lunch and supper combined. Once again, she thought how much she enjoyed the freedom to eat when she felt like it, not when a husband expected to eat.

When Steve came around the next day to clear away some of the built-up snow banks at the foot of her driveway, she called him in for tea.

"A dance? You want me to go to a dance? In town? This town? Are you out of your freakin' mind?"

"You do know how to dance, don't you?"

"It's not the dancing. It's all those silly women that are always at those things."

"Not all women are silly. Stay home then. I'll go by myself."

"Where's it at. In case I change my mind?"

"Legion Hall. Friday. 7:00 PM."

At 6:30 Friday evening, Steve's truck pulled into Tory's driveway. She couldn't keep from smiling. *Maybe one of these days he might even surprise me and agree to do something without arguing first.* She came downstairs as he was letting himself in the back door.

She had seen him in a suit at her aunt's funeral, but this time there was something different about him. He looked almost... pleasant. "Well, don't you look nice. Going somewhere, Steve?"

"Don't give me a hard time, woman. Here."

She almost fell over when he handed her a box of chocolates. Trying to keep a straight face, she thanked him and put them on the kitchen table. "I'll just get my coat."

When they arrived at the hall, she apologized, but asked anyway, "Should I be getting your truck keys from you now, or will you be OK to drive later?"

"If you're worried about me getting drunk, why did you ask me to come?"

"Because you're the only single male I know and I understand they're in short supply at these dances." As solemn as she kept her voice, she couldn't keep the teasing out of her eyes.

"I guess you won the lottery then."

She laughed and warned him, "I was already told, if I found a man to bring, I have to be willing to share."

He groaned. "Maybe I'll drop you off and come back for you later."

Grabbing him by the collar of his buckskin jacket, she warned him that no man had ever stood her up and lived to tell about it. It was his turn to laugh. He came around and opened her door then took her arm to guide her into the hall. Everyone noticed them immediately and the hall went silent.

Steve leaned forward and whispered. "See? They know what a mean bastard I am. You wouldn't listen."

"That's OK. I won't have to share you then."

Liz broke the silence by coming over and hugging Tory. She shook Steve's hand and insisted they sit at her table. Steve hung up their coats. When he returned to the table, introductions were made then Steve offered to get drinks.

As soon as he was out of earshot, Liz leaned over. "How in the world did you get Steve Turner to come to a dance?"

"I just asked him. Why?"

"He's a woman-hater. He'd cross the street to avoid talking to one."

"Maybe you just have to get to know him."

"Trust me, women have tried."

"Watch carefully. You may even see him laugh before the evening's over."

"Tory! You surprise me. And you've also upset Dr. Needy over there. I've never seen him looking so glum."

"Well I don't care. You can go comfort him, OK?"

"No way!" laughed Liz.

During the evening, Tory sensed Steve's discomfort in trying to make small talk. She knew he would rather be in the bar with a rum and Coke, so she was pleased when they served the meal promptly. Next to drinking, Steve liked eating. He did the buffet justice, commenting that the prime rib had been cooked just right. He was attentive to her, making sure her wine glass was full and even brought dessert for her. Of course, when she couldn't eat it all, he cleaned off her plate. There were a few speeches, but it wasn't long before the band was set up. As soon as the music started, Steve stood up, pulled Tory's chair out and led her to the dance floor.

He was an excellent dancer and led her around the floor in the two-step. When the music changed to a slower waltz, he held her close and moved smoothly once again around the dance floor. She caught Liz staring as they glided by and she couldn't help but wink at her friend. When Steve whispered in her ear and made her laugh as they went by the next time, Liz's mouth fell open even farther. After another waltz, the next set changed to the twist. Steve asked if she minded if they stopped for a breather.

There was no end to his surprises that evening. They did the polka, the rumba, the tango, and when a jitterbug started, he pulled out her chair once again. They were the center of attention. All the food he had eaten must have fueled his energy. When she begged off the second set of polkas, to her surprise he asked Liz if she were free for it and led her onto the floor.

During the last dance of the evening, he stared Tory straight in the eye and said, "You lied to me."

"What do you mean? I never lied about anything."

"You told me not once, but twice, that you would keep it secret that I can be nice once in awhile. Now the whole damn town knows."

"How is that my fault? You didn't have to be nice. You could have been your usual ornery self."

"I was going to be, but when I saw you looking so nice tonight, I just couldn't do it."

"Liz is going to wake up tomorrow morning positive that she was drunk and imagined the whole thing."

Steve laughed out loud just as Liz was dancing by with one of the town's volunteer firemen. The shocked look on Liz's face prompted Tory to grin at her and say, "I told you."

"What'd you tell her?" demanded Steve.

"That if she listened, she might even hear you laugh—out loud."

He laughed again and Tory spotted a glint in his eye that should have warned her that something was to come. The next time they passed

Liz, Steve snuggled his mouth near Tory's ear and nibbled on it. With that, Liz left the dance floor, grabbed a drink from their table, and downed it.

When the dance ended, Steve held Tory close and gave her one last squeeze before he led her back to their table.

When they arrived back at Tory's house, Steve thanked her for having invited him.

"I'm glad you enjoyed yourself. Had I known I was going out with Fred Astaire, I would have taken dancing lessons."

"I hope my reputation ain't ruined for good," he muttered as they pulled into the driveway. The truck stopped and he took her hand and looking down at it, said, "I think you were the best looking one at the dance."

Tory couldn't think of anything to say, not even a sarcastic comeback. Instead, she pulled her hand away and got out of the truck. She couldn't make eye contact with him but allowed him to walk her up the stairs and see her safely inside. When she finally did look up, she saw an amused smile.

"What?"

"Nothing." This time it was he who kissed her on the cheek. Then he left.

Sleep didn't come easily that night because Tory kept wondering what Steve had meant when he had warned her to be afraid of him. Was it too late? Had she led him on too far? Maybe she shouldn't have invited him to the dance? But deep down she was glad she had and she finally dozed off.

8

"JUST LIKE A WOMAN," STEVE'S voice crackled through the phone. "Is there an unwritten law somewhere that says it has to be thirty below outside before Christmas lights can be hung? Why didn't you ask me to hang them in October?"

"That's far too early. Besides I didn't think of it until this morning." She glared at the pile of lights on the table. "Why didn't you *offer* in October?"

"Christmas lights are the last thing on my mind in October. Getting wood and winterizing the house and the vehicles are on my mind. Along with getting the cattle in, shipping the ones sold to the packing houses, and getting the plows and snowmobiles in shape."

"There you are. You would have been far too busy in October."

"Holy old jumped up… Cripes, woman! Can it at least wait until I get my cattle fed?"

"Never mind. I don't need your sarcasm, I'll do it myself." She hung up.

Fifteen minutes later, she was on the front porch unraveling the long cords when he pulled into her driveway. He clumped up the steps and bodily lifted her out of the way.

"Get inside. No point both of us getting pneumonia."

She didn't comply but instead watched as he stomped off the steps and went behind the house to return moments later with a ladder.

"What can I help with?" she asked.

"You can help by staying the hell out of my way is how you can help."

It was her turn to storm and stomp away. *That ornery little runt better put them up where I want them, or else. Who the hell does he think he is talking to me that way?* Breathing deeply, she forced herself to calm down, then went inside to watch out the window.

He had barely started up the ladder when he climbed back down and opened the front door.

Tory turned away. She had calmed down, but refused to get involved in another argument. Besides, tears were threatening and there was no way she wanted him to see those.

"Sorry, OK?" He shut the door behind him. "I don't even know how you want these damn things set up."

She didn't respond.

"OK. So I need your help." He pulled her to him and put his arms around her.

"I hate being dependent. This is the part I don't like about owning a house. At least in my apartment I can do everything for myself. And I didn't mean that you had to stop everything you were doing and come running right this minute, you know."

"I know you didn't. I was worried you were going to do something stupid like going up that ladder by yourself. And you were, weren't you? I was right, wasn't I?"

"I was just trying to show you that I don't need you."

He lifted her chin and kissed her. "Well. I need you."

He was about to take her in his arms again but she took a step back and pushed him away from her.

He appeared stunned. Was speechless for a moment then, "No, no.

I didn't mean it like that. I don't need you in my *bed*. I need you in my *life*. If I didn't have you to growl at, who would I have?"

"So what you want is somebody to verbally browbeat daily?"

"Maybe not daily."

"You confuse me. You warn me away from you. Tell me to remember you're not a nice person. Then you tell me you need me. What am I supposed to believe?"

"Put the teapot on, Tory. We have to talk."

She took her jacket and gloves off while he removed his boots and put his gloves by the fireplace to dry. Then he followed her into the kitchen and sat at the table. He noticed the opened box of chocolates and helped himself to one. When the tea was ready she poured some for him, then stood leaning against the sink.

"Come here," he said. "Sit down by me."

She hesitated, but he pulled a chair out for her and moved it closer to him. She sat slowly, eyeing him warily.

"I'm not going to bite you. When I told you I'm not nice, I meant it. I'm an old drunk, totally unreliable. Just when you think you can rely on me, I'll let you down. That's a given. I've been in and out of jail all my life.

"My father died when I was still in diapers. My mother kept me for a while then dropped me at an orphanage. I'm told she became a whore and eventually she died, too. I was in and out of a bunch of foster homes. The ones I didn't run away from, the foster parents usually ended up bringing me back to the orphanage. I took off for the final time when I was a teenager and worked on the west coast boats. I worked my way inland. Ended up here. Miss Lottie was the only person ever believed there was something more to me than troublemaker. She gave me work, then I worked the farm I now own. She co-signed the loan that helped me buy it when the owner died." His breath caught and his voice wavered as he continued. "She stuck by me all these years. There isn't anything I wouldn't have done for her."

"Do you hate women because of your mother?"
"Partly."
"Were you ever married?"
He hesitated. "For a while."
"What happened?"
"I killed her."
"You... killed your wife?"
"Yes, and I would do it again."
Tory pulled back, repulsed.
Steve stared into his teacup.
Tory sighed. "What happened?"

"It was while I was working the boats. I met Trixie in Vancouver. I was hardly twenty. She used to let me stay at her place when I was in port. She got pregnant. We got married. We had a little boy. His name was Jimmy. He was only about a year and half old when I got a call on the fishing boat I was working. I had to get back to port. My son was in the hospital. A helicopter picked me up and brought me back. By the time I got to the hospital, he was dead. I found out she'd been entertaining a boyfriend who got drunk and didn't like Jimmy crying so he punched the little guy in the head. At the trial, Trixie testified on behalf of her boyfriend, saying he didn't know what he was doing because he was drunk. The guy got three years for manslaughter. He was out in two.

"When I went to our apartment and confronted Trixie, she laughed at me. She asked me what the hell I thought she was supposed to be doing with her spare time while I was gone. I asked her how she could testify for the bastard who killed our son. She told me not to take it too hard, that she had never been sure if Jimmy was even mine. She said it probably weren't any of my business anyway."

Steve looked at Tory through tear-drenched eyes. "I knew he was mine. I had a picture of me taken by a foster family I stayed with for a while when I was real little. Jimmy was the spittin' image of me. I lost control. I started slapping her around. She fell and hit her head. Hard. Never woke up. I was charged with second-degree murder but it got changed to manslaughter. I got seven years for it. If that ain't a crock of shit! The guy that killed an innocent kid gets two years. I kill a heartless bitch and get seven.

Tory put her hand on his arm and squeezed.

He continued. "I spent my time in the medium security in Edmonton and when I was released, found my way down to Red Deer. Worked in a gas station for a while. Owner—the asshole—was audited by income tax and was skimming the daily take. He pleaded innocent and his wife testified I done it. Because of my previous record, I got five more years. Halfway through my term he was caught again and finally admitted I was innocent.

"I saw an ad in the Calgary paper for a handyman needed to work for room and board and a small allowance. I phoned and asked if it was too late to apply. I hitched a ride and got here by noon the same day. It was Miss Lottie's ad. When I saw her, my first thought was 'Now here's a lady who'll never hire a guy like me.' No way was I going to tell her anything about my past. She got it out of me, though. She knew just the right questions to ask and fixed me a look I'll never forget. She asked me to give her one good reason why she should hire me. I told her I would work harder and faster than anybody else. She thought for a minute then told me to take her car into town and get a haircut and some clean clothes, that I was to start the next morning and she didn't want me looking like a bum. I worked for her for four years. Then she retired. Didn't need me full time anymore so she spoke to Mr. Godfrey who owned my farm back then and he hired me four days a week. I stayed with him and came two days a week to Miss Lottie's. When he died a few years later, she knew how much I wanted the farm and offered to co-sign a loan. She even gave me a character reference at the bank. Imagine that! I worked hard and made the ranch better than it ever was. I got the mortgage paid off in half the time. The only thing is I started finding the winters long and I'd come into town and get drunk. I started seeing a waitress at one of the restaurants down closer to Calgary. I thought we had a thing going and just when I was about to pop the question, I find out she took off with a transport truck driver. I started drinking heavier and ended up in jail more than a few times for getting into fights. Or just being plain old drunk and disorderly. Miss Lottie had to come bail me out a few times. And she never judged me. Just asked me to take better care of myself. She wanted me to join AA but never nagged about it. She knew everything about me, but nothing ever got passed on to nobody. She's the only woman I ever trusted. I don't have much use for females. Now you know why."

"Now I know everything about you."

"Now you know everything about me."

"Why have you revealed all this to me now?"

"I got a feeling you and me are going to be neighbors for a long time. I can't see you giving up this house. I figure we get along OK. You don't scare easy and I miss my old neighbor. I miss having someone who knows me and accepts me anyway. I need a friend and I guess you're it. When you started kissing me on the cheek and all, I got real uncomfortable. I thought you were another female who was going to take off one day. Then I realized kissing's just your way and you don't mean anything by it."

"But I do mean something by it." When his head came up swiftly to look at her, she explained, "I am an affectionate person. You're right, I do tend to hug and kiss—but only people I like."

"You're saying you like me then?"

"Steve, we get along well. More or less, anyway," she smiled. "And you are right, I don't scare easily. I miss having people around me that I care about. I still think you're an ornery son-of-a-bitch but I need a friend, too, so I guess we're stuck with each other."

"You don't care that I killed a woman and done hard time?"

"What I care about is how you treat *me*. You get mean with me, our friendship is history."

"I thought maybe you were trying to manipulate me into doing things for you. I hate women who try to trap men. I mean *especially* that kind of women." Tory could see the hint of a grin on the corner of his mouth.

"I think we have a pretty good thing going here," she said. "You like my cooking and baking and I like your muscles when I need them. If you think I'm going to be staying, next year you can put my lights up in October or whenever it damn well suits you. Just don't wait till December and then holler at me if I ask you to do it. But it doesn't matter, because I won't be here anyway."

"You'll be here. You like the way I dance."

Tory burst out laughing and Steve followed suit. They stood and headed arm in arm toward the front door again.

"Just promise me that if I can't get here when you snap your fingers, you won't go climbing any ladders or using any chainsaws or such."

"Promise. But I am coming out to tell you exactly where you can put the Christmas lights."

9

THE NEXT DAY STEVE ROARED in on his snowmobile towing a toboggan. "Get dressed up warm then climb on behind me."

"Where are we going?"

"No way I'm picking out a Christmas tree for you. There'll be no pleasing you."

She bundled up quickly and jumped on and they took off for the bush in the high country behind her place. She loved weaving in and out around the fir trees and trying to spot animal tracks in the snow. The absolute quiet was overwhelming when they stopped and Steve had turned the motor off. Several seconds passed before she realized she had stopped breathing.

"Nothing quite like it, is there?" His voice was thunder echoing around them.

"I understand why men live alone in the mountains. I could stay here forever." She was whispering.

"We'll come back again."

It didn't take long before they found the tree. The sound of the axe chopping through cold, hard wood echoed back from the hills around them and after the tree was tied to the toboggan, they headed home, Tory reluctantly.

Back at Tory's, together they nestled the tree in the area between the corner windows on the opposite wall from the fireplace.

By Friday, Tory was so wound up waiting for her family to arrive in their rented SUV, she couldn't concentrate on anything. She had rearranged the decorations so many times—except for the tree, which was a family event—she was afraid she was wearing them out. She kept peeping out the window, imagining she heard vehicles coming into her yard. Finally, they arrived with horn blaring, and hooting and hollering through rolled-down windows.

Tory ran onto the front steps to greet them and Josh and Maggie came running up with arms extended for a giant hug. Both started talking at once, each wanting to be the first to tell her everything. Ian and Becky were left to bring everything in from the vehicle as Tory set milk for hot chocolate on the stove and helped the children get out of their winter outer garments. Two hours later there was still so much noise and commotion that no one had noticed Steve at the back door.

"Hello. *Hello!* Are you all deaf?" he called out. "Hey."

Ian was the one who heard him and held out his hand to introduce himself.

"I'm Tory's neighbor," said Steve. "Just wondering if maybe the kids want to go for a snowmobile ride. Put some hay out for the deer."

Eight-year-old Maggie, the older child, called out. "We'll be able to see them?"

"Some days they're around and other days not. No guarantees."

Josh didn't have to be asked twice and ran for his ski suit.

Their mother, Becky, however, was skeptical and whispered to Tory, "Is he a safe driver?" Tory reassured her that she need have no qualms about that at all.

When the children were dressed and safely tucked into the sleigh hooked on the back of the snowmobile, Steve drove off, promising to return them in an hour or so.

"What a nice neighbor, Mom. He's not that mean old guy you were telling me about then."

"One and the same. He has his moments. He was a wonderful neighbor to Aunt Lottie and he's been very kind to me. Helps me with a lot of things around here. I'm afraid he doesn't have a lot of patience with city women. Any women, really. He barks a lot but it's definitely worse than his bite."

"You don't think he'll frighten the children, do you?"

"Never. He loves children."

True to his word, he had the children home again in just over an hour and Tory asked him to stay for supper. He declined saying he didn't want to barge in on their first evening together but Tory stared him down. "That's hog wash. I wouldn't ask if I didn't want you to stay."

He still declined so she shrugged and told him to suit himself. "Just as well. We're only having stew with dumplings and deep dish apple pie for dessert, anyway."

Ian let out a hoot. "If you can pass on that, you're not human."

"Please stay, Mr. Turner," said Josh, his big brown eyes looking up at him.

Steve relented. "But I have to leave right after."

This promise he did not fulfill as he ended up eating his usual two helpings of everything and staying until 10:00.

Tory walked him to the door, kissed his cheek and thanked him for taking the children for a snowmobile ride.

"If the weather's nice one of these days, I can hitch up the big sleigh to the horses and take 'em for a sleigh ride into town. Think they'd like that?"

"They would. Absolutely. Now as for you, you have to come over tomorrow afternoon for the tree trimming party."

He seemed at a loss for words at first but left the house mumbling something that sounded to Tory like, "Christmas used to be much quieter around here."

The following day, all the Christmas tree decorations were sorted and new hooks put in the ones that were missing. Tory ended up teary-eyed several times as she recognized ornaments from childhood Christmases she had enjoyed here. Memories of her parents, grandparents and of Aunt Lottie came flooding back. She couldn't help but wonder whether someday her grandchildren might look back on this particular Christmas with fond memories of its being special. She hoped so.

Around 3:00, Steve arrived with a bag full of pinecones that he'd picked around his yard earlier in the season. While the women decided how to decorate with them, the men strung the lights on the Christmas tree then the children took over to place what ornaments they could reach up to hang. Then they all took a break for hot chocolate and Rice Krispies squares. By the time the tree was bedecked in all its splendor, it was already dark outside. Four-year-old Josh, because he was the youngest, was allowed to turn the tree light switch on to everyone's delight. Tory switched bulbs until she was happy with the final color arrangement.

A supper of lasagna and cheesecake dessert ended the evening.

On the afternoon of Christmas Eve, Steve came with the horses and sleigh and enough warm blankets for everyone. Tory and Becky filled Thermoses with hot chocolate and coffee, and Ian filled a wineskin for him and Steve. The day was warmer than the previous few but some clouds were moving in as well; the sun managed to break through just often enough to keep the day from being gloomy. Ian sat up front with Steve and the women and children faced each other in the sleigh. The two big work horses trotted proudly in front, jingling the bells Steve had hung from their harnesses. It wasn't long before the singing started and by the time they had run the gamut of most of the carols they knew, the hot chocolate and wine had run out. A couple of hours had passed and the sun was slowly sinking behind the mountains in the west. The snow had held off and the children were red-cheeked and giggling when Steve lifted them onto the horses' backs for picture taking while there was still enough light.

Ian read a couple of Christmas stories that he had found on the Internet and they watched a Christmas special on television. Then it was time for the children to don their pajamas and hang their stockings before singing the bedtime Christmas carols. Tory had knit Becky a large stocking when she was a child and when she married Ian he also received a hand-knit stocking. The tradition continued with the birth of each of the grandchildren and they had insisted that Grandma knit one for herself. Each stocking was personalized in some way: Josh's had a racecar stitched into it and Maggie's had a figure skater. Because Tory always spent Christmas with them, they kept the stockings at their place but had remembered to pack them with all the things they brought. One by one, they hung them from little ornaments placed across the mantel.

When Josh had hung his stocking, he turned to Tory. "That's not fair. We all have a stocking except Mr. Turner."

"I don't live here, Josh," he smiled. "There's no need for a stocking for me on your mantel."

"But Grandma said you found our Christmas tree and you put the lights up outside and you took us for a sleigh ride. You *almost* live here."

"Josh," said Tory. "Do something for Grandma?"

"Sure," he nodded.

"Go look on the shelf under the end table. Open the box there."

Josh did as requested and as soon as he opened the box, his eyes lit up and he grinned from ear to ear as he pulled another Christmas stocking from the box. He ran over and climbed onto Steve's lap "Look,

Mr. Turner. A stocking for you, it has your name on it and everything. Let's see what picture Grandma knit for you."

Steve turned several shades of red before he paled somewhat. He couldn't take his eyes off the stocking that Josh was holding for everyone to see. Knitted into the side of it was a cowboy sitting on a black horse, with a snow-capped mountain in the background and two fir trees near the rider.

"Grandma must like you a lot, Mr. Turner. You got the best one."

It was Tory's turn to blush several shades of red, but Maggie broke the moment by announcing it was time to sing some carols and then put out a plate for Santa and the reindeer. This was the time reserved for religious carols about the birth of Christ and peace on earth. They wanted to remind the children that it wasn't all about gifts. There was a reason for the season.

Steve took out his hanky and blew his nose several times before Becky and Ian took the children into the kitchen to fix the plate for Santa. While they were in the other room, he finally moved to sit beside Tory on the sofa. "I don't know what to say. I never expected to be included like this with your family and... the stocking..." He turned away but not before Tory saw the tears on his cheeks.

She reached for his face and turned it toward her. "You're family, Steve. Like Josh said, you almost live here. How would I get by without you?"

Just then Josh and Maggie came in to say good night and to kiss their grandmother.

"Now you gotta come back in the morning to see what Santa put in your stocking," Josh told Steve.

"I have to look after my animals in the morning, Josh."

"Then we have to wait. But can you maybe hurry?"

Steve laughed then looked over at Tory for help but she shrugged and said, "You heard him. We'll wait."

Becky led the children upstairs but Josh came flying back down. "I forgot to give Mr. Turner a goodnight kiss." And he climbed back up onto Steve's lap, wrapped his arms around Steve's neck to plant a kiss on his cheek.

A few coffees and sweets later, Tory walked Steve to the back door and after he had donned his jacket and gotten his boots on, he turned to her and tried to mouth some words that just wouldn't come. She smiled, leaned into him and kissed him on the mouth. "Merry Christmas, Steve. We'll see you in the morning."

He stared, then walked out mumbling something about "… cattle and Christmas don't mix."

It seemed to Tory like she had just put her head down when she was awakened by shrieking and hollering, and fists pounding on a door. She lifted her head and realized it was her door that was being attacked and little voices begging her to come downstairs.

"Mom says we can't open anything till you come and join us, Grandma. Can you hurry?"

"Right away, Josh. Just give me a minute to comb my hair and put on my robe."

Tory washed her face and ran a pick through her hair and trundled off down the stairs. "What time is it anyway? I feel like I just went to bed."

Ian answered sarcastically that it was very late, already 5:15 AM. "The children think they slept in. It's two hours later here."

"Oh, no," moaned Tory. "I forgot about the jet lag. And hey there, Josh. I thought you told Mr. Turner you were going to wait for him before you opened your gifts."

"Oh, Grandma, he's so late. Could you phone him? Tell him to hurry up?"

"No, I won't." She shuddered to think what Steve might say to her, telling him to get over here right this minute. "But you can. His number is by the phone."

Josh jumped up and ran into the kitchen and soon they could hear his voice but not the words. He came skipping back into the room with the news that Steve would be here in half an hour. All the time he was talking, he was looking at the gaily wrapped parcels spread around the tree.

It wasn't long before Steve's truck pulled in and Josh ran to open the door. "Put your boots on the mat. Put your jacket on the chair. Grandma'll hang it up for you. C'mon, Mr. Turner. Let's go."

Steve, his arms loaded with wrapped parcels, did his best to comply as Josh ran back and forth to the tree with the gifts. "I'm a disgrace to all kids my age sleeping in on Christmas morning, aren't I?" laughed Steve.

When the stockings were opened, a smile from Steve told Tory that her choice of Old Spice toiletries had been a good one.

"My dad says Old Spice is for old men," offered Josh. "Grandpa Hardisty uses it. You're not old, Mr. Turner. Santa must of made a mistake."

Steve winked at Ian. "No. Santa didn't make a mistake. He knows that wearing it makes all the old ladies want to kiss me on the cheek."

"Yuck," spouted Josh, then quickly lost interest in the subject. "Can I open this one now?" He patted one of the large packages.

"We'll open them one at a time," said Tory. "Daddy will choose."

Ian made a big production about which parcel he was going to choose next for each person so even the children were interested in what the adults received.

When he handed Steve one from Tory, Steve seemed quite taken aback. "I thought the stocking and the Old Spice *in* the stocking were my presents. What's this now?"

"Everyone gets their stocking filled *and* a present, Mr. Turner." This came from Maggie.

When Steve lifted the lid off the box and saw the sweater, he was clearly pleased. "I'll be wearing it to the next hockey game." He refolded the sweater and as he was placing it back in the box, he paused, picked up a photo-sized package that had slipped into a corner, and opened it. His gasp was audible.

"I found it in one of her photo albums," said Tory.

"What is it?" Josh asked.

Tory could tell that the photograph had affected Steve to the point of silence and almost regretted giving it to him in front of everyone. She pitched in for him. "It's a picture of Mr. Turner and Great-aunt Lottie. It was taken a few years ago."

"Lemme see. Lemme see," said Josh moving to Steve's side and looking at the photo.

Steve took the opportunity to look over at Tory. His eyes had morphed into a soft shade of blue the color of mountain skies. If his could ever be called warm, they were at that moment. When his lips turned down at the corners, she again eased the situation by saying, "You're welcome. Whose turn next?"

"It's for you, Mom."

Tory took the large parcel from Ian. The sticker said TO TORY FROM STEVE. "What in the world...?" Upon opening the box, she burst out laughing. Inside a lidded picnic basket was all the equipment necessary for a roadside emergency, including a first aid kit.

"You're stubborn," said Steve, recovered from his brief moment of emotion, "just like Lottie was. Neither of you thought of equipping yourself for driving."

Tory examined each item, thanking Steve profusely and making him squirm. "But all I really need is a cell phone—to call you." And she winked at him.

This made Steve turn beet red but he covered with: "I still say women should never be allowed behind the steering wheel of any vehicle."

"Mom?" piped up Josh. "Does that mean you can't take us to McDonald's anymore?"

"Of course not, honey," said Becky. "Mr. Turner's just teasing Grandma. Who's next?"

Ian handed Tory the last parcel which was a small one done up in the same wrapping paper as the emergency picnic basket Steve had given to her. Steve shifted in his chair as she opened it. It was her turn to gasp. Nestled in tissue was a wrought-iron pin that clearly had been worked by a skilled blacksmith. It was a tiny horseshoe fastened to a bar with a small amethyst covering the little spike. It had been the symbol of the Lucky Bar Ranch, the ranch that her aunt's house had been a part of two generations before.

"Who made this, Steve? It's beautiful."

"Um. Me."

"I'll treasure it always. Did you know that amethyst is the provincial stone for Ontario?" Becky helped pin it to her housecoat and she stood up proudly, turning so everyone could see it. "It's beautiful," she repeated. "Thank you."

"That's the last of them," said Ian.

Becky clapped her hands. "Go wash up. Breakfast, then church."

With minimal grumbling, the children ran off.

Steve rose. "Not for me. I have chores to do." He started for the door. "But since you insist…" he laughed. "I *will* stay for breakfast, though."

After breakfast, the children went back to examining their Christmas presents while Becky and Ian collected the dishes. Tory walked Steve to the door where, as they both reached for the other's hands at the same time, what started as a simple brush of the lips ended up as a full-blown kiss.

It was only a few moments later that Tory got a phone call from Steve.

"After you're done with church and supper…" he started.

"You don't have to wait for an invitation, Steve. Of course, you're coming for Christmas dinner this evening. I thought that was understood."

"Yeah," he responded. "I know. And I'll be there. It's just…" He paused again. "Would you come with me after supper? While I go visit a friend?"

"Go out with you after supper? It might be quite late. We have to clean up, do the dishes…"

"He's a neighbor. A long-time neighbor."

In the background, Becky was waving and nodding frantically at Tory, telling her to *go go go* in hand signals.

"Well. OK. What should I wear?"

"Women! Doesn't matter what you wear, dammit! You'd look beautiful in sackcloth and ashes. I'll see you later." And he hung up.

10

ALTHOUGH THE DRIVEWAY WAS WELL plowed and the steps and front porch were all neatly shoveled, the house they pulled up to was rather neglected and there was only one window showing any light, all lending the place a forlorn ambience. Steve reached for a parcel from the back seat of the truck and came around to open Tory's door.

On the porch, Steve knocked then entered. He took Tory's coat and hung it with his on a coat tree in the vestibule.

"Awfully quiet. Are you sure your friend isn't in bed?" she asked.

"He's expecting me." Steve guided her, hand under her elbow, into a small parlor off the front hallway. Cowboys and Indians chased each other on a black and white television screen while a very old man slept in the chair in the opposite corner. Tory guessed him to be over ninety.

"Alfred?" said Steve. "Hello, Alfred. Wake up, man. You've got company."

The old man's eyes connected to Tory's face first and he was startled.

"Alfred, I brought a pretty lady to brighten up your Christmas for you."

Alfred smiled.

"This is Tory Hardisty. She's Miss Lottie's niece and has moved into the old farmhouse. Tory, this is my old friend, Alfred Potter."

"Merry Christmas, Mr. Potter."

"Well, my Christmases are quiet these days but it sure is nice to see a fresh, pretty face come around to visit. This your girlfriend, Steve?"

Steve didn't hesitate. "She's a lady friend, Alfred. Just a lady friend. I'm too old for girlfriends."

"Well you always were a bit slow on the charm. I'm surprised this one puts up with your miserable disposition. She must be deaf and blind. Are you, girl?"

Smiling, Tory sat near the old man and replied, "No, just a little meaner than he is, that's all." She had brought one of her gift baskets filled with Christmas baking and put it on the table.

Alfred's grin widened. "Steve, make this smart lady a drink and get something for yourself while you're at it." To Tory, he said, "I'm afraid I don't have any fancy booze, just rye and rum."

"Rye happens to be my favorite, Mr. Potter."

Steve put the drinks on the table between their chairs and handed Alfred the gift he had brought. The old man issued only a mild protest before sliding his fingers under the tape. It was a rolled-collar, heavy-knit cardigan fastened with Velcro in the front. Tory guessed it had come from a specialty store for people with disabilities. As Steve helped the old man try it on, Tory saw that the old man's fingers were deformed into arthritic claws.

"This is a good one, Steve. I'll be able to do it up by myself. Dang manufacturers keep making zipper tabs smaller and smaller all the time."

Again she was amazed by Steve's thoughtfulness. They sat and talked for over an hour with Alfred regaling Tory with stories about the old days in the area. Then rather abruptly, he stated that while he had enjoyed their visit, it was time for them to go.

Steve laughed. "I might not be much of a charmer according to you, Alfred, but you yourself could never be accused of having tact."

The old man insisted on walking them to the door. "Have to lock the house up, anyway."

Tory kissed his cheek and told him she was very happy to have met him while he held her hand and thanked her for brightening up his Christmas and for bringing the baking.

After he and Steve shared a warm hug and a prolonged handshake, the old man took out his handkerchief and blew his nose. "Run along now, you two, and don't hold that door open too long."

Back in the truck, Tory asked how old the man was. She was floored when Steve said, "Alfred? He's ninety-nine."

"And he lives here all by himself?"

"Yep. Won't give you the time of day if you mention nursing home to him. Says he was born in that house and he'll die in that house. He's begged me not to let anyone take him away."

"But who looks after him?"

"Guess I do mostly. I arranged for someone to come from town once every two weeks and give his house a cleaning, change the bedding and do his laundry. I help him with a bath once a week and try to bring him some warm meals. He manages to make himself porridge in the morning and I open a bunch of cans of soup for him whenever I go see him. Keeps them in the fridge. I drive by every evening and make sure there's a light on. He doesn't want me coming every day and babying him so I try to do some things without him knowing."

"You did that for Aunt Lottie, too, didn't you?"

"Neither one had anybody."

"You scared the heck out of me that one night sitting on the road in front of the house. I thought you were a peeping Tom or something."

"Old habits die hard. Sorry I scared you." He gave her a sheepish grin.

They rode home in silence. When they pulled into Tory's driveway,

Steve took her hand before he got out of the truck and just stared without speaking while he held it. Finally he said in a quiet voice, "I've never had a Christmas like this. Miss Lottie and I used to eat together, or I'd go over to old Alfred's, so I was never alone. But this is the first time I've felt like it really was Christmas. Your kids and grandkids are great. But so's their grandmother. I used to think it was all lost in gift giving but I can see that with your family, even the giving is done in a special kind of way. I'll never forget this holiday, Tory. Thank you."

He pulled her hand to his mouth and kissed the inside of her palm. Then he cleared his throat and jumped out of the truck.

Tory's eyes had filled up by the time he opened her door. "Thanks for helping me realize just how lucky I am," she said, looking Steve directly in the eye. "And thank you for introducing me to Alfred. This was a wonderful way to end a wonderful day."

Steve put his arm around her and gave her a warm squeeze then saw her inside the house. She watched him back down the driveway and wished that all the people in town could know him as she did. To them he was the town drunk, just a miserable old man who drank too much. If only they knew.

11

Tory's family stayed until the morning of New Year's Eve. She had tried to talk them into staying through that holiday as well but Ian had to work the day after. "It'll take us a whole day just to put all this Christmas stuff away," Ian laughed. "Even without the things Steve is shipping for us." To Maggie he said, "You have your Barbie?"

"Yeah," Maggie answered pulling Barbie out of her jacket. "Grandma's boyfriend's really nice. Isn't he, Mom?"

"We're all set then?" Ian asked.

"Wait a minute, young lady," Tory added quickly. "Mr. Turner is not Grandma's boyfriend. He's a very good neighbor and a close friend. That's all."

Maggie's smile broadened.

"He used to take care of Aunt Lottie and now he's taking good care of me."

"That's too bad. I was hoping it was more than that, Mom," said Becky.

Tory couldn't believe her ears. "What do you mean that's too bad?"

"He's such a nice man and you've been alone for so long. I was hoping you might have found someone to share the rest of your life with."

"I had a man to share part of my life with and you know how that turned out. I don't need, nor do I want, a man. I am quite capable of living on my own. As you well know. Why would I want to start cooking and cleaning for somebody at this stage in my life?"

"Don't you get lonely?" asked Becky as Ian began taking parcels and luggage out to the car.

"I have friends. I go out when I want company. Steve's available when something comes up. We've even gone dancing. I do not want to be tripping over a man on a daily basis. Thank you for your concern but I'm quite fine. I'm not even sure I'll be staying here. I said I'd try it for six months and I meant it."

"How are you liking it so far?"

"I'm liking it fine. I'll see what January and February bring before I say any more."

"All packed," said Ian. "Let's go, kids."

"Well, I miss you being just a couple of hours away, but I can see that you fit in here better than in Peterborough. You have more going on here for one thing. Everybody thinks you're terrific. Every time I went into town they were asking if I was Tory Hardisty's daughter because they want me to talk you into staying."

"You and your gang better get going or you'll miss your plane." Tory prodded them toward the door. "Phone me as soon as you get home. Love you, and love you, too, little Miss Muffet. Give your grandma a kiss." After hugging and kissing Ian and Josh, too, then rushing out with Josh's Game Boy that he had left on the hall table, they were finally on their way.

Tory knew the house would be awfully quiet for a week or so, but hoped she would be able to settle in to a routine once she got over the "missing" part.

She had sent several containers of turkey soup and a couple

containers of turkey stew over to Alfred's with Steve. She made up her mind that she was going to make sure she took him a casserole a couple of times a week, and baking too. *Poor old guy, living on porridge and soup. Why the hell hadn't Steve said something?*

January turned bitterly cold and Tory was glad when Steve offered to take her into town for her groceries and things. At least his truck was warm by the time he got to her house and she didn't have to walk far in the cold. He would just drop her off at the door to the supermarket and come back an hour later. Her wood supply, which she thought was going to last at least two years, was getting down close to the ground. If it stayed this cold for much longer, she'd have to think about getting another load in. She worried about old Alfred in this cold, but knew that Steve was checking on him regularly. All it would take would be his furnace going out and that old uninsulated house would cool to dangerous levels in no time. She shuddered at the thought of him freezing to death in his bed. He was hard of hearing so refused a telephone which he said he couldn't hear anybody on anyway. He also refused to leave his house even when Tory invited him for Sunday suppers.

Toward the end of January, Liz called to invite Tory to a girl's weekend in Calgary. Two other women from town wanted to spend a day and a night. "We'll all have facials, manis and pedis, and do some shopping. Take in a movie. Maybe even a play. What do you say? You'd make up the foursome."

"Exactly what I need to dispel the January blahs," Tory answered.

She alerted Steve of her upcoming absence in case he noticed inactivity at her place.

The four women, Liz, Tory, Linda (who had made their appointments in Calgary) and Mary Ann were on the highway by 9:00 on Friday morning. The day was sunny with intermittent cloud and still quite cold.

The afternoon was filled with taxi drives to a full body massage, a facial and a manicure for Tory and saunas, hair colorings and pedicures for Liz and Mary Ann. Linda opted for a hair styling make-over and she had been able to get tickets to a symphony performance of Broadway tunes which would follow one of the hotel's famous prime rib beef dinners. The hotel was also known throughout Calgary for their desserts.

"What more can any woman want, except a good man?" asked Mary Ann, setting her dessert fork down on her empty plate.

"Show me a good man and I'll show you a married one," exclaimed Liz. "You know there are no good single ones around."

"Who said he had to be single?" giggled Mary Ann.

After the Broadway performance, they stopped in the hotel's piano bar planning for one nightcap. But the piano player sang and a bass player added an extra flourish to the entertainment which consisted of plenty of Johnny Mercer tunes. And they even took requests so the women stayed until the bar closed.

The next morning Tory slept in until 8:30 which was unusual for her, but an hour later at breakfast, the other women all admitted to having slept in, too. And couldn't wait to get shopping.

Tory took advantage of the opportunity of being in the big Calgary stores and picked up a lot of Easter-oriented craft materials to work on and donate to the hospital and her church's annual Spring Tea.

"You should buy something for yourself," chided Liz. "You never do."

"I don't need anything."

"When we go on these weekends, Tory, we don't buy what we *need*, we buy something we *want*. That's part of the fun."

"OK. I'll get some work socks for Steve. Every time he takes his work boots off, I swear the holes are bigger than the last time."

"Get something for yourself," said Mary Ann.

"This is for myself," Tory laughed. "I'd rather bake bread for a man than darn his socks."

"I hear you," said Mary Ann and both Linda and Liz smiled agreement.

Tory was back home with her parcels by late afternoon and was surprised to see that the note she had left for Steve was still propped against the canisters on the counter.

Friday's mail had been nothing but flyers and she used these to start the fireplace, even though the furnace was running. Then she called Steve but there was no answer. *He'll be around as soon as he's finished doing whatever he's doing.*

After putting all her purchases upstairs in her sewing room and unpacking her suitcase, she checked the freezer for what might be there to heat up for her supper. *I'll take out this big container of stew,* she decided. *Steve will be over later.* She made tea and turned on the TV but there wasn't much on except reruns so she soon dozed off, not waking until after dark. Her stew had defrosted so she called Steve again. Once more, the phone rang with no answer. "I'm glad I like stew," she said aloud, looking at the big container of it on the counter.

She slept fitfully, waking often and wondering if something had happened to Albert or if Steve had spent the whole afternoon and evening drinking in town. By morning she had her answer.

At 6:45, the phone rang and she grabbed it. "Steve?"

"No, honey. It's Liz."

"Liz. What— what is it? Has something happened to Steve?"

"No. He's fine but he's in big trouble."

"What do you mean by big trouble, Liz?"

"He's been arrested for murder."

12

T ORY ALMOST DROPPED THE PHONE. "Murder? Who?"
"Do you remember when we were at the bar one night us telling you about those two little girls whose father had abused them and their mother?"

Feeling an unease in the pit of her stomach Tory waited for Liz to finish.

"The mother was found murdered in her home the day before yesterday. It looked like she put up quite a struggle. I can't tell you any more than that without breaching hospital policy on privacy."

"Why would they arrest Steve? What about her husband?"

"They took fingerprints and Steve's were the only ones they found. It seems he has a record, Tory. He was in prison a long time ago for a murder similar to this one."

"I know."

"You know? And you still let him come around? Tory, were you not afraid? When I think of him being around there when Miss MacArthur was alive... well, I'm glad nothing happened to her."

"Liz, please don't judge prematurely. Where is he now?"

"He's being detained in a cell down at the RCMP office."

"Thanks for calling, Liz."

Tory was shaking by the time she hung up the phone. *Well, that explains why you're not answering your phone, Steve.* After a shower and a cup of coffee, Tory decided to go into town to find out what was going to happen to Steve, and whether she might be allowed to see him.

A tall, lanky Mountie guided her to a large room where Steve sat with his wrists in cuffs and his ankles in irons. He looked up when the door opened but those cold gray eyes immediately flashed with anger when he saw that it was Tory coming in. The Mountie told her to sit on the opposite side of the table.

Steve's eyes lowered to the floor.

"I can't go away for two lousy days without you getting yourself into trouble," she whispered harshly.

"This is no place for you. Go home."

"And what am I to do there?"

"I don't want you here. I don't want you involved in this."

"I'm your friend so I'm already involved. Do you have a lawyer?"

"I don't know any lawyers."

She hoped he was being a little more cooperative with the police than he was with her. She wished she knew exactly what had happened.

Tory turned to the Mountie and asked what was happening. She wanted to know what Steve was being charged with and why.

"Can't tell you much, ma'am, other than we're holding him for the murder of Joanne Dimmery."

"Has he been charged? Is he allowed bail? Will he be staying here?"

"He hasn't been formally charged, but there will be a bail hearing as soon as we can get a Justice of the Peace here. I'd be surprised if he's granted bail though. Because of the criminal record. Probably depend if he's charged with first- or second-degree. So most likely he'll go to Calgary. Heard you asking him about a lawyer. He's got a court-appointed one for now. Until he decides if he wants to be represented by one of his own choosing."

Tory moved toward Steve but the Mountie instructed her to keep her distance.

"That's good advice, woman. Keep a big distance away and don't be coming near here at all."

"Steve. Please. Let me see about getting you a good lawyer."

"I can take care of myself. I don't need you meddling in my affairs."

"If you're trying to scare me off, forget it. I told you before, I don't scare easily."

He looked over at her then and asked why she was there.

"Because I don't believe you did it, and I can't sit at home doing nothing while they've got you locked up in here for something you didn't do."

"How do you know I didn't?"

"Did you?"

"Hell no! But you don't know that."

"I know you, and if you say you didn't do it, then you didn't do it."

He mumbled something about damn stubborn women and got up and paced the floor. The Mountie never took his eyes off Steve.

"You're probably the only person in town that believes me. Pretty soon nobody will believe you either."

She wanted to shake him and hug him simultaneously. How could one man look so mean and ornery and so forlorn at the same time?

"Let me see about a lawyer, Steve."

"Damn it, Tory, no!

"And who's going to clean my driveway with you sitting in jail? I've got a vested interest in your freedom, Steve Turner."

He shook his head. "Don't you understand the word no? Get the hell out of here and get the hell out of my life. The last thing on my mind right now is your damn driveway."

The Mountie took Tory's elbow. "I think you better leave, ma'am.

Don't want him getting violent with you."

"Steve would never get violent with me." But she let him guide her through the door with just a quick look back. She noticed Steve had walked to the back wall and stood facing it.

"I'll bet that's what the victim thought, too."

"Oh, I see. You have him already tried and convicted. I think I *will* see about getting him a good lawyer."

All the way back home her hands shook on the steering wheel. She didn't know who she was angrier with, Steve, the Mountie, or herself for letting him get away with being so stubborn. When Tory got back to her house, she checked her address book for her lawyer's phone number in Peterborough. It was two hours later there, but still only early afternoon. She dialed the number. After two rings a female voice answered, "McCubbin, Johnson and Albright Law Office, good afternoon." Within a few minutes Jack Albright's voice was booming over the line asking about the winter weather in Alberta.

"Hi, Jack. The weather has been pretty cold but I understand the possibility of a Chinook is always looming in the mountains."

"It's great to hear from you, Tory. What can I do for you?"

"I'm hoping you might be able to recommend a really good criminal lawyer for a friend of mine. He seems to have gotten himself into a whole mess of trouble out here." Tory went on to give him an abbreviated version of Steve's predicament without giving him the man's whole life story.

The lawyer let out a low whistle and Tory could almost see him running his hand through his curly red hair the way he always did when he was thinking. A very big man, Tory always wondered how many chairs he broke in a year by leaning as far back as they would allow while his hand went automatically to his thick head of wavy hair. More than once she had seen him grab his desk as the chair tilted too far back, ready to tip.

"Are you at your aunt's house right now?"

"Yes, it's the same telephone number I gave you last fall."

"There's only one name comes to mind right at the moment. I'll check with my partners and see if they agree, or if they know anyone better. I'll get back to you today."

"Thanks, Jack. I'll be waiting for your call."

It came within the hour and a lawyer by the name of George Stefurak was the one that Jack felt was the best for a murder charge. "He practices in Edmonton, Tory, and he has handled some pretty nasty cases, almost all of them successfully. Would you like me to give him a call?"

"I would really appreciate that, Jack."

"I'll call you after I've spoken with him."

"Thanks again."

At 5:00 that afternoon, Jack called back and told her that George was waiting for her call and gave her the number. Tory dialed it immediately and realized while she was waiting for an answer that her stomach was in knots. "That stubborn little runt better appreciate this—and cooperate," she found herself saying out loud. Her thoughts were interrupted by a female voice stringing off a number of names and a pleasant good afternoon at the end.

"Is Mr. Stefurak there please? This is Tory Hardisty calling."

"Just a moment, Ms. Hardisty."

Then a deep, silky voice greeted her, "Mrs. Hardisty, good afternoon. Your friend, Jack Albright, just called me."

"Thank you for taking my call, Mr. Stefurak. I'm sure Jack explained the situation to you already, but you must have some other questions."

"Actually, I took the liberty of calling the RCMP office in your town and talked to the sergeant in charge. He answered a lot of my questions but of course I will have to talk to Steve Turner himself. I understand he doesn't have a lot to say in his own defense though."

"I will pay whatever it costs for you to acquaint yourself with the case. Jack tells me you are one of the most successful criminal defense attorneys in Alberta, so I hope you will represent Steve."

"I'll have to thank Jack for the compliment, and yes, I do want to come down and talk to Mr. Turner in person. He may not even want me for his defense and if so, I can't force myself on him. My services do not come cheap, Mrs. Hardisty, win or lose. So unless I'm absolutely sure that the defendant and I can work together, I'd rather not take the case and waste my time and your money."

"That's fair. Do you want me to tell Steve you're coming?"

"No. I prefer to talk to him myself. After I've seen him, perhaps you and I could meet and I'll be in a better position to let you know my decision. You understand that due to lawyer-client privilege, I won't be able to discuss the case with you."

"I understand. I only want to ensure that Steve has the best defense. He's his own worst enemy because of his stubborn nature. He told me that he's innocent and I believe him. Because of past confidences I know he would not lie to me now. Whatever passes between the two of you is no business of mine. All I want is for you to give him the best defense possible."

"You must care for him a great deal."

"Steve hasn't had many people he could trust or call friend. He's been there for me many times when I needed him, and now he needs me. Why would I not be there for him?"

You better bloody well cooperate, Steve Turner.

13

It was hard for Tory to concentrate on anything over the next couple of days. She would pick up her crafts then find herself staring into space wondering if Steve was eating, or cooperating, or even sleeping. She would try to lose herself in a pocket novel then read the same page three or four times before she finally gave up. She decided to turn her energy into something productive so taking a stepstool into the pantry, she started washing kitchen shelves. There was a box in the pantry with several rolls of shelf liner and it was time to put it to good use.

It was late afternoon the next day when her phone rang and she heard George Stefurak's voice on the other end. "Mrs. Hardisty, would it be possible to meet with you for a short while before I head back to Edmonton?"

"Certainly. I'll come in right away."

"Better I come to your house," he replied. "More privacy."

It took him only half an hour to brief her on exactly what Steve was up against. He had decided a change of venue to Edmonton would be in Steve's best interest even though it would mean having him moved to the district jail there. Surprisingly, Steve had been very cooperative and appreciative of the lawyer's efforts on his behalf.

"Mr. Stefurak, would it be possible for me to see him before he's moved?"

"Since I'm in your employ, Mrs. Hardisty, I'd like it if you would call me George."

She smiled at that. "I will, but then you must call me Tory."

He nodded. "Whether you can see him or not is his decision. I would like to drive out to Steve's just to take a look around and get the feel of the place. I've already visited the house where the woman was murdered."

The next morning, while dressing to go into town, she couldn't believe her nervousness. She wanted to look nice for Steve even knowing that he wouldn't notice. She had called the office to see if he needed anything in the way of clothes or toiletries, but was told that everything was supplied for him. When she arrived and saw him in faded blue shirt and pants, she realized it was the standard issue for occupants of the jail.

He seemed somewhat embarrassed and found it difficult to look at her when he was first brought in. At least he wasn't manacled any longer and they were left alone in a little room with a couple of straight-back chairs, an ashtray stand bolted to the floor and another small table, bolted as well, with a calendar and plant on it. Tory had been told to leave her purse and coat in the outer office and had been subjected to a search of her pockets and a frisk by a female staff member.

She put her hand on one of Steve's arms and held it there until he looked at her. When he did, she could see something in his face she had never seen before. It was a mixture of shyness, embarrassment and what? Uncertainty? Loneliness? Fear? She wasn't sure. Suddenly, she felt his arms envelope her and he was half sobbing on her shoulder. She slid her arms up his back and held him close for several minutes, not saying anything. When she pulled away a little and looked at him, she saw the torment on his weathered face. While kissing him tenderly on the mouth, she told him she would do everything and anything she could to help him.

"Why?" He looked at her incredulously.

"Isn't that what friends are for?"

He leaned his forehead on hers and took several shaky breaths. "Your lawyer friend was in to see me. I thought I told you to stay out of this?"

"I'm afraid I don't listen very well."

Steve moved away from her and leaned against the wall with his hands in his pants pockets. "He seems to know what he's doing."

"He should. I'm told he's one of the best criminal defense lawyers in the country."

"Sounds expensive."

"He is."

"Guess I better cooperate then, eh?"

"Guess you'd better."

"Tory, I've never had anybody do anything like this for me before. It's a bit overwhelming and kind of hard on a man's ego to have a woman looking out for him."

"Not hard for most men, Steve. Just you, because you think now you're going to have a hard time hollering at me next time I put the car in the ditch."

"Next time? *Next time?* Cripes, woman, you've already done enough vehicle damage to last most women two lifetimes."

She tried to look indignant but they both ended up laughing. It was good to hear his deep belly laugh. She thought the Mountie outside the door must be wondering what they possibly could be laughing about.

"Steve, how do you feel about going up to Edmonton?"

"Hopefully, it won't be for too long. Stefurak is going to arrange a bail hearing and maybe I'll be able to come home to wait for the trial."

"You sound as if there definitely is going to be one."

"It will take a miracle for me not to be charged."

"Do you want to talk about it?"

"She was a great or grand niece of Alfred's, his kid sister's granddaughter. Her mother died at a pretty young age and since she had no daddy to speak of, her grandmother raised her. When Alfred's sister passed on he started helping her out. He asked me to check on her from time to time as he was her only kin. So I did. I brought her groceries once in awhile or gift certificates for her to take the kids to the bowling alley, maybe the movies. I helped with some of the heavy chores around her place. She was a pretty good kid, but she still had feelings for that no good piece of shit she was married to."

"Did the police check him out?"

"Seems he was at a new girlfriend's in Calgary that night."

"What happened?"

"She called me that her television wasn't working so I promised to come and fix it. She said she was working the evening shift at the restaurant and for me to come after eleven o'clock. I went to The Roadhouse and had a few drinks and then to her place. I fixed it the best I could—it's an old junker of a set—then I left. The next morning the cops came looking for me because somebody saw me leave her place around midnight and that's around the time the coroner set the time of death."

"Well, Steve, you didn't do it, so somebody else did and the police just have to find this person."

"The police don't seem to be looking too hard, seeing as how they've got a suspect in custody, one with a murder record to boot."

"I have a lot of faith in George. He'll get them moving."

"George?"

"Yes. George Stefurak."

"You're on a first name basis with him? I didn't know you knew him before now."

"I didn't. He reminded me that I am his employer. And as such, should call him by his first name. Steve, if you're in Edmonton for any length of time, I want to come and visit you. Will somebody let me know when your bail hearing is so I can be there to bring you home?"

"I can catch the bus."

"Yes, you can, but I would rather drive you home. Quit looking at me with that why-are-you-doing-this look on your face."

There was a knock on the door, then it opened. "Time's up."

"Tory?"

"Yes?"

"You look real nice."

Tory hugged Steve again and this time he initiated the kiss. He told her again that he would prefer she didn't come to his hearing but she insisted on being there.

What's really going to happen to him? she wondered. A log truck rumbled through the intersection on the corner and old man Rutledge was sweeping the snow away from the doorway to his gas station. She saw one of the nurses from the hospital going into Betty's beauty salon. How could everything appear so normal when Steve's world, her world, was falling apart? Would he really have to go to trial? Surely, they won't stop looking for other suspects just because they had him in custody. If they convicted him and he went to prison, well... he was already an old man. He probably would never come out. Tory felt sick inside, and realized she cared a lot more for Steve than she had ever admitted, even to herself.

She finally drove home and when she checked her telephone messages, there was one from George telling her that Steve's bail hearing was set for the following Monday in the provincial court house in Edmonton. She would be wise to be there early if she was coming, he had said, because he had no idea where they were on the docket. Taking a deep breath, she hoped she wouldn't be driving back alone on Monday evening.

She phoned George and left a message on his machine that she would like to come north on Saturday and hopefully visit with Steve on Sunday. If this was not possible he was to call her back, otherwise she would arrive late on Sunday and would call him then. The next morning

George's secretary called with the message that there was a hotel reservation for Tory at the Constellation Hotel in downtown Edmonton for Saturday night. Arrangements had been made for her to visit Steve at the district jail on Sunday afternoon. She thanked the young woman and found herself planning what she would wear.

14

Saturday, Tory arrived in the late afternoon and found a message from George at the desk, telling her that if she had no plans, he would meet her in the hotel dining room at 8:00 for dinner. He wanted to update her on the case so far and brief her on what to expect Monday in court. His cell phone number was included so she called her affirmative reply.

At exactly 8:00, Tory found George waiting in the bar adjacent to the dining room. She refused a drink and they were shown to their table. Tory knew she had never been what most people would call beautiful, but she had always known how to play up her best features which were her white hair and her long slender figure. Her wardrobe had always included well-made, exquisitely cut suits and dresses. It was better to have three or four really good outfits than a dozen inexpensive ones. Her real weakness, though, had always been fine leather shoes. She felt guilty when counting the number of pairs she owned, so in recent years she had stopped counting. Her guilt was eased somewhat because she gave a number of them annually to a shelter for abused women. Some young woman would step more confidently when going into the work market and sitting for job interviews.

So when she walked into the dining room with George Stefurak who was wearing an expensive suit, silk shirt and Italian leather shoes, she knew she looked just as successful as he did. His appearance belied the fact he had just completed a hard week in court; he was clean-shaven and appeared as fresh as if he were just starting his day. Wearing shoes with a three-inch heel, Tory was almost as tall as he was and they presented a striking picture moving gracefully across the room. His well-manicured hands held her chair and when she faced him across the table, there was not a hair out of place on his gorgeous head.

He ordered a bottle of white wine and suggested she might want to try the baked, stuffed salmon for which this dining room was notorious. Always having enjoyed fish, she took his suggestion and also ordered an appetizer-size Greek salad. George was surprisingly easy to talk to and she found herself enjoying his company.

"Did you know that Jack and I went through law school together?"

Surprised to learn he was probably only a year or so her junior, she listened while he continued. "Jack was always a genius with figures so he went into tax law. I never liked sitting in an office and thought I had more to offer in a court room, hence criminal law."

Tory could understand how he might charm a jury with that smooth-as-silk voice and his suave good looks. What a true waste those attributes would have been stuck permanently behind a desk somewhere.

Listening to his stories about some of his difficult cases, and some funny ones as well, she was surprised when the dessert tray was parked beside their table. Almost two hours had passed and they hadn't even started to talk about Steve's case. Tory declined dessert but accepted a coffee refill. George suggested they could move to the small bar, but Tory was feeling the stress of the day and just wanted to hear about Steve. He told her how the day probably would go and not to get her hopes too high. She, of course, would not let him dampen her spirits any more than they already were.

On Sunday, she and Steve were allowed thirty minutes of visiting time. He seemed rather nervous and ill at ease when he was brought in, only making brief eye contact with her. When she asked if he wasn't feeling well, he shrugged and said he was getting too old for sitting in jail cells. They chatted awkwardly for a few minutes before Steve told her he was uncomfortable having her come to visit. He really wanted her to leave.

"I'm not about to leave until my thirty minutes are up, Steve Turner."

Finally, after struggling to keep the conversation light, they were told they had one minute more.

"Tory, I don't want you to come to the hearin' tomorrow. In fact, I don't want you making the trip up here for any of the trial."

She was crestfallen. "Why?"

"It's too humiliating to have you see me like this. Be easier for me if you don't come at all."

She tried to assure him that she was coming because she wanted to see him and it didn't matter if he were in a jail uniform or not.

He finally raised his voice and said, "It matters to me, woman. I don't want you here and if you insist on coming I'll just fire your lawyer and find my own. I don't want you here."

With that, he walked out of the visitors' room without looking back.

The next morning she was stubbornly sitting in the courtroom when it opened, hoping Steve's case might be heard early and it was only mid-morning when his name was called and he was brought into the little courtroom. The Crown Attorney read the charge of second-degree murder being leveled against Steve. He asked that no bail be allowed stating it had been a brutal and vicious attack that had taken the victim's life. He continued that Steve had a history of brutality and had served time previously for the murder of another young woman.

The judge asked Steve how he was pleading and Steve answered "Not guilty."

Immediately, George asked that bail be set at $50,000 as the previous murder had occurred forty years before and he reiterated there were personal circumstances surrounding the previous murder conviction. He added that Steve owned his own ranch in central Alberta and had lived there quietly and productively for over thirty years and therefore was not a flight risk. The judge asked a few more questions and set bail at $500,000.

Tory cringed. She didn't think it would be possible to raise the required amount, at least not within the next week or so. Or that he would even let her help. She hoped he hadn't noticed her sitting among the spectators.

She went back to the hotel and within the hour George phoned to tell her that Steve had seen her in court. "He instructed me to tell you that he won't cooperate any further unless you go back to Weston and stay away from the court house."

She thanked him, packed up her travel bag, checked out of the hotel and headed back down Hwy 2. She tried to understand Steve's feelings but her own kept getting in the way. How could she stay in Weston day after day while he was on trial for murder just a few hours away?

Four days later, George called. "Steve's raised bail and is on his way home. He'll have to report regularly to the RCMP office, however."

Tory thanked George and asked him to let her know as soon as a trial date was set. He warned her about Steve's threat of non-cooperation, but she insisted she just wanted to know how much time they would have together. Hanging up the phone, Tory wondered whether Steve might call her. She finally decided if she hadn't heard from him by noon the next day, she would take a drive over to his place with some fresh baked bread.

The air was definitely warmer than the day before, considerably warmer. Could this be the beginning of a Chinook? Never having experienced one, Tory was not sure what they felt like.

At 2:00 the following afternoon, Tory turned into Steve's driveway. The truck was parked near the kitchen door. Hoping he would not turn her away, she picked up the freshly baked bread from the seat of the car and started toward the steps. She'd only been in his house a very few times, but could not remember the stairs making so much noise. It was as if every step she took trumpeted her arrival and allowed Steve time to think of some reason to send her away. However, no reason was given. He simply did not answer his door. When she tried to open it, she found it locked. So he was going to play this kind of game was he? Well, he would find out she didn't give up easily on a friendship.

She drove back home feeling heavy disappointment. Was he ashamed to see her? She didn't know why that would be, but when she thought back over the events surrounding his arrest, Tory realized he had never called her. Never asked for her, or even wanted her near him. He had in fact threatened non-cooperation with the authorities and his lawyer if she insisted on seeing him. But she could not just give up on him. She had to see him, to make sure he was all right. She wanted him to know he was not alone. *You stubborn, old fart.* Tory slammed her fist on the steering wheel.

She was just about to go inside when she noticed a snowmobile come over the rise behind her house. She laughed and cursed at the same time. *Steve, I knew you wouldn't let our friendship just fade away.* By the time Steve pulled up to her deck, Tory was crying as well as laughing and cursing. She almost knocked the wind out of him when she hugged him so hard they bumped against the railing on the deck.

"I was just at your place."

"I'm not home."

"I know that, you old fool."

"What did you go to my place for?"

"I brought you some fresh baked bread."

"Well, give it to me and I'll go."

"Not so fast." Tory grabbed him by the collar of his parka and dragged him toward the door. "You're going to come in for tea."

"I see you had a bit of snow. Good thing I got bail or you'd have to rely on a Chinook to clear your driveway."

She hung up her jacket and went to the kettle and started filling it with water but before she had it half full, she dropped it in the sink and let the tears come.

Steve was beside her in a second, turned her to him and held her close. "Women. If I'da thought you were going to end up sniveling like a female, I wouldn'ta come. What the hell are you crying about?"

She put both arms around him and hung on. "Steve Turner, what an old fool you are! Don't you know women cry when we're happy too?"

"Well, what have you got to be so happy about?"

"I was afraid you were shutting me out. You told George if I didn't butt out you would not cooperate with him, or the officials either. It has been hell sitting here knowing you're in a jail cell up there in Edmonton. When he phoned to tell me you were on your way home, I gave you till noon today to call. When I went to your house and your truck was there but you didn't answer your door I thought... well I thought... hell... I thought what a selfish old fart you are." The tears came again. Talking between sobs, she said, "When I saw your snowmobile coming over the hill... I was afraid to believe it was you... until I could feel you in my arms again... I don't give a damn whether you need me or not... I need you. I've been scared out of my mind they're going to... convict you and I'd be left here all alone. I'm really quite selfish you know. I don't know what I'd do without... you. Oh, damn." The sobs took over completely.

"Miss Lottie would turn over in her grave if she heard you swearing so much."

"Promise me... you'll cooperate with the authorities."

"If you promise you'll stay away from Edmonton."

"Why? Why can't I come and be there for you? For me?"

"It's too hard on me knowing you're sitting there seeing me like that. Listening to all the horse shit they'll be bringing up about me. If they find out we're friends and call you to testify... that would kill me. No,

Tory. I definitely do *not* want you anywhere near Edmonton. And that's final. I mean it! Allow me some pride here."

"You and that goddamn pride."

He pushed her back.

"OK. I promise. Let me get this coffee made now or next thing I know it'll be suppertime and you'll be expecting an invitation to stay."

"Gotta do something first," he said then went about refurbishing her fireplace wood supply all the while mumbling about helpless women freezing to death and not having the good sense to look after themselves.

When he finally sat, she cut him an extra big slice of chocolate layer cake and put it in front of him and kissed his forehead. "Thanks for saving me from death-by-freezing." She poured coffee.

"How was Calgary?" he asked.

"Calgary?"

"When you went with your friends. Had a good time?"

She had almost forgotten about her weekend in the city with the girls. "It was a lot of fun. We did silly female things like manicures and massages then we went to see a musical thing and shopped all the next morning."

"It's good you got lots of friends. I knew you would. Soon's the people got to know you."

She wasn't about to tell him that these same friends had been mighty quick to condemn him so she didn't care if she saw any of them again. All they called her for was to hear the latest gossip about their resident killer. He was their small-town news now and they tried to use her as the conduit to all that was juicy up in Edmonton. Tory knew that once he was proven innocent—*and isn't that a switch,* she thought, proven *innocent*—they would be apologetic and insist they knew all along that he hadn't murdered anyone. She knew she would forgive them eventually and all would be forgotten. He would go back to being the town drunk and she would continue to have her evenings and weekends with her new girlfriends. She said nothing. Was she the only person, besides her late aunt, to see the kindness behind that homely face? No, old Alfred knew what a good man Steve was, also. She realized with real shame that she'd been so wrapped up in herself and Steve that she hadn't even been over to see the old man. It was his niece after all who had been the victim here. She wondered how he was surviving.

"The old man's doing OK."

"Pardon?" Tory realized that Steve was answering her as if he had read her thoughts.

"I went to see old Alfred last night. Spent most of the night with him, in fact. I wasn't able to talk to him until then about Joanne's murder. I didn't know if he thought I done it or not."

"And?"

"Seems he has faith in me, too."

Did Tory detect a shy smile?

"Says he knows damn well I'd never hurt anyone or anything of his."

"And the law will too before long."

"With no witnesses except the lady that saw me leave, I can't see how."

"I trust George. I understand everything is circumstantial at this point. They have no DNA evidence. It would have helped your cause had she been raped. They'd at least have that to go by. George is the best. He'll come up with something."

"We'll see."

Steve stood saying he still had work to do with his livestock before dark. Tory made him promise he'd come back for a hot supper.

"Just so you remember," he said. "I didn't ask anything about an invitation."

"I thawed a roast that's too big. I can't eat it all myself. I don't know where my head was."

When he came back for supper he brought news of the trial date being set for late April. She was at the sink rinsing out pots, the food laid out steaming-hot in the dining room. She took her apron off, wiped her hands, walked straight over to Steve and kissed him, first on the cheeks then on his mouth. He grabbed her and held her close.

"Nobody but Miss Lottie ever cared a hoot before. Somehow that makes me ready to face anything."

Supper was eaten in silence, they removed the dishes together and at the sink, Steve picked up a dishtowel.

"Steve! I can do that. They can dry in the rack."

"If you can drive all the way to Edmonton to visit me, the least I can do is dry dishes for you."

That night, she lay in bed staring at the stars blinking at her through the window. Two and a half months—she would have him nearby for two and a half months. She would make them the best two and a half months of his life. If he were going to spend the rest of his life in prison, he would at least have this time to remember. She could not imagine a life without having had her family close when she needed them. How could someone go through life without one single person who cared? Thank God he had found her aunt. Too bad it wasn't until life had dealt him all those bad blows.

She would cook for him, support him, clean his house, be his friend. *Hell,* she thought *I'll even go to bed with him if it comes to that.* The laugh came from deep inside as the thought of coupling with him made its way through her mind. Then the tears came and she found herself rubbing the cold, empty space on the other side of the bed. *Maybe it wouldn't be so bad, couldn't be any worse than it was with Doug.*

She had always envied the women who talked warmly about the time spent in bed with their husbands. With Doug it had never been anything more than a release for him. Sex had never been anything beautiful or warm. She had felt the need and desire when she was first married. When she realized it was never going to be satisfied, she learned the art of ignoring her needs until she no longer felt them. The love she once had felt for her husband, she re-directed to her daughter. By the time Doug eventually left her, she was quite able to live without him and not experience any great loss. Could she ever revive those feelings? They say if you don't use it, you lose it. Would she be just a dried up old prune? Oh, hell, Steve was an old man. They had been in compromising situations and he had never once shown any inclination toward anything sexual. *Why would he want to jump your old bones anyway, Tory Hardisty?* She ran her hands over her stomach and her breasts. *Well, I'm not that bad. I've kept in pretty good physical condition and most married women my age are still sexually active.* George Stefurak certainly had given her an approving look when she'd met him in the dining room at the hotel. Why wouldn't Steve find her attractive? She smiled again at the picture of her and Steve in bed together. She ran her hand again over the empty space beside her. *Steve, oh, Steve, it is lonely in this bed.* Something stirred deep within, something warm and…

Oh, hell, how am I going to fall asleep now?

She went down to the kitchen and heated some milk. She laughed again as she sat in her warm housecoat. *Tory. Look at you, girl. Sitting here drinking your warm milk when there's a perfectly wonderful man right up the road.*

15

THE NEXT DAY, TORY TOOK stew to Alfred and sat with him, playing checkers, for an hour. He was genuinely concerned for Steve and he harbored some guilt since he had asked Steve to look out for his niece. "If Steve hadn't been helping Joanne, he wouldn't be in this trouble. Please, Tory, do everything you can for him. I have money, you know. It's hidden away. For emergencies. You know. Does Steve need some for his lawyer? I got some if he does."

"Steve has the best lawyer money can buy. If anybody can prove his innocence, George can." She hopped two of Alfred's checkers in a single move. "King me."

"Dang," said Alfred. "If I'd known you were this good, I wouldn't have asked you to play a game."

She promised to return again next week and give him a chance to beat her.

As the days passed, more and more often, Tory found herself watching the clock and looking out the window as the light faded and evening set in. Never knowing what time his chores would be done, she tried to cook meals that would "wait" well. She wanted the food fresh and hot whether he came early or late. The weather warmed and the days lengthened. Steve never came through the door without logs for the fireplace or without having chopped a few more pieces to be ready. These things grew into habit, like married couples kissing each other quickly when he came in then eating in silence, discussing the day's events during the dishes, watching the late news on TV, but ending the night with his departure.

Several weeks passed this way. Besides his chores, Steve had to report regularly to the RCMP office in town. Tory found the hours were getting unbearably long. Finally, one evening, she approached the subject of cleaning Steve's house for him.

"It's almost time for spring cleaning. Why don't I come and do your curtains for you?"

"Are you crazy, woman? I won't have you spring cleaning two houses at your age."

"I think it would be a fair trade for you cultivating my garden and offering to help me get it planted. After all, that's two gardens you're having to worry about—at your age."

Being careful not to invade his privacy, she started with his curtains and then offered to wash and air his blankets and bedspread. She was pleased to find that for a bachelor he was a spotless housekeeper. She should have known, she thought, by how neat his yard was. After she finished with his cleaning, there would be no need to come on a regular basis. Once again, her days became long with just the care of her own house and waiting for him to arrive for supper each night.

One evening in mid-March, they were watching the late news, when Steve asked if she wanted to go to Edmonton for a hockey game. "I have a meeting with George. Thought maybe you'd want to see the Oilers. Maybe get some shopping in?"

It would be a more-than-welcome change to the daily routine of waiting for Steve and waiting for something to happen. She thought it would be good for him, as well, as he was not allowed to leave town and she knew he was getting bored. He had not been into The Roadhouse since his murder charge and she realized he had avoided the townspeople as much as possible. Knowing how everyone stared at her whenever she went in, she could imagine how it must have been for Steve. She always tried to pick up some groceries for him so he could avoid that, at least.

When he was ready to leave for home, she asked, "Is this just a routine visit or is there something special that George wants?"

"Nothing special far's I know," and he leaned in to kiss her.

She held him close.

"Something wrong?" he asked softly.

"No. Yes. Oh... damn. We haven't talked about your trial. I keep hoping it will go away. This means it's still there."

"Get it through your head, woman. It's not going away. There isn't a day goes by I don't hope George is going to phone saying they've found new evidence. Every time the phone rings I think, 'Is that my freedom call?' Then it's the feed store, or the garage with news on my tractor part. It's not going to go away."

"I'm being selfish. This isn't making it any easier for you." She straightened up and wiped her nose.

He pulled her back against him and kissed her hard, then again more softly. Holding her against him, he whispered. "I never thought I would ever tell a woman again that I love her, but I never met a woman quite like you before. I have no right even saying these things to you. I'm probably gonna end up in prison. But... hell, woman, I do love you. All I can think about is what my life mighta been like if I'd met you when I was a young man. But we can't go back and you probably wouldn't have looked at me twice anyways. Your husband was such a big, good-looking guy and you probably had lots like him wanting you."

"He couldn't tie your shoelaces. And you're right. He was my big handsome hero. But it didn't take too many years of married life to find out that big and handsome were his only attributes. Big and handsome don't mean diddly squat when you're sitting at home alone night after night. Big and handsome don't mean diddly squat when you're the only one going to your child's concerts and sporting events and tucking her in at night. No, if I had it to do over again, I'd choose short and scrawny and probably have a lifetime of happy. Of course," she laughed, "my daughter might not have turned out so beautiful with no big and handsome genes in the pool."

"I don't think big and handsome had much to do with the genes in that young lady's makeup. She's the image of you." He stepped out the door but paused on the bottom step. "I guess I should hitch up the tag-along trailer for your shopping parcels, eh?"

16

DRESSED IN THE SWEATER SHE had given him for Christmas and his sheepskin jacket, Steve looked almost... cool, but the ever-present Stetson was perched on his head. His white hair was probably his most redeeming feature so she wondered why he, like many men, insisted on keeping it covered.

They stopped close to Red Deer for steak and mushrooms and baked potato. Tory enjoyed a glass of red wine while Steve had a beer. Dessert was included so Tory let the waitress bring one for her, but Steve ate it. *If he was nervous at all, it certainly hasn't affected his appetite,* she noted, wondering what the meals were like in the provincial jail. *Don't let yourself go there, Tory. Not until you have to. IF you have to.*

Once again in the truck, Steve asked what had brought about the change of mood in the restaurant.

"You're much more observant of women than I thought," she answered quietly.

"Well? Tell me. And I'll know if you're not telling the truth."

"I wondered how the meals were in the jail. You have such a healthy appetite, I can't imagine it being satisfied in there."

"They're not bad. The cuisine isn't... Well, you couldn't even call it 'cuisine' on a good day. It isn't all that tasty, maybe not even healthy. But it's filling." He reached over and put his hand on hers, "You gotta stop thinking all the time. We've got ourselves a couple days in the city. We're going to enjoy them."

They arrived in Edmonton very late and Steve carried their bags up, commenting it was probably going to be a much bigger chore carrying all *her* bags back down again.

Tory's room was a two-room suite with a king size bed and a sitting room with a full size hide-a-bed. *What a waste of money,* she thought. *We could have shared the one suite. Well... I won't be the one to initiate that conversation.*

Steve left her and returned fifteen minutes later with ice, canned pop and a bottle of rum. He mixed their drinks while she opened a bag of Cheetos and put it on the coffee table. She switched on the TV.

The news was full of dire warnings of possible drought conditions and Tory expressed her concern that it might affect Steve's feed crops and her garden.

"She's worried about her garden." Steve put his arm around her shoulder and pulled her closer. "I guess this means you're staying."

"What are you talking about?"

"Last I knew—when was it? Ah. Christmas—you were talking about only staying six months, just putting in the winter, you called it."

She saw Steve's amused expression but before she could punch him, her own look of stunned bewilderment caught her eye in the mirror over the bar sink. "You purposely distracted me to make me forget about going home. You thought if you were nice enough to me, cleaned my driveway and carried in firewood, I would stay and keep on baking bread for you. If you aren't the sneakiest, most conniving man I ever met, Steve Turner, why I... I..."

He cut her off with a kiss. "It wasn't your bread I was thinking about." He whispered in her neck.

"No?"

"Nope."

He kissed her ear.

"Then it must have been my home-made soup."

"Nope." His lips moved to her eyelids.

"My chocolate cake?"

"Nope."

"Then... what?"

"Your popcorn. You have to make the best darn popcorn this side of the Rockies. I don't want to have to go all the way to Peterborough to get a decent bowl of popcorn." He started to laugh as she punched him again.

She faked a sore fist and leaned into him. Why could he not show this side of himself to others? Everyone saw him as a miserable old drunk—worse!—one who hated women. She feared it would be his reputation that would bring him down in the courtroom. She snuggled in close, slid her arms around his waist and leaned against his chest. He kissed her temple. Neither said anything more and they fell asleep like that, in the comfort of each other's arms.

Tory woke to a late-night commercial and stirred. Steve emitted a grunt and snort so it was apparent that he, too, had fallen asleep. She tried to ease herself from his embrace without waking him but he opened one eye.

"Is it morning already?"

"Take the bed," she whispered. "I'll take the sofa."

Half asleep he followed her direction. When she could hear no more sound other than a smooth rhythm of heavy breathing, she went into the room and retrieved her bag with her pajamas and toiletries. Standing with the light from the hallway casting soft shadows on the bed, Tory took time to study Steve in repose. Free of any distractions or stress, his face seemed to lose some of its hardness. His wrinkles and leathery lines were less pronounced. He was still verging on ugly, but a masculine, been-kicked-around-but-I-survived kind of ugly, an ugly that in a puppy would be described as cute. The kind you want to hug and protect from the world. She realized that's exactly what she wanted to do. Hug and protect Steve from the world. Who were they to judge him anyway? They didn't know him. Nobody knew him. Not his accusers, not his lawyer, not the jurors in whose hands his fate would lie. His own mother hadn't even known him. His wife hadn't known him. Aunt Lottie had... but she was dead. Now Tory knew him. She was the only one who did. How she wanted to hug him and protect him. If only he knew how much…

Maybe he did.

Her cheeks were wet with silent tears. She moved quietly into the bathroom and put her pajamas on.

When Steve woke up in the morning, Tory was snuggled against his back with her arm around his waist. "Good Lord, I wasn't drunk when I went to bed. How did this happen?"

He turned slightly and Tory rolled over and turned her back to him. He slid out of bed and went to the washroom. He was wiping his face dry when he came back into the bedroom and Tory was lying on her back looking at him. He sat on the bed staring right back.

"God help me, Steve. I don't know what I will do without you if... I hate to even think about it."

He lifted her shoulders off the bed and held her to him. She grabbed him like she was drowning and he was her lifeline. It took everything she had not to cry. If she were going to hug and protect, she mustn't cry, but who was going to hug and protect her?

They rocked together on the bed clinging to each other. "Why did I find you only now?" she asked. "What kind of cruel joke is this? You can't go to prison. I just won't allow it!"

Steve found her mouth and silenced it with his. She did cry then. He let her sob until she had no sobs left. Then he returned to the bathroom and turned the shower on for her. "Enjoy the refreshing water while I arrange for breakfast to be brought up."

Later, she sat in her housecoat and ate the ham and pancakes he had ordered for her. They drank several cups of coffee. All the while, he had hardly taken his eyes from her.

He was genuinely worried about her. She was a strong woman but even strong people have a breaking point. He hated himself. He hated himself for causing grief to one more human being. He had warned her. He had told her he would let her down. He had told her he was unreliable, undependable. But all that didn't alter the fact that he had caused pain one more time. Shit! Why the hell had he let her into his life? Why the hell had he forced himself into hers? Now what? What was that big time lawyer doing to earn his big time fee? Hell, hell, hell.

Somebody killed that young woman. It wasn't him. But she was damn sure dead, so somebody had to have done it. Why couldn't they find him? And who the hell was he? Where was he? Would they ever find him? The thought of rotting in prison was unbearable. Then there was Tory on the outside, probably having to move back down east to get away from the townsfolk feeling sorry for her—her pickin' a loser and all. He never should have gotten involved with her. But how was he supposed to know he was going to get charged with somebody else's crime? *Because it happened before, you dummy.* Why did these things keep happening to him? *Because you're a loser, always were, always will be.* Isn't that what everyone in authority always told him? That's what the guard told him when they let him out of prison last time. "You'll be back," he had said. "Your kind always comes back."

"You're not going back." Tory's arms slid around his neck. Her statement shook him.

"How did you know what I was thinking?"

"The same way you always know what I'm thinking. We're two of a kind. We belong together."

He pulled her arms from around his neck. "Tory, we're the farthest thing from being alike as the devil is from Angel Gabriel."

"We may have come from different backgrounds but that doesn't mean we're not the same. Some tomatoes are grown underground in hydroponic gardens and others are grown out in the sunshine in fields. They couldn't have come from two more different environments, but they're still tomatoes. That's us, Steve, we're just a couple of tomatoes that ended up in the same supermarket."

Shaking his head he smiled at her, "Just a couple of tomatoes, huh? Well, some tomatoes go into the soup and some go into the sauce. Unfortunately, they don't all end up in the same place."

"We will. You wait and see." She kissed his nose. "Now I have some heavy duty shopping to do, then we have a hockey game to see. By the way, I have a better place to put that hundred and fifty bucks you're paying for that other room so you may as well cancel it for tonight." *So much for not being the one to open that door.* "I have to put on my face then I'll meet you downstairs."

They wandered around downtown from store to store. They held hands. They laughed and made faces at their reflections in the windows. They acted like a couple of young lovers and they enjoyed every second they were together. All Tory's big shopping spree netted her was a new waste basket for her bathroom and a scarf to wear with her spring coat. She was going to buy some tomato seeds but Steve told her he had already started plants in his greenhouse. They decided to change clothes and go to the rink early. They would snack there and have something later after the game.

If anyone had asked Tory about the game, she would not have been able to tell them a thing. She watched the action and cheered and shouted at the right times, but it was all by rote. The puck went in, the good guys scored and she hollered. The referee blew his whistle and their players went into the penalty box and she shouted. Who scored and who got penalized were not important. All that was important was the man next to her. She loved him. Really loved him. And she was going to lose him. She was going to be alone once more. Only this time she would feel alone. Last time, she hadn't really lost anyone. The man who showed up once in a while just quit showing up. This time, however, she was in danger of losing the one person that she waited for every single day. If he was late coming for dinner even one day now, she would count the minutes listening for his truck to pull into her driveway.

How had this happened? She hadn't been looking for a man. She hadn't even wanted a man. Her life was complete with her daughter and grandchildren. A man would just infringe on her freedom, on her independent lifestyle. Now, here she was wanting, actually wanting, this man to be part of her life, wanting him to worry if she weren't home when he called, wanting to plan her day around his. A year ago, six months ago, she would have fled from this scene. Fled as if the gates of Hell had opened and the fire was about to consume her.

"You want me to get you a sleeping bag?"

"What? Oh, I didn't hear the horn."

"Then I guess you didn't hear my stomach growling either. I'm starving."

"Well, why not? It has to be at least two hours since you ate."

They were quite pleased to find an Italian restaurant not far from their hotel where Steve ordered meatballs, ribs, lasagna and Caesar salad. Tory settled for a small order of spaghetti. The meal ended too soon. The evening ended too soon. Tory did not want the morning to come. It was foolish of her to think of the appointment with the lawyer in the morning as the beginning of the end. She knew this, but they had been able to avoid thoughts of the trial—and the possible outcome—by just not talking about it. If they were younger, she knew she could deal with this better, but time was running out for them. What was the best sentence he could hope for, fifteen years? Twenty years? He would die in there. Something had to be done. She did not find the best attorney around just to have Steve convicted of a crime he did not commit.

When they were once again in their suite, she managed a more upbeat mood. She joked about bringing her best lingerie and pulled out her cotton tailored pajamas that she had worn the night before.

"Cotton or satin—they all look the same piled on the floor beside the bed," he told her.

Startled, she wondered whether this was such a good idea after all. She lingered in the bathroom, harboring second thoughts. This is ridiculous, she decided, and opened the door to find Steve sitting in the bed, bare-chested, watching the news. He had mixed their drinks and hers was sitting on the night table on her side of the bed. She could feel Steve's eyes on her as she rounded the bed and lifted the sheets on her side. Steve's chest wasn't all that was bare. *I'm too old for this. Why did I invite him into my room? Into my bed?* Suddenly, she felt like she didn't know him at all. He was a total stranger. Why had she thought she was the only one who knew him? She gulped her drink and realized he was speaking to her. What was he saying? What had he said already?

"They're showing a fire in the mountains up on Pinecrest Ridge."

"Where's that?"

"About thirty miles up the mountain from our places."

"What?"

"They figure they got it contained now, but they're worried about a wind shift."

"Could it reach your place?"

"It could if all the conditions were right."

"Do you want to go home?"

"I can't. I have that meeting tomorrow. Anyways, not much I can do about it. They brought firefighters all the way from Northwestern Ontario. My cattle are still on the ranch so I don't have to worry about rounding them up."

"Oh, Steve. That's all you need on your plate right now."

"Hey, life's a bowl of cherries. Didn't anyone ever tell you that? They look great, nice and red, taste fantastic, nice and sweet—but sooner or later, a bad one shows up in the basket. Nothing you can do about it. Just happens." He brushed her hair from her forehead and kissed it. "Tory, darlin', you are the nicest, sweetest one in the bowl."

She snuggled closer and leaned her head on his shoulder after she kissed it. "I would think you've had more than your share of bad cherries, Steve. You don't deserve any more."

His lips brushed one of her eyelids then the other. "I love you, Tory." His mouth found hers. She moved one arm around his waist and the other smoothed the hair on the back of his head. He gathered her into his arms as his lips dusted her throat with soft kisses. His arms were muscular and his body sinewy—not an ounce of fat. His stomach was flat and hard. Tory whispered lovingly as she kissed his ears. He pulled her beneath him and all thoughts of forest fires and ranches were replaced with another fire. How long had it been since she had felt such ecstasy? She probably never had. Love and tenderness has to accompany the passion, neither of which she had ever been offered before.

As she lay in Steve's arms listening to his even breathing, she knew she loved this man with her whole being. No one could ever be more loved and she would make sure he knew it every day of his life. She watched his chest rise and lower with each breath. It started as just a little kiss on his shoulder—a simple display of affection, then it moved to a nibble on his ear, followed by a barely perceptible shift of position. Steve opened one eye, then the other.

"Tory, love, what *are* you doing?"

17

They had breakfast together in the hotel coffee shop before Steve went to his meeting with George. They had arranged for a late checkout so Tory could wait for him in the comfort of the hotel. They had no idea how long the meeting was going to take or what his lawyer even wanted to discuss. Tory wanted to go with him but Steve was adamant about her staying clear of the court, the lawyer, and anything remotely connected to his trial. He would not have it any other way, no matter what she threatened.

The morning dragged. Every time Tory looked at the clock she was sure it was wrong, but when she checked her watch, it was ticking as slowly. It was almost 1:00 when she finally heard Steve's key card in the door. He was poker faced. She moved into his arms and kissed him. He told her it did not look good. Apparently, the only hope they had was the girlfriend of Joanne's husband, but she was remaining firm in the alibi she had supplied. George had his private investigators checking out all leads, questioning again all the neighbors and every one who had come into contact with the victim in the final couple of weeks. It looked like their only defense would be to weaken the circumstantial evidence the crown attorneys would be using to convict Steve. George Stefurak would have to create a very strong case of reasonable doubt in the minds of the jurors. But by Steve's own admission, he had been there and had left the premises around the time of death as determined by the medical examiner.

Tory felt like she'd been punched in the stomach. *What must Steve be feeling?* Her arms found their way around his waist and she held him close. Then moving back, slightly and wordlessly she brushed her hand over his hair like a mother does to her small son when he's about to face the dreaded needle in the doctor's office. Just as a mother feels the needle, Tory was feeling the depth of Steve's pain.

As they were leaving the outskirts of the city and passing the Leduc exit, Steve smiled at the thought of this wonderful woman whose love he was lucky enough to have. He felt like he was twenty again—only better. When he was in his twenties, life wasn't as good is it was now, even with a murder conviction pending. Now, he had a successful ranch, the best woman a man could ever hope to find, a good old friend who needed him and believed in him no matter what. He had never ever thought he would find a woman like this. All the women he had ever known had used him, stepped on him and then left him. Except for Miss Lottie, of course. He wondered if she were happy about the way things turned out with him and Tory. Maybe Lottie had hoped Tory would find a man who would be around to take care of *her* in her old age. By the time he got out of prison, if he ever got out, they would both be too old to really care. *Better just enjoy what you've got right now, Buster, cause it ain't going to last.*

They stopped for a late lunch along the highway near the Millet exit. Tory wondered out loud how the fire situation was near their farms.

Unsuccessful in their attempts to pick up something on the radio, they realized they would have to wait until they were south of Red Deer for the local radio station reception. After downing bowls of bean with bacon soup—plus a turkey sandwich for Steve—they jumped into the truck and continued their drive home.

South of Red Deer, they could see the haze in the sky from the distant fires. Once on their own road, the haze and the smell of fire were all around them. Steve dropped Tory off at her house and told her if he wasn't back for dinner it would be because he had to move some of his cattle and not to worry, he had a couple of good hands working for him this spring. He would call her later when he got home.

He showed up shortly after 10:00, filthy dirty and smelling of smoke, but the fire was keeping its distance. It looked like they were safe for now. He wouldn't come in to eat but would take some stew back for himself and the boys. Tory would start making enough food for the others on a regular basis, most certainly while Steve's trial was before the court. It would give her something to fill her time and she'd be helping him in some small way. It was good to know there were four hungry men, Steve, Alfred, and the two hands now, depending on her for nourishment.

Steve told her, "I usually ran a tab for the men's suppers at The Roadhouse and I always cooked breakfast and lunch for them."

"No need for that anymore," she told him. "I'll cook supper for all of us. I have to cook anyway and it's no fun cooking just for myself. Besides I enjoy cooking."

He took her hand in his dirty one and looked at her crooked fingers. "You can't tell me that kneading bread every day isn't painful."

"Au contraire. It's good therapy."

He lifted her hand and kissed it. "Bullshit." He continued mumbling something about stubborn women and not arguing anymore as he walked to the door with the big pot of stew. "I'll call you tomorrow."

"Tell the boys I'll have supper ready at 6:00. That should give them time to clean up and still have time to go to town later—if that's where they're heading."

"Come on, Tory! I won't have you cooking for them every day."

"You have no say in the matter."

"Who the hell put you in charge?"

"Can you tell your crew where to eat? I don't think so. If they choose to eat here, then that's where they'll eat. I'll put my cooking up against The Roadhouse any day and I'll win hands down."

"Maybe I want you to myself."

"You'll have me to yourself—after they've finished eating."

"You feed 'em fast and get 'em out of here."

"I'll take the weekends off. Saturday and Sunday they can go into town. I think I want you to myself, too. Sometimes."

"Tomorrow. At 6:00."

The next day Tory baked sweet rolls, made a giant lasagna and baked spareribs. She found some frozen borscht in the freezer and heated it as well. It was clearly enjoyed—if the empty dishes were any indication.

"That's got to be the best meal I've had in a long time, Mrs. Hardisty," Tom, one of the hands said. "I'm stuffed."

"Oh. That's too bad. There's apple pie and you have no room."

"Hmm, maybe I can find room for just a small piece."

"Ice cream on the side?"

"Maybe a small scoop."

Somehow a whole pie was eaten and Tory promised she would send the other one home with Steve for their lunch the next day. The young men left uttering a mantra of thanks as they headed out the door. Steve in the meantime had started the fire in the living room and was reading the paper. Tory picked up the dishes and put them in the dishwasher. She had already scrubbed the pots by hand.

When she finally sat beside Steve on the sofa, he pulled her to him and planted a big kiss on her cheek. "I don't know how I got so lucky, but I will be eternally grateful, Tory Hardisty."

"I never had any sons. It does my heart good to cook for healthy young appetites. Healthy old ones, too, for that matter."

"Don't think for one minute they don't appreciate it either. Tom and Skip have never had much of a home life. My ranch is about as good as it gets for them, and with my future up in the air, I don't know what will happen to them. I'm trying to do the best I can for now. Your meals are more than they—or me—could ever hope for. If it gets too much I want you to tell me right away. Promise?"

"Sure."

"They know I'm up on murder charges and they don't ask questions. They just come in, slap me on the back and get right to work."

"They must know you, Steve. Just like I do—and Alfred."

"Like I said, how did I get so lucky?"

They watched the final episode of *Law and Order* and then the news. Steve asked, "Tomorrow's Saturday, right?"

"Yes. You know that."

"The weekend. Your days off right?"

"Already? Seems I just got started."

"If it's nice out, let's go for a motorcycle ride to the city."

"Motorcycle?"

"Yeah. I've got a big old Harley that's just waiting to be taken out."

"Steve Turner, you never cease to amaze me. A motorcycle. Who would have thought."

"Ever been on one?"

"Never."

"Then, missus, you are in for a real thrill. You haven't lived till you've ridden on the back of a Harley."

Laughing, Tory said, "Next you'll be wanting me to go sky diving."

"No, next comes whitewater rafting while the spring runoff is still going strong. Then comes sky diving."

"You're serious. You *are* serious."

"You only go around once, might as well enjoy it."

"Enjoying sky diving is an oxymoron."

"Whatever you say. Regardless, we're going for a ride on a Harley tomorrow."

"What does one wear for riding on the back of a Harley? I wouldn't want to embarrass anyone."

"Well, my guess is you don't own leathers. You don't, do you? No, didn't think so. Well, just wear your jeans and a sweatshirt—and a leather jacket if you have one. No? Then I'll lend you one. Now a real biker chick would wrap her head in a bandana but for you anything that covers your ears will be fine. No babushkas though. I won't have my chick looking like she's planting cabbages."

He pulled her down on the sofa and raised his eyebrows a couple of times like a villain in an old play while he held her hands above her head. "Too bad you don't have leather. Leather is a real turn-on for a biker."

"*Now* you tell me. I could have bought some in Edmonton."

"No problem, we'll pick some up for you in Calgary. Red ones. Or maybe pink. Yeah, pink."

Before she could answer, his mouth covered hers and her now-free arms slid around his neck but she couldn't help but laugh so hard she shook.

He lifted himself from her and slid to the floor. "Tory, what is it? What's the matter?" Her tears made him frown. "What's the matter?"

She was laughing so hard she was crying.

"Dammit, woman. Don't do that to me. I thought I hurt you."

She was gasping for air and couldn't say anything. Finally, she sat up and took several deep breaths. "I'm sorry. I am so sorry. I can't help it," she said, fighting for control. "I was just thinking about how frightened I was of you that first night when you stopped me on the road. You scared the living daylights out of me. You knew how scared I was and you played on that. If I had only known then what a character you are. You know what you are? A big phony. I called you that once before but now I know what a truly big phony you really are."

"I'm not a phony, Tory. I really don't like women. You know that. I was angry that night. Angry that you would drive home alone down a country road to an empty house in a car whose tires weren't safe. I thought you were stupid. I found out you're just too trusting. You're used to driving your car in the city, knowing there's a gas station on the next corner if you have a problem. Or maybe you have a cell phone at home that you can use to dial CAA. As you've since found out, gas stations are few and far between and cell phones don't always work out here. If that happened now, I would be even angrier, loving you the way I do. I would be sick if anything happened to you."

Tory ran her finger along his jawbone. "You are a complex man, Steve Turner. So serious. Yet so spontaneous. I can't think of any other man who might want his woman in pink biker-chick leathers, yet would worry about her arthritic fingers. Only you. I'm sorry I laughed at you. I just can't believe I was frightened of such a caring, loving man."

He kissed her hand and stood up, pulling her with him. "I have to go. With the guys in town, there's no one there to take a fire call if conditions change. Tomorrow they'll both be working and then Sunday I'll have to hang around here with you again."

She went to bed wondering what Josh would think about his grandma going for a ride on the back of a Harley, wearing pink leathers.

18

IN THE END THEY SETTLED for deep purple leathers. She was unable to believe she was doing this. It was something to go for a motorcycle ride once, but to actually buy a leather suit meant this was going to be a regular thing. How ridiculous could she get? *Oh God, please let me continue to be ridiculous all summer and all next summer,* she prayed, hoping that "ridiculous" was not going to be replaced with unspeakable.

She had come downstairs in her jeans and sweatshirt and her black leather jacket, with a bandana tied around her head, across her forehead and behind her ears, just as she had seen in that full-page cologne advertisement in *Vogue*. She even wore black leather gloves and dark sunglasses. Hoop earrings finished off the outfit. She didn't know if she looked more like a gypsy or a cabbage planter. Steve had watched her come down the stairway and the way his eyes slid over her, she knew she wasn't going to embarrass him.

"You look twenty-five years old."

"Well, these bones will let you know how old I *feel* when we come back."

She had held on for dear life when they hit the highway even though she had been surprised when she climbed onto the machine how comfortable it really was. She felt vulnerable the first time they passed a car on the freeway. The helmet on her head helped but she knew her legs would be mincemeat if they made contact with anything, especially the pavement. Before long, she was enjoying the feeling of being free, the feeling of riding the wind. All too soon they were in the outskirts of Calgary. She knew she would never enjoy a ride to the city as much as she had this one. When Steve turned into the parking lot of a restaurant, she wanted to tell him to keep going as far as they could possibly go. He shut the engine off and removed his helmet. She kissed the back of his neck and squeezed his middle before climbing off the machine.

"That much, huh?"

"It was everything you said it would be. More."

"Then let's eat first, then go leather shopping."

He took her to the shop where he had bought his own leathers. She could not believe the prices. Her first instinct was to refuse, but Steve was enjoying this too much. She tried on several outfits, green, black and red. When she saw herself in the purple one, they both knew immediately that was the one for her. It was so dark, it was almost black, but her platinum hair brought it to life. Steve insisted she wear it home so the clerk wrapped up her jeans and black leather jacket which they stowed in the saddlebags. They rode around town a bit, enjoying the warm spring weather before hitting the highway once more. When they turned onto their road, she motioned for him to slow down. "What's the matter? Getting sore?"

"No. I just don't want to get my new outfit dirty on this gravel road."

He laughed and moved off the road and into the field beside it. When he was approaching her property, he took off cross-country and came into her yard from the back. At the creek running through the corner of her yard, he slowed almost to the tipping point as they bumped over the rocks in a shallow spot. Tory held her feet out.

"If I'd known you were training me to be a stunt rider, I would have put cushions on the seat."

"Well, all you have to do is eat more of your own cooking and put a little meat on your ass."

"I work very hard to keep the meat off my—my buns."

"Thank you kindly. I appreciate it. The result of your efforts really shows in those tight leather pants. I saw those big guys looking at you at the gas station— Uh uh, don't deny it. You saw them, too. I think you even gave a little wiggle for them."

"Do you think they noticed? I hope I wasn't too obvious."

"Too obvious? I betcha the pilot in the Air Canada jet going over noticed." He hugged her from behind then gave her bum a pinch. "That's OK, they can look all they want, as long as they all know that gorgeous little behind is for my hands only."

She looked at herself in the hallway mirror and asked when she could show off her new outfit again. "When we go up the highway to do some rafting."

"You're serious, aren't you." It was a statement rather than a question.

"Yep. We are going to do it all. Then, when you go back east, you can tell your grandkids, 'Old Steve and I, we did it all. We packed a lifetime of living into two months. There isn't anything we didn't do.'"

"When I go back east?"

"I don't think you'll want to stay and try to look after this old place by yourself."

"Of course not. I'll have you to help me."

He didn't say anything more, just smacked her backside and told her he would be back after he checked at the ranch and changed his clothes.

During the next weeks, Tory cooked, baked, and cooked some more. She was in her glory. Her relationship with Steve grew with such depth that anyone observing them would think they had known each other most of their lives. They never talked about moving in with each other. She knew that she really didn't want that. They were together on weekends and almost every evening, that was plenty. She still valued her free time. She also noticed that when Steve was not with her, she worried about him. When they were together everything seemed fine. They did go white water rafting, but not skydiving—to Tory's great relief. They talked about taking downhill skiing lessons, but decided the conditions at this time of year were not great for beginners. It was something they would save for later.

"How old are you Steve?" They were sitting watching a hockey game on television.

"Sixty-six. Why, are you afraid you're robbing the cradle?"

"Robbing the...? What an awful thing to say to a lady in her prime."

"What, you mean I'm *not* ten years younger than you?"

"I'm sixty-two but feel like thirty-two since I met you." She smiled at the surprised look on his face.

"Why?"

"I was looking ahead to a dull retirement. The volunteer work I did was satisfying for the most part, but some of it was just to put in time. The ladies I played cards with were a nice bunch, but they would be shocked to learn I have a man who takes me motorcycle riding." She laughed. "You have added a whole new dimension to my life. I now have exciting interests to look forward to and someone to do them with. I'm glad I let you talk me into staying here."

Steve continued watching the hockey game without speaking. Just when Tory thought he hadn't paid any attention to her, he took her hand in both of his. "I never found the things I've done particularly exciting. I rode a motorcycle when I couldn't afford a car and still find it a good means of transportation. I like to dance but it's hard to do that by yourself. I wouldn't trade a single minute that you and I have spent together, Tory, but I am sorry that I talked you into staying."

"Now it's my turn to ask why?"

"Because now you're tangled up with an ex-con who's got himself involved in another murder rap. I don't see any possibility of me getting off. Whoever did it got clean away with no witnesses and I happened to be in the wrong place at the wrong time. I could be put away for a long time. Too long for us to have any future at our age. I told you I want you to go home to your family and just forget about me. In fact, I'd be happier than a pig in shit to see you gone and settled while I'm still around to help you pack."

"Don't be so negative, Steve. You know I am not going back east and you are not going to jail. So just get those ideas out of your head right now. I don't even want to talk about it anymore. When I testify about how kind you've been to me and to my aunt and to Alfred, the jury will know what sort of a man you are—one that doesn't go around killing innocent women."

"You are not testifying. You are not coming into that courtroom. You are not going to be anywhere even near Edmonton."

"I most certainly am!"

"I won't allow it."

"How are you going to stop me?"

"I told George that if you were not kept away, I will not cooperate."

"Steve, I—"

"No! That's it. Final! Nothing more to be said."

Tory knew there was no sense in arguing further. So it was, that a week later, Steve left by himself to stay in Edmonton to prepare with George Stefurak for his trial.

He had stayed with Tory the night before and they had held each other all night. He was convinced he would never see her again and he wanted to savor every last minute with her. There was no way on God's earth he would allow her to come into that courtroom and hear everything that the Crown Counsel would be digging up about him. The trial was going to be hard enough without living through the humiliation of her sitting there while they went on about his lack of education, his bad upbringing as a child, his whoring mother, his first murder conviction and the many nights he spent in jail for being drunk and fighting. He was sure they would have witnesses testifying how he had hated and verbally abused women. They might even bring up his conviction for robbery even though it had been overturned when they found him innocent after a long time in prison. He knew all this was going to work against him and nothing that Tory could say would make any difference. The only chance he had would be for them to find the real killer and it didn't look like that was going to happen.

He thought all night about how it had been in prison. It had been damn near unbearable and he had been a much younger man. The chances of him living out a long prison term were impossible. At that thought, he rolled over and pulled Tory in close to him and just breathed in her scent. She always smelled like peaches. That would be something he could cling to during those long days and nights, the fragrance of Tory and her peaches. He wanted to cry at the thought of leaving her and never seeing her again, but he couldn't. He had to be brutally strong or his resolve would weaken and he would welcome her coming up to Edmonton. He couldn't allow that. Not for her and not for him.

Tory was already awake when the sun came up. Knowing that the next time she would see Steve might be through prison bars, she could not close her eyes and lose herself in sleep. She had dozed, but mostly she had listened to Steve's uneasy breathing. A couple of times she thought he had been on the verge of crying but perhaps it had been her imagination. He appeared ready to accept whatever his fate would be, and he seemed to think it would not be good. She had faith in the system, however, and hoped that the circumstantial evidence would not be enough to convict him. They had made love with the urgency of knowing there might be no tomorrow. It began with tenderness then blossomed into heated passion erupting in a raw craving for satiety. Afterward, he had reached for her a couple of times and pulled her close to him as if he were hanging on to life itself.

She knew he was adamant about her not going up for his trial and she had promised to abide by his wishes. It would be extremely difficult staying behind, not knowing what was going on up there, whether things were going his way or not, but she had given her word and she would live with it. However, he had not said anything about her not visiting if he went to prison and she was not going to bring it up. If he didn't think about it, he couldn't force her to make promises that she knew she wouldn't keep. Whatever his background, he was the best damn man she had ever met and she would stand by him. *Whether the stubborn old fool wants me to or not.*

Now she had to pull herself from his side and make him some breakfast and coffee, then see him on his way. How was she ever going to get through a day without him? Blast his hide. Why did he have to come into her life anyway if he couldn't stay? She punched her pillow and jumped out of bed before she started to cry.

Steve woke and moved into the shower so she went down to get the coffee started and use the toilet in the little washroom off the kitchen. She was standing looking at her face in the mirror, wondering how she had aged so much overnight, when Steve wandered into the kitchen and saw the devastation in her eyes. As soon as she saw his reflection behind hers she took a deep breath, determined to make this last half hour together as pleasant as possible. She smiled and turned to kiss him. He took her face in his hands and rubbed noses with her, telling her that he wanted to remember her just as she was. That he wanted to remember her beautiful platinum hair suffering the ravages of their lovemaking; her one eye underlined with a little left-over mascara; her pajamas buttoned crooked so one corner hung down lower. She laughed, and after a kiss on the neck, he sent her upstairs with a pat on the bum.

Half an hour later he was gone and she was alone. So alone. She sat at the living room window, buried her face in her arm and cried the forlorn, deep wailing of a woman left to mourn. Her eyes were almost swollen shut when she finally lifted herself from the chair. Some lingering sobs sneaked up uninvited and when she put her hand to her mouth to stifle them she felt her badly swollen lips. She ran cold water in the sink and squeezed a washcloth under the tap then held it repeatedly over each eye and against her lips. Now her mascara was very badly smudged and her hair was an absolute mess. She giggled to herself remembering Steve's words.

It was mid-morning and she hadn't thought about supper for Tom and Skip. She realized that life goes on and that two very hungry young men would be counting on her to give them a hot, filling meal. After checking in the freezer, she decided on chicken and dumplings and lemon meringue pie. She didn't want to cook anything that would remind her of Steve. It had to be something she had never cooked for him and she knew he was not fond of anything with lemons in it. She decided to add some peas to the chicken pot just for good measure.

Steve must have had a talk with the young ranch hands before he left because they at no time brought Steve's name into the conversation. They talked about the ranch and the cattle and the scores of the semi-final rounds in the hockey. They even talked about one girl in town who had caught Tom's eye. After several years of working at the same ranch, near the same town, this was the first time this particular girl had gotten his attention. They lingered a bit over a second piece of pie and seemed almost uncertain whether to leave or stay. Finally, Tory let them off the hook by telling them she had sewing to do and needed the kitchen table to work on.

When they had gone and the dishes were all put away, Tory decided to take control of herself and pulled out some sewing she had started months earlier but hadn't finished.

She took her machine-finished product into the living room to complete the hand sewing and turned on the TV to watch one of the hockey games. Her mind kept wandering, however. She kept picturing Steve all alone in a hotel in Edmonton. Wishing she had never promised to keep away from him, she felt utterly useless. Finally, she picked up the phone and called Becky just to have someone to talk with. They chatted awhile about the grandchildren and finally the topic came around to Steve. Tory explained that Steve had gone to Edmonton that morning to get ready for his trial. Becky was sympathetic with her mother's wanting to be with him, but she was glad that Steve had made it impossible. Sitting in a courtroom watching the progression of a murder trial in which her boyfriend was the defendant was not something that Becky wanted her mother to experience.

"Why don't you come down here for a while, Mom?"

"Thanks, honey, but no. I want to stay around in case Steve's lawyer calls. He may change his mind and want me to testify. And besides, I have to cook for Tom and Skip. And Alfred. Who would look after that old man if I went away?"

"Mom, you can't take on the plight of the whole world. You have to think of yourself once in a while."

"I am thinking of myself, Becky. I would be a wreck if I left here right now. Please understand that I *must* stay—for me."

"I understand that you want to be close by, but please don't overwork yourself taking care of all those men."

"I love you, darling. Give Josh and Maggie a big hug from their grandma and give that awful man you're married to a pinch from his wonderful mother-in-law."

Laughing, Becky replied, "I will, Mom. Take care. I love you, too."

Tory barely had the phone back in place when it rang. Quickly picking it up hoping it was Steve, she breathlessly answered, "Hello."

"Hi, Tory."

Second best. "Hi, George. What's up? Did Steve get there OK?"

"We spent the better part of the afternoon and evening together. I've been trying to talk him into letting me get a taped deposition from the girl's uncle but he is as stubborn as a mule."

"You mean you want old Alfred to testify?"

"He's the only one that can help. If he testifies that he asked Steve to check in on his niece and help look after her, it would go a long way to help his credibility as to why he was in her house in the first place. But Steve won't hear of it. Says it might kill the old man if reporters got wind of the old guy's connection and started bothering him for a story. Apparently the old guy doesn't go anywhere? Never leaves his house?"

"That's correct. Alfred is pretty crippled up and almost deaf. Steve has been looking after him for years. I understand when the old man's sister died he was concerned about his niece's welfare. He knew she was married to a guy who liked to slap her around and he was worried, especially after her husband was free again. George, how is Steve?"

"He's OK. Stubborn like I said, but he's OK. He's one hell of a guy. I've taken a liking to him. He's a little rough around the edges but I believe he's honest. I hope that comes across to the jury."

"Will you keep in touch? Keep me informed?"

"As much as I can without violating client privilege."

"Just let me know how it's going. I don't imagine the news programs will follow it very much. Steve is just a small rancher and Joanne was only a waitress so they're not very newsworthy."

"It will all depend on what else is happening in the news. I'll call you from time to time. Let you know where we're at."

"Will you tell me where he's staying?"

"No."

"I didn't think so."

"Good night, Tory."

"Good night, George, and thanks for calling."

That dumb, stubborn little runt! Why the hell won't he let his friends help him? She knew that Alfred would not want to see Steve in jail, that he would rather have the real killer captured and punished. Why couldn't Steve understand that?

19

THE REST OF THE WEEK went by so slowly it seemed like Steve had been gone for a month. On weekends, the boys would go into town for their suppers. Tory found that planning their meals gave her a reason to get up in the morning. Without that motivation, who knew how her depression might have overtaken her. She knew that Steve had arranged for a cleaning lady to come in once every two weeks. He would not hear of Tory working like a cleaning woman, no matter how much she had argued that it would do her good and help fill her days. He told her that visiting her grandchildren would also fill her days.

One Saturday afternoon she decided to go into town to get her groceries for the following week. She had planned a menu and written a grocery list. When she walked into the supermarket, she could see heads turning as if synchronized. As she traversed the aisles, everyone smiled and nodded but she could feel the chill. She knew they were curious about Steve, but she supposed she was to be shunned for her association with a known criminal. Everyone had him guilty and executed without even knowing the details. Poor Steve had the biggest, kindest heart of anyone she knew. He was head and shoulders above anyone in this town. Let them stare; she would be polite and smile but they could rot in hell before she would tell them anything.

They had all been so nice to her when her aunt was sick and dying. Now they treated her like she had the plague. Even Liz had not called. When the real killer was found, they'd be embarrassed that they hadn't been nicer to Steve and to her. And he will be found. Of that she was confident. She finished her shopping and stopped at the library for some fresh reading material before heading home.

Steve had taken her car into the shop for a tune-up and an inspection before he left. After a few minor repairs, the mechanic had told her it was as good as new. She drove with confidence, but Steve had told her in the event that it should give her any trouble, she was to leave it in the garage and drive his pick-up truck. He added that it would still be better if she would go back east, then he wouldn't be worrying about her. He kept mumbling about her being a stubborn, selfish woman.

Finally, the trial was under way. The jury selection came first and then the pre-trial motions, et cetera. She still wasn't sure what the preliminaries were before they actually got started with the witnesses and the testimony. She knew a jury trial was far different from court hearings in front of a judge but that was as far as her knowledge of courtroom procedure extended. She wished she could be there to see for herself that everything was being done right for Steve. George had said he had taken a liking to Steve, that he was an honest man. Maybe that would make him go that extra mile. She felt helpless. There was literally no news about the trial, only the gossip she had heard in town before everyone clammed up when she came near them.

George finally phoned after the end of the first week of testimony and said the Crown had been really hard on Steve. They had pulled up everything from his past and then some. He didn't go into detail with Tory because most of it was quite demeaning to Steve. He had been right in keeping her away. Her testimony wouldn't have done him that much good anyway; she had been out of town herself on the night in question. The Crown would have torn her apart and made her look pathetic. The only thing he felt that could truly help Steve was the old man's testimony but Steve was remaining adamant about that not happening. George had very few witnesses to call. His whole case lay in cross-examination and trying to discredit the Crown witnesses. Then he hoped he might instill some doubt about the circumstantial evidence in his closing argument. It would not be enough, he knew that already, but he had to give it his best shot.

The trial lasted only ten days. The jury was out for less than an hour. Steve was found guilty with no recommendation for leniency. He seemed to have already accepted his fate and appeared to be relieved it was all over, George told her. George himself felt like hell. He knew in his gut the man was innocent.

When the phone rang, Tory had stood with her hand on it for several rings before she could bring herself to answer. "Hello?"

"I'm sorry. The jury didn't believe us."

"Oh, God. Oh, God. No. How is he? Will he let me come and see him now?"

"They have him in custody again, awaiting sentencing. He seems OK. He actually seems relieved. I think he knew what the outcome was going to be and he just wanted to get it behind him."

"Will he let me come and see him?"

"No."

"How long will it take for the judge to sentence him?"

"A week. Maybe two. There isn't a lot of evidence for the judge to go over. And there were no character witnesses for him so the judge doesn't have a lot to weigh."

"You're saying he's going to get a long sentence?"

"Tory, I don't know. Just when you think a judge is going to throw the book at someone, the judge lets him off easy and other times they're tired of certain crimes and decide to set an example. Maybe his age will work for him but each judge and each case is different."

"What do you think he'll get?"

"Tory, don't ask."

"What do you think he'll get?" She was not going to be put off.

"Honestly? I'll be surprised if he gets less than twenty."

"He's sixty-six years old. He'll never come out."

"I'll certainly use his age as an argument. As I said, each judge is different, and we may get lucky. I'll call you when the sentencing is over."

"Is there an address where I can write to him?"

"Not yet. I'll let you know."

She went through the motions each day. She got up and showered, ate her breakfast and cleaned her house until she had taken a layer of paint and wax off along with the dirt. She cooked supper for the men and read and watched the hockey playoffs on TV. She wasn't even aware of which teams were playing.

A week later George called to tell her that Steve was sentenced to fifteen years with no chance for parole. He would be eighty-one years old, and Tory would be seventy-seven. She could write to him at the medium security prison at Drumheller for now, she was told, but he would probably be moved. And no, he definitely would not see her.

A week later, George called again. He wondered if Tory could make a trip up to Edmonton as he had some papers of Steve's for her to sign.

"What kind of papers?"

"Because his prison term is long, Steve is thinking he has no likelihood of getting out. He asked me to draw up some papers concerning his personal assets."

"His personal assets?"

"He has signed everything over to you, Tory. He wants you to sell it all and donate a portion of it to a foundation for the education of homeless boys that he talked to me about."

"He wants me to sell his ranch? I can't do that. He worked too hard to build it up. I can't sell it. I *cannot* sell it. Besides, what if he gets out? What if they find the real killer?"

"That's always a possibility, but not likely. I think he wants all these loose ends cleaned up. He'll be happier if he knows all this business has been taken care of. Can't you give him that peace of mind?"

"Peace of mind? I'll give him a piece of mind all right. *My* mind. If he would've let Alfred and me testify, he wouldn't need to sell his ranch."

"Tory, that's all behind us. No one feels worse about this than I do. I was his defense attorney for God's sake. Both of you were counting on me to win this case, but I didn't. Do you think I feel good about seeing a sixty-six-year-old man go to prison for a crime he didn't commit? It won't do you or him much good to second-guess what might have happened. It didn't happen, and now he just wants to be left in peace."

The tears came. She hung up with a promise to call George in a day or so. This couldn't be happening. Steve was going to come home. She just knew it. How could she sell his ranch? How could she live here knowing that strangers were on Steve's property? She couldn't. She would have to move. Where? If she stayed and Steve got out, at least he would have a home to come to. But would he be happy here when his own place was right next to it and strangers now owned it? She slumped to the floor. What was she to do? She knew it was Steve's way of trying to get her to leave. He knew she wouldn't be able to stay if she sold his place. But she couldn't leave. She just couldn't.

She would ask Tom and Skip if they were willing to stay on indefinitely. How would she pay them? She had enough money to pay them for a while, but for how long? She decided to take the drive up to Edmonton.

The next day, she called George's office and made an appointment for the following week. In the meantime, she had a long talk with the two hired hands. They were willing to work for this summer but wanted to wait before making a decision about the fall. Used to having the winter off and heading south, they told her they would have to think about staying on past October.

When George's secretary called her into his office, Tory squared her shoulders, all set to do battle. He greeted her with a warm smile and a hearty handshake. After discussing the outcome of the semi-final hockey playoffs, they got down to business. Copies of the deed to Steve's ranch and the legal descriptions of all of his vehicles, farm equipment and a broad coverage of the furnishings and contents of his house were all laid out for her.

"Steve had a bank account and some investments that will also be signed over to you, minus the legal costs of the trial and our office services pertaining to the disbursement of Steve's assets. Steve wanted to maintain his own investments separately from the insurance policy Lottie MacArthur had given him—for a future time when he might be released. You will have his power of attorney for these in case he should fall ill. Steve says he'll need something to live on in his old age."

"I'm relieved to hear that last sentence because up to this point, it had sounded like we were dealing with a deceased person's estate. Are there any written conditions associated with my acceptance of Steve's property?"

George assured her that they would be hers to do with as she pleased, but he hoped she would respect Steve's wishes and dispose of the property the way he wanted. She asked how much the property had been valued at. When he told her, she asked how much Steve had wanted donated to the foundation.

"One hundred thousand dollars," George replied. "That's if you get a fair price for the property. He didn't want you running yourself short. He knows you'll have certain taxes to pay on all of this."

Tory smiled and shook her head at that. She had enough money of her own to live comfortably but it was just like him to make sure she was well cared for.

After signing the necessary papers, she asked, "How long will it take before all the legal documents are taken care of?"

"It's a clean deal. All that will be necessary is to file the papers with the Alberta government and pay the filing fees associated with that. A survey may be required but my guess would be that it could all be taken care of in a matter of weeks."

"Can I see Steve?"

"Definitely not. Don't even waste your time going to the prison. Steve will only refuse to see you. He wants you to get on with your life. I'll call you when the papers are all in place and the deed and monies transferred."

She gave him her bank branch and account number so the funds could be transferred electronically. "I'll send them to Weston and you can sign them in front of a notary there if you like. It'll save you another trip up here."

"George, the fewer the people in Weston who know Steve's business and mine, the better. I'll come back to Edmonton and sign everything. My only regret is that the township will now know I'm the owner of the ranch through the municipal tax registry."

"Do you have a real estate lawyer to help you with the sale?"

"I'll worry about that when the time comes."

When he called her a few weeks later, she drove to Edmonton, signed the papers, left him a check for one hundred thousand dollars payable to the foundation Steve wanted to support. She thanked him for his help and walked out. Inside her car, she took several deep breaths and turned her car south.

Her mind was made up. At 62 she was now a proud ranch owner and come hell or high water, it was going to remain a successful ranch until Steve came back to live on it—whether he wanted it or not. If it were to be sold, he would be the one to do it.

Maybe she couldn't visit him, but she was damn well going to write to him. If he tore up her letters without reading them, that would be his problem.

Once a week, faithfully, she sat down at her kitchen table and filled him in on each week's events. She got into a routine between her house and his. At first, looking after two houses was overwhelming but it wasn't long before she found it wasn't impossible. She kept the cleaning woman that came bi-weekly to his place. All she had to do was keep the kitchen tidy for the men who ate their breakfasts and lunches at the ranch. They continued coming to her house daily for supper. She got the hang of the riding lawn mower and the rototiller for weeding the gardens. Her days were full and she was thankful for that as it kept her from dwelling too much on the man sitting in Drumheller prison. He hadn't answered any of her letters, but he hadn't sent them back either so she hoped he was reading them.

Three times a week, she went to visit old Alfred. She was grateful for his knowledge of ranching and farming and the many tips she picked up from him. He would always tell her to make sure those young fellows remembered to do this or that. It seemed to please him that he was helping her in return for all she was doing for him. She assured him that she passed along his greetings to Steve and remarked that hopefully one of these days Steve would write back.

She routinely had to sit down with the two boys and go over some of the financial matters. The health of the cattle was constantly monitored, the pastures checked for adequate food supply. The water was a source of some concern but so far the wells and creeks were holding their own. There had been no mechanical breakdowns because Steve had checked all of his machinery pretty thoroughly before his trial.

At night, after all the work was done, she would sit in the living room and turn the TV on. This was the time of day she felt the loneliest. Her thoughts would automatically wander to him sitting in a cell. *Are you already asleep, Steve? Can you feel the love I'm sending?*

She was sure they rose pretty early in prison, not that they were eager for the start of another wonderful day, of course. She wondered why in the world they had to get up so early—just part of their punishment she guessed. Was he getting enough to eat? She would have loved to take him some chocolate cake, or an apple pie. A number of times the tears came and then she would curse him for not having allowed Alfred or her come to his defense. She could understand his reasoning, but she could not forgive him for it.

There were so many things she wanted to talk to him about. Would he be angry with her for not selling the ranch? What would she do if the boys decided not to stay on for the winter? Could she find someone experienced to stay on? She was learning something about cattle from the young fellows and from having to make the decisions. Knowing what to do and actually doing it were two different things, though. Steve had stayed on the ranch alone all winter. Perhaps she could talk one of them into doing it as well. He could stay right in the house where it was warmer and more comfortable. Or maybe they'd be willing to split the winter, one stay for the early winter and the other for the late winter. That was a thought. She would talk to them soon.

The summer dragged on and the little rain that fell was not even measurable. The farmers in southern and central Alberta—and even into Saskatchewan—were talking about a return of the Dust Bowl, the years during the hungry '30s that the prairies were so dry, the topsoil blew clean away. It wasn't that bad yet, but some of the creeks were almost dry. The fire hazard was extremely high. Fortunately, Tory had enough well water to take care of her vegetable garden so she was able to fill her freezer with produce. As July turned to August, she worried about the fall and winter for the animals. Feed prices were already high and they would go much higher. Perhaps she *had* been foolish hanging on to Steve's place. Well, it was do-or-die now. Skip had agreed to stay the winter for room and board and a reduced salary. He had no place to call home so he welcomed an opportunity to stay put for a winter. He also agreed to look after the snow plowing at both places as well as at Alfred's. Tory also suggested that he could pick up extra money plowing elsewhere; he could do that as long as he maintained the equipment.

With that worry behind her, Tory left the men in charge of the sale of the beef and getting it to market. The prices were pretty fair this year as their stock was healthy and well fed. She was confident that the ranch would turn a profit, a small one, but a profit nonetheless. Not bad for an eastern city woman who didn't know a steer from a cow. Of course, without the young men, she would have been lost and made a mental note to pay them a good bonus after the cattle were delivered and the money received.

September had always been her favorite month and now it was almost over. She loved the crisp, clear air and the fragrance of the wooded areas. A lot of the forests in the mountains comprised fir trees so the colors didn't change quite as dramatically as back east where the deciduous trees were abundant. There were just enough maple, birch and poplar to give a grand enough show to appease an autumn lover like Tory. Every once in a while, depending on the weather, the far off mountain tops, normally a smoky blue, would deepen to a mauve or purple—*deep purple*, she thought, like her leathers that she'd probably not wear again.

She knew she would miss having Steve around to help with the firewood. When she looked at the load of cut logs that was neatly stacked in her yard, she remembered the reaming she had received from him the year before. With the knowledge that for an extra charge they would stack it for you, she had been wiser when she ordered the wood this year. *God, has it been almost a year since I came out here?* Sitting on a chair on the back deck she looked out over her yard and remembered how he had taken charge of her affairs. He had made sure there was always a neat store of logs by her fireplace, kept her driveway clean, put up her Christmas lights and took over any other labor that might be classified as a man's work. They had argued like cat and dog last fall and if she were really honest with herself, she had started loving him even then. It had taken her until Christmas to realize it, but once over her initial fear of him, she realized she respected the kind, honest man that lived inside that hard, gruff exterior.

Again she cursed him for being so stubborn. The tears didn't come as often anymore but as she sat taking in the fall landscape around her, she couldn't help but wonder if he were sitting in his cell remembering last autumn as well. The teardrops started rolling down her cheeks. "Damn you, Steve. I hope you are as miserable as I am!"

She had shouted out and shook her fist in the general direction of Drumheller, without realizing she had voiced her despair out loud. She started sobbing and didn't hear the movement of someone coming around the corner of the house. When he came close enough for her to catch the sound, she jumped, startled and embarrassed that someone had caught her crying.

"I was hoping you might have been through cursing him by now." It was George Stefurak.

20

"Every once in a while I seem to remember something and lose control. Most times, I'm OK."

"I see you're still here. Did you get a good price for Steve's place?"

"I didn't sell it."

"I'm not surprised. You are one stubborn woman."

"Steve used to tell me that quite regularly. What brings you here, George? Checking up on your client's interests?"

"Actually, I'm just on my way back home from Drumheller. I thought you might want to hear about Steve."

Panic fluttered in the pit of her stomach. "What about Steve? He's all right isn't he? Nothing's happened to him?"

"He's doing OK. Complaining about the food, but looks pretty good. He's grown a moustache."

"He didn't say if I could come and see him, did he?"

"Actually, if justice prevails, you might. And I want to impress the *might*, see him released this winter."

Tory's knees weakened and she slumped onto the deck chair. "He's... he's OK? He's not sick or anything?"

George sat in the chair opposite hers and took both her hands in his. "I don't want to get your hopes up, Tory, but the alibi for the only other suspect may not be so ironclad anymore. It seems that Joanne's ex-husband beat up his girlfriend one too many times. She turned herself into police custody in Calgary claiming she gave false testimony to the police. Alec Dimmery, Joanne's ex, had threatened to kill her if she didn't back his story up. The girlfriend was in love with him, thought he was the best thing that had ever come into her life, and she didn't want to lose him. God knows, if he's the best, I hate to think about the previous scum she's been with. Anyway, last week he came home not only drunk, but high on something and damn near beat her to death. When he passed out in the bedroom, she made it outside and fell in front of a passing car. The driver swerved and avoided hitting her, then called the police on his cell phone. She gave the police the story but has demanded protective custody until Alec is put away."

Hardly anything that George had said penetrated Tory's conscious mind. The only thing she heard was that Steve might be freed. "How long?"

"Pardon?"

"How long before he can come home?"

"*If* he can come home, it will take a while. The police have to check out her story to make sure she's not just angry and trying to get her man put away for spite. The court has to be convinced there is a possibility Alec may have committed the crime. I'll fight for a new trial for Steve, or at least for him to be released on bail pending a new hearing based on this evidence."

"How long?"

"I'll try to get an early hearing. If her story checks out and they take it to trial, it could be early in the new year."

"He'll be in there for Christmas. Oh, God, I want him home with me."

"He asked about you. He said you've been writing."

"He reads my letters then?"

"He lives for them, he said, but I wasn't supposed to tell you that."

"Can I write him that you were here and have given me this news?"

"I told him I would be stopping in. I felt you deserved to hear this. You've been so loyal to him."

"Loyal? I love the man, for God's sake! It's not loyalty. It's love."

After assuring her he would keep her abreast of the proceedings, the lawyer gave her a hug and left. No longer feeling miserable, her love of the month of September was renewed. Steve would be freed. He would be coming home. She had to go and tell Alfred the news.

The old man was sound asleep in the chair when she let herself in. "Alfred, I have some wonderful news. Steve will be coming home." He must be sleeping very soundly she thought. When she gave his arm a shake she realized his face was contorted and his arm was curled into his side.

"Oh, no. Oh, no! Alfred, you've got to be all right, do you hear me?" She felt for a pulse and checked his breathing. They were both there, but weak. Tory whispered that she had to get help and after tucking an afghan around him, she drove home to call for an ambulance.

The paramedics were quick in coming and she followed the ambulance in her own vehicle. She knew he was like Steve in that he had no family. His only relative had been his niece, the one that Steve had been accused of killing. When she arrived at the hospital, they had taken him into the small intensive care unit where her aunt had been. The doctor finally found her in the waiting room and confirmed what she had suspected. Alfred had suffered a massive brain hemorrhage. The doctor thought it probably had happened the evening before and that the damage was quite extensive. He offered to notify Alfred's family for her so they could decide on the next course of treatment. When informed he had no family, the doctor asked if anyone had been given his power of attorney concerning his medical care. Tory was about to say no, but wondered if possibly Steve knew. She told the doctor she would find out and get back to him as quickly as possible. He told her there really was not much that could be done for him, but someone in charge of his care may want him transferred to a larger facility. They also required his medical insurance information.

Tory knew that George would not be back in Edmonton yet and wondered whether she might be able to get through to Steve herself. It was worth a try. She drove home and put in a call to the prison in Drumheller. It was almost an hour later when her phone rang and someone asked for Mrs. Hardisty. When she confirmed her identity, she was told to stay on the line. The next voice she heard was Steve's. She was stunned into silence when she heard him say *Hello, Tory.*

"Tory? Are you there?"

Shaken, her voice was strained when she replied, "Steve, it is so good to hear your voice."

She thought she detected a tremor in his reply, "How's the most beautiful woman in Weston?"

"I'll ask her the next time I see her."

"They tell me that Alfred's in the hospital."

"Yes. He's had a really bad stroke. They're asking for next of kin or anyone who might have his power of attorney. Do you know of anyone?"

"Joanne was his only kin. He told me he had a box in his dresser drawer with all his instructions about what to do if he died or wasn't able to look after himself anymore. I guess you can dig it out and give it to the doctor. Or to Old Man Atkinson, the lawyer. They might have something on file there. That's about all I can tell you."

"Steve, are you doing OK? I think about you all the time."

"I'm OK. They don't give a fella much chocolate cake but other than that it's not too bad."

"I check the mail every day. Maybe someday I'll find a letter has arrived."

"You were supposed to go back east."

"I feel closer to you here. George came to see me today. That's why I went to see Alfred. Steve, I'll be waiting right here for you when you get out."

"Don't get your hopes up, girl, there's a long way to go before that chance becomes a reality."

"My hopes are already built up." Hearing someone tell him that time was up, she quickly told him she loved him and heard a soft "I love you, too" before the phone was placed back on the receiver.

She had to sit and savor the conversation for several minutes. His voice sounded good. *Of course it sounded good, you silly goose.* Trying to picture him with a moustache, she could only come up with a grandfatherly image. Actually, he was about the size and age she remembered her grandfather being.

She took the picture of the two of them from the mantel, the one taken last Christmas. Wiping non-existent dust from the glass, she smiled through her tears and whispered, "Soon, Steve. We'll have you home soon."

Once again in her car, she drove the few miles to Alfred's. The key was where she had hidden it after locking up the house. When she found the cigar box in his drawer, she took it to the kitchen table and looked for the paper she hoped would give the doctor the information he needed.

She had found a small leather case on his dresser with his health insurance card in it. She didn't see anything among the papers that would help the doctor but there was a sealed envelope with Steve's name on it. Should she open it? Would it have the papers inside? Perhaps she should give it to the lawyer to open. But if Alfred had wanted the lawyer to have it he would have given it to him, wouldn't he? Not sure what to do, she took the envelope out and dropped it into her purse. Perhaps she could ask George later what she should do with it. She took the box and his little wallet of sorts and drove into town, hoping to catch Robert Atkinson in his office.

"Mrs. Hardisty, what can I do for you today?" Robert's friendly voice interrupted her thoughts about Alfred alone in the hospital.

"Hello, Robert. I need a few minutes of your time, if you can spare them. I understand your father was Alfred Potter's attorney."

"Was? Has something happened to Alfred?"

"I used the past tense because your father is retired now. Do you have Alfred's file?"

"I will have my secretary pull it. Come into my office, Mrs. Hardisty, and tell me what this is all about."

When she explained what had happened and the urgency of her visit, he opened the buff-colored folder his secretary had retrieved, and started to shuffle through it. He found a copy of a will and also a power of attorney for Alfred's care. It seems Steve was the man in charge of both. She asked the lawyer to please call the hospital and give the doctor some direction since Steve was in prison and not in a position to execute Alfred's wishes.

By the time Tory made her way back to the hospital, it was early evening and the shadows were quite long. She parked in the visitors' area of the lot and went straight into the ICU. She was surprised to see a flurry of activity around Alfred's bed. She waited near the door until one of the nurses spotted her and came over. "He has suffered a second event, Mrs. Hardisty. It's not looking good for him right now."

Tory told the nurse to call her if she could see him, even for a few minutes. She would be waiting in the visitors' lounge. About ten minutes later, the same doctor who had looked after her aunt came to tell her she could see the old man. He was in a coma but he might be able to hear her.

She took the old man's hand in hers and pressed it to her cheek. She sat by his bed and leaned over his ear whispering loudly, "I came to tell you that Steve will be getting out. Your son-in-law's girlfriend confessed that she lied about his whereabouts that night. They are checking on her story now and then Steve can come home. Isn't that wonderful news? I thought you'd want to know that Joanne's murderer is finally going to be punished. I even spoke to Steve on the phone today! He sounded great! He asked about you, wondering if you were eating OK." She thought she saw some moisture in the corner of the old man's eye that hadn't been there before. Could it be a tear? She squeezed his hand and told him to get some rest. She promised to come back the next day when he might be feeling more like company. Giving his hand another squeeze, she kissed his cheek and stood. She was no sooner heading down the hallway when she heard the nurse call her name and realized that staff were rushing into his room. The alarm was sounding at the nursing station and she remembered all too well from the year before what that meant.

Steve was allowed to come home for the funeral. He was escorted into the little chapel at the funeral home by a prison guard minutes before the service. Tory was waiting for him in the front pew. He was dressed in a suit, one she didn't recognize. He was not wearing irons but he was not allowed to touch her, nor she to touch him. She watched him and couldn't help but think how much his moustache really did resemble her grandfather's. It gave his face some dignity she thought, kind of softened the hard lines. How she wanted to hug him, and even more, she needed him to hug her. As she sat beside him in the pew, she whispered that she had the envelope addressed to him from Alfred's cigar box. She asked what she should do with it.

"Tory, everything I have is yours. Open it and deal with it accordingly. I have no idea what it contains. Alfred never gave me any indication that it existed."

"I'll open it before you leave. Steve, it's so good to see you. I can hardly keep my eyes off you."

"The hard thing about being allowed out, is going back."

"The next time you're allowed out, there will be no going back."

"I understand you didn't sell my place."

"No, I couldn't. I knew you'd be back. The boys helped me and we'll even turn a profit. Not as big as you would have done, but a profit all the same."

"You are the most stubborn woman I have ever met."

She giggled. "I know, but you love me anyway."

The service began then. It was very brief, there were few mourners. Some came out of curiosity. It wasn't public knowledge that Steve would be there, but a few had guessed he would be since he and Alfred were like father and son. After the service, Tory quickly opened the envelope and found a penned note naming Steve the sole beneficiary to Alfred's estate. It was dated after his niece's death and had been witnessed by one William Wronosky—Skip. Tory had sent the boys over to check on Alfred a number of times and had given them hot dishes to take. She walked over and asked the guard if she could talk to Steve in private as they were leaving the cemetery. The guard could stay but she didn't want anyone else to hear their conversation.

When she told Steve what was contained in the envelope, he shook his head and said he could not understand what the old man was thinking. He advised her to take it to Robert and let him deal with it. All too soon, the guard told him it was time to head back. Tory put a hand on Steve's arm and quickly kissed him on the lips. The guard was about to protest but allowed it. "Go ahead." He smiled.

Steve quickly put his arms around Tory and kissed her gently at first then more firmly. She liked the feel of his moustache and his arms, especially his arms. Then he released her without looking at her and climbed into the police car. She watched it move away until it was out of sight.

Later that afternoon, she went into the post office and made copies of Alfred's last will and testament then she crossed the street to Robert Atkinson's office and waited until he was free. She had no idea what Alfred's estate entailed, but she was going to make sure that Steve got what was rightfully his. When she left Robert's office, she went home and wrote a letter to George and enclosed one of the copies she had made. Another copy she put into her desk drawer in an envelope marked S. TURNER.

The boys had said they would eat in town that night. They knew she would be at the old man's funeral and didn't want to put her to any bother. She made herself a sandwich and sat on her sofa looking at the photo album from the Christmas before and praying that she would have new pictures of her and Steve this year. George had said it would be into the new year before he would be released but she was hopeful things might fall into place more quickly. She ran her fingers over her lips and smiled. The old bugger sure could kiss. She had to give him that.

A week later, George called to tell her that Robert Atkinson had called him regarding Steve's inheritance. He had phoned Steve and was now passing along the message that Steve wanted to give Tory the power to execute Alfred Potter's estate. This was all getting very confusing for Tory.

"What am I supposed to do with it?" she asked.

"Steve said he felt the house should be sold and the money put into a program of some kind for abused women. He said he'd leave that up to you, Tory, but he wanted the house put on the market now before the snow comes and it has to be heated all winter."

"What about the furnishings and personal chattels?"

"Steve said if there is anything you want just to take it, otherwise hold an auction and get rid of it all since his niece isn't alive anymore."

"What a shame."

Tory remembered the high-quality crystal in which Albert had given her drinks and the china teacups he had insisted she use when she came for tea. Perhaps she would keep a couple of the cups and saucers just for the memories. *Well,* she thought, *better get a move on.* She had lots to do before snow came. George told her he would forward the necessary papers to Robert's office and she could sign everything there. She thanked him and told him to pass her love along to Steve next time he was talking to him.

Tory asked an auctioneer from Calgary to come out and give her an appraisal of Albert's household effects. She was surprised to learn that some of his wooden furniture pieces, paintings, china and crystal were worth a fair amount of money. They had been in his family, they guessed, for so long that no one had ever given them much thought. They chose the articles worth auctioning and the man advised her to have a garage sale for the balance. When she went through Albert's personal effects, she found he had cash stashed away in a number of places. When she had cleaned out all his pockets, humidors and old wallets, it totaled over fifty thousand dollars. She could not believe it. Then she remembered one of her friends speaking of an aunt who did not trust banks and had stashed over two hundred and fifty thousand around her house.

The auction was held in Calgary and netted close to seventy-five thousand dollars. She put all the money into the estate trust fund and when the sale of the house was completed a month later, that also went into the trust fund. Robert Atkinson then had her sign a check written on that account for one of the agencies in Calgary that sheltered abused women. Thinking of Joanne, she made sure the shelter was one that had a widely distributed 1-800 number and provided emergency transportation from the outlying communities.

The day after the house deal closed, it snowed. Not a blizzard like she remembered the first storm of the year before, but a decent snowfall. True to his word, Skip showed up early the next morning with the plow on the front of the jeep. A week later, Tom left, and she and Skip settled into a kind of togetherness that two neighbors, one young and one old, could call a friendship. It made her think of her aunt and Steve. She remembered to ask him, while it was still relatively warm out, if he would mind stringing her Christmas lights up for her.

Becky told her she was very disappointed that Tory was not coming east for Christmas. The grandchildren especially were reluctant for her to stay out there and have Christmas by herself. She assured them that she would not be by herself, that Steve would probably be out by then and they would have a nice quiet holiday, just the two of them. Perhaps, if Steve agreed, they would come east in the new year for a visit. Becky told her she was just being stubborn. "Have you put a hold on your remaining years in the hopes that he'll MAYBE be released? You're wasting your life waiting for a man who may never be allowed to come home. I like Steve, but… I *love* you."

21

Tory was relieved to see a blanket of snow. It would help relieve the still-dangerous forest fire situation. They had been lucky in their area: outside of the one in the spring, nothing more had developed. The fires up north in the mountains had raged out of control almost the whole summer.

She hoped the early snow was an indication of the winter to come. She had her wood, she had a young man to shovel her out, her house was warm and snug, and she had Steve coming home. The winter had prospects of being a grand one.

George was non-committal any time she phoned him about the progress with Steve. Apparently, Steve was upset that George had spilled the beans to Tory in the first place. He knew she would get her hopes up and he didn't want her disappointed, so he asked George not to tell her anything further until they knew for sure if he were being released, and when. George had been right: it was a long slow process. It was proving to be difficult to find witnesses who could corroborate the woman's confession. But George assured Tory, they were not leaving any stone unturned.

One night, when she was watching one of the Oilers games on TV, her phone rang. It was Liz.

"Well, a voice from the past," Tory replied to Liz's greeting.

"Oh, Tory, I know I should have called before but I didn't know if you were staying or going. Some of us are going to The Roadhouse tonight and we thought—for old time's sake—you might like to join us? Have a couple of drinks? Dr. Needy's found himself a girlfriend so you wouldn't have to deal with him." Liz attempted a light laugh.

"Thanks, Liz, but I'll pass. I'm still rather defensive when it comes to Steve and I wouldn't want to spoil your conversations."

"Tory, you're not the type to hold a grudge are you?"

"Hold a grudge? Me? Why would that be? Surely not because the whole town had Steve guilty before he even went to trial. You included, Liz. Thank you for the invitation but I'm in the middle of something here and I don't want to leave it."

She hung up the phone. *Of all the nerve. What? Have they heard rumors and want to get the lowdown? Well, they can call somebody else. I should have given her George's number and let him answer her questions. Maybe she'd get more out of him than I've been getting.*

She knew she shouldn't be bitter, and that some day she may need her former friends, but she found the immediate condemnation of Steve hard to stomach. They hadn't even given him a chance. As soon as the murder had been committed and Steve picked up, he had been tried, found guilty and condemned to die by the whole lot of them. Well, she would wait and see if they apologized when he came home.

She continued to cook supper for Skip every day. She found him to be an intelligent young man who seemed to have an interest in everything. His education had not gone beyond high school. He said if it hadn't been for the constant prodding of his father, he would have quit and joined the rodeo circuit on his sixteenth birthday. As soon as he had that graduation diploma in his hand, he moved north and started working at a large ranch east of Calgary. At one of the cattle auctions a few years later he had met Steve, the two men had sat down and had a few beers, "And I've been working for him ever since." He liked Steve a lot and never, for one minute, felt the old man was guilty, or even could be guilty of anything like that. Especially not of murdering Alfred's kin.

Tory asked him what he found so fulfilling about ranch life and he said he liked working outdoors, that it would kill him to work indoors all day. He really liked the animals. He had been brought up in the city and in the sixth grade his class was taken on an outing to a farm outside of town. He never forgot how much he enjoyed that visit. He said the cows were especially interesting, then the horses. He knew, from the age of 11, exactly what he wanted to do when he grew up: ranching.

He expressed a sorrow that he didn't know more about the animals' make up. There were times, he said, when he felt helpless. A sick or injured animal really upset him.

"Why don't you take a correspondence course on animal husbandry?"

"I never thought about it to be honest with you. I always head south every winter and never gave much thought to continuing my schooling. Do you think it's possible?"

"Let's take a look on the computer and see what we can find."

"I never worked a computer, Tory."

"Then let this be your first lesson. Let's take a look."

After researching and finding little in the way of distance-learning university courses in animal husbandry, Tory offered to browse the library in town for him. She wanted to look for any books that might get him started and then if he felt he wanted to continue, they might find something with courses starting in January. The young man seemed genuinely grateful to Tory for her interest in him and for her help.

Her Christmas lights were strung and she was determined to have her house decorated and ready for Steve's return. Christmas last year had meant so much to him, and while they would not have the children around this year, she was going to make it just as meaningful. Tory was determined that Steve would be home for the holiday. At the beginning of December, Skip took her out and they found Christmas trees for both houses and she promised to come and help him decorate his. His young sister and her boyfriend had promised to come and spend a few days with him over the holidays. She told him that she would cook Christmas dinner for all of them. He had devoured the books she had found for him and had registered for one biology course through a distance learning program in Calgary.

Christmas was drawing closer and there was still no word from George on Steve's release. He was very evasive when she called and she was not happy about it. Maybe she would just have to face up to the fact that justice could *not* be rushed. Damn it though, she did not want Steve spending Christmas in prison. If only he would let her come to visit him. She missed him terribly and thought perhaps it was going to be harder on her than on him to be apart this year. Again she cursed herself for letting him into her life.

On Christmas Eve, she received a phone call from her family in the east and they chatted and sang Christmas carols together. Josh told her a Christmas story his class had read together at school about a homeless child who was found by a childless couple on Christmas Eve. They told her they would call again in the morning and they could all open each other's gifts while they were on the phone. She hung up, turned on the TV and mixed herself a drink. She knew she should have gone into town for the Christmas Eve service but she was reluctant to leave just in case... Dammit, he wasn't coming after all. She set her glass down on the coffee table and reached for a tissue. She blew her nose then looked at the small present she had placed under the tree for Steve and cried all the harder.

The phone rang again and at first she ignored it. She was not in the mood to chat with anyone. *Oh, but what if it's the kids again?* she wondered and picked it up.

"Hello."

"You don't sound very merry, it being Christmas and all."

"Steve? Steve, is that you? Oh, I just knew you'd call. How are you?"

"I'm fine, Tory. And you?"

"Much better. Now."

"Can you come get me?"

"Get you? Where? Where are you?"

"The bus depot. In town."

She couldn't answer. Her breathing had stopped.

"Unless you don't want to."

"Don't you move! I'll be right there. Don't you dare move, you hear?" She hung up the phone, grabbed her jacket and ran out the door without even looking in the mirror.

The ride to town had never seemed so long. Steve, her Steve, was home! Deep in her heart she'd known all along that he'd be home for Christmas. As she turned the corner and pulled up in front of the bus depot, she could see him inside drinking a cup of coffee. She pulled into a parking spot and watched him through the window. He wore a denim jacket and jeans, no visible hat or gloves. He didn't see her until she sat on the stool beside him and placed a hand on his arm. He patted her hand, not looking at her.

Finally, he turned and kissed her without saying a word. Her tears came and he grinned, "You got black stuff running down your cheeks."

She quickly wiped her eyes with the sleeve of her jacket. "If I had known all I had to do was cry to make that phone ring, I would have started earlier in the day."

He stood up and put an arm around her shoulders. "Let's go home and mess up your hair."

They rode in silence most of the way, stealing glances at each other, grinning and winking. She wouldn't let go of his hand except to turn the ignition off when they arrived in her driveway. Once inside the house, he grabbed her and wrapped his arms around her in a bear hug. Then his tears fell. They clung to each other in the warm kitchen for several long minutes and finally he released her.

"I can't believe you're still here."

"You always said I was a stubborn woman."

"I never knew how stubborn. George told me you were a real pain in the ass."

"Speaking of George, why didn't he tell me you were coming home?"

"Because I told him not to. I didn't want you to know until I actually walked out the front door of that place. Only then I could be sure they were actually letting me go. Then when I got outside this morning, I phoned him and told him that I wanted to surprise you."

"Damn you, Steve. I knew you would be home for Christmas, but did you have to leave it till the last minute?"

He laughed and pulled her to him. "I don't know why I came back. All you do is swear at me."

"Come into the living room and sit down. I want to get a good look at you, Steve Turner. I can hardly believe you're here. Can I get you a drink?"

"You sure can, a good strong one."

"Have you eaten?" She called from the kitchen.

"What have you got?" He called back.

"I don't suppose you've lost your taste for chocolate layer cake?" As she was speaking, she came in with a tray of cold cuts, cheeses and some cold canapés. In one corner sat a glass with rum and Coke, and a small plate with a big slice of chocolate cake.

"How did you get that ready so fast?"

"It's been ready all day, just waiting for you to call."

"What the— Did George call you after all?"

"No, he did not. I just knew you would be here. I felt it in my bones."

She placed the tray on the coffee table next to her unfinished drink. He took her hand and kissed it. "I don't deserve you, Tory. I've brought you nothing but grief and here you are—still."

"You've given me nothing but happiness. It's the law that's given us both grief. Nothing matters now, though. You're home and that's all that counts. Just hold me for a while. It feels good to have your arms around me."

She put her arms around his waist and leaned against his chest. He put one arm around her shoulders and the other around her waist. She sobbed while he kissed her forehead repeatedly.

"When's the last time you had a decent meal?"

"Last April."

She pulled away and looked at him in dismay.

He laughed, "Prison cooking is filling but I wouldn't call it decent. I certainly will look forward to whatever you've got on the menu for tomorrow."

"Skip, his sister and her boyfriend will all be here for dinner tomorrow. I hope you don't mind."

"Are they all staying at the ranch?"

"Yes."

"Do you mind if I stay here then?"

"You're not getting out of my sight for a long time, Steve Turner." Under her breath she mumbled, "If ever."

"Well, I think I'll try to do this tray of goodies some justice. I'm a little bit hungry."

That proved to be an understatement as he cleaned off the whole platter, had a second piece of cake, then coffee after he had downed his drink. Tory sat smiling while she watched her man eat.

Steve carried the tray into the kitchen for her. He leaned against the counter while she put the dishes in the dishwasher and wiped the tray off.

"It looks like Skip's been taking care of you OK. Your driveway looks pretty good and I see you've got kindling cut and wood stacked."

"He's been very good to me, thanks to you."

"Why thanks to me?"

"He has nothing but the utmost respect for you, Steve. He told me that I must be a pretty good woman for you to have taken a liking to me and he has thanked me several times for standing by you. I think he's grateful for the opportunity of taking care of your ranch for you."

"When I went away, I didn't think I'd ever get out, let alone have a ranch to come home to. And I certainly didn't expect you to still be here." His eyes filled with tears again and Tory drew him to her.

She put her arms around him and patted the back of his head while whispering soothing words into his ear, like comforting a baby. "I never thought I would ever love a man the way I love you, and especially not at this time in my life. You would think I'd get smart in my old age but here I am, grateful as hell to have you back. I was so afraid you wouldn't come here when you got out. I thought that was why George wasn't telling me anything."

"Woman, I didn't want you sitting out here waiting for a man that wasn't ever going to come home. I just don't get it. I don't know how I ever got so lucky to have a good woman like you care about me. When George told me you wouldn't sell my ranch and that you were staying put, determined that I'd be back, I couldn't believe what a damn stubborn filly you are. I guess I knew then that I had the best woman God ever placed on this earth. It didn't make it any easier for me in there, that's why I wouldn't let you come and see me. When I had to go back after Alfred's funeral, it tore me apart to leave you. I couldn't bear going through that same thing every visiting day. I know I'm selfish, but if I couldn't have you full time, I didn't want you at all."

"I don't understand, though. I never heard of a second trial, is there one still pending? Are you free for good, or what?"

"Alec Dimmery finally confessed to the murder. He tried to make the police believe his girlfriend was drunk and couldn't remember anything clearly, but before long he realized he was only digging himself in deeper. If she couldn't remember anything, then her original testimony wasn't worth the paper it was written on. When he realized his alibi was blown, he then wanted to plead self-defense saying that Joanne came at him with a knife. By the time the police were finished with him, he just gave up. It took a long time but it's done and he's in custody waiting for the judge to sentence him... and I'm here with you. Free as a bird. Once he confessed, George practically sat on them till they got me out. He told them if I wasn't out before Christmas, his was the next murder they were going to read about. Don't suppose you know what he was talking about."

He had pulled back from her a bit and was looking at her sideways with a mischievous gleam in his eye.

"Well, I might have mentioned once or twice that it would be nice to have you home for Christmas."

"Tory, if it wasn't for you, I'd probably still be in there and I know I would definitely not have a home waiting for me. How am I ever going to make it up to you?"

"By taking good care of me just like you did before."

"Well, I don't know who took care of who, seems to me you were pretty good in the cooking and cleaning and mending department."

She laughed and told him that now she really had her work cut out for her. She had to get some meat back on his bones so he could get back to work. He frowned and wondered whether Skip might resent his coming back and taking over the ranch again. "On the contrary, I think he'll welcome some free time to continue with his college studies."

"College? Skip? What are you talking about?"

"I'll let him tell you all about it tomorrow. Let's go to bed. I have a feeling I'm going to get an early morning phone call. My grandchildren sometimes forget there's a two-hour time difference and they want us to open our presents together over the phone."

"I don't have a gift for you, Tory."

"What? You silly old man. You gave me the gift I wanted more than anything else in the world—you. You're all I've ever wanted and now

I've got you. Come on. Let's go upstairs. I want to remove the gift-wrapping and take a look at my present."

"Lord, woman, no one could ever accuse you of being shy." He shut the lights off as they went upstairs.

22

THE SKY WAS STILL DARK when Tory awakened, but at least the phone hadn't rung. She rolled over and looked at the man in bed next to her. Her man. Would she have chosen him from a line-up of possible suitors? Never in a million years. *What foolish things we women are,* she thought. She would have walked right by this diamond. Her ex-husband had been everything in physical appearance that Steve was not. He had been tall, well built, and gorgeous. Steve was barely taller than she was in her high heels, thin, and no one would ever call him handsome. On close study, she did admit, he had a rugged attractiveness. A strong, leathery face. He had to smile before a person was able to see how kind his eyes and mouth could be. But smiling did not come easily to Steve. Tory could get him to smile.

She could get him to do a number of things that surprised other people. She lay there remembering the night a year before when they had gone dancing. He had surprised her and everyone else in the hall. He'd been a regular Fred Astaire. They would have to go dancing again. Lord, how she loved him. Her breath literally caught when she thought about it. This man, her man, had been put through the wringer so many times in his life it was no wonder he had a hard time smiling. But he was a survivor, and this time she was going to see to it that his remaining years, his golden years, would be the happiest of his life. He had suffered through sixty-six tough years, but his next ten, fifteen or twenty would be pure sunshine if Tory Hardisty had anything to do about it. She slid over and kissed his cheek. She was about to sneak out of bed when his arm snaked out and drew her to him.

"Merry Christmas, Tory." He kissed her softly but with the passion of a man desperately in love.

"Merry Christmas, Steve." She kissed him back while she ran her finger around the outline of his ear and jaw. "Aren't you just the best thing to wake up beside on Christmas morning."

"Snuggle in a little closer. I wanna give you the rest of your Christmas present."

"Why, Steve Turner, what have you got up your sleeve?"

"It ain't anywhere near my sleeve, more like my pant leg if you're going to get territorial."

"But you aren't wearing sleeves or pant legs."

"No. You removed them last night, remember? Called them gift-wrapping, if I recall. In fact, you kind of enjoyed getting a sneak preview of what's to come."

"If that was a sneak preview, I can hardly wait for the real thing."

He pulled her closer and she felt her "present" throbbing between his belly and hers. He kissed her chin then slid his lips along her jaw line to just behind her ear. She drew her head back to give him full access to her neck and breasts. Their lovemaking was slower and more tender than it had been the night before. He played his hands over her hips and gradually feathered them over her stomach. She responded by moving her hips in rhythm to his finger strokes. Steve devoured her breasts with his eyes then paid homage with his lips. When she didn't think she could wait a moment longer, he moved his lips to her eyelids and gave her the relief her body was seeking.

"Steve Turner," she whispered. "I love you and your Christmas present more than anything on this earth. Nothing is ever going to separate us again—nothing."

Before he could answer, the phone rang. "Well, at least they let you sleep in a little bit."

"You call what you just did to me sleeping in?"

He grinned as Tory reached across him to pick the phone up from the table by his side of the bed.

"Merry Christmas to all you little sugar plums!" She exclaimed into the phone.

"Merry Christmas, Grandma. You didn't open your presents yet, did you?" Josh's voice asked.

"No, pumpkin, I waited for you. Can I call you back in two minutes after I get my dressing gown on and run downstairs?"

"Sure. Two minutes, Grandma. I'm going to start counting right now." She could hear Josh singing out the seconds as she hung up the phone and reached for her dressing gown behind the door. Calling to Steve to join her when he was ready, she hurried down the stairs.

When Steve joined her ten minutes later, he went into the kitchen and turned the coffeepot on. He could hear Tory exclaiming over something she had opened and he felt a tug of jealousy. They had given her gifts to make her happy and he had given her nothing.

He would make it up to her somehow. He watched her through the doorway and wondered how he had lucked out. What a woman! She was as beautiful as he was ugly. What the hell did she see in him? It certainly wasn't his looks or his charm. He knew everyone thought him an ornery son-of-a-bitch. Yet she had found something in him to love. Maybe she was near-sighted and just didn't let on. He snickered to himself. Hell, she would have to be blind as a bat not to see how ugly he was. Well, she loved him—he knew that much for sure, and he sure as hell loved her. He would treat her the way a precious gem should be treated. He would spoil her rotten. He was going to make damn sure she never regretted for one second that she had waited for him. The coffee finished perking and he brought her a cup and kissed her cheek as he set it down. She took his hand and smoothed it over her cheek in return.

Almost an hour later, with gifts opened at both ends of the conversation, Tory hung up the phone and turned her attention to Steve. He had noticed gifts under the tree for the young people who were coming for supper and wondered what in the world she would have bought for people she had never met. Tory reached under the tree, picked up a small flat parcel and handed it to Steve. He opened it and found a round trip ticket to Australia. Looking at her with a curious expression he asked, "What the hell is this? Are you tired of me and sending me away already? I just got home."

"I have a matching one in my desk. I was hoping we might enjoy a nice long holiday together, as far away from here as possible."

"You must have some kind of travel agent to deliver these on Christmas."

"I purchased them for the spring as soon as I knew you were getting out. I've had them for a while."

"So you want to go away?"

"I had so much time to think—and nothing but think—while you were away. It bothered me that you had such a zest for life and there you were locked up in prison. There is so much of the world to see and to experience and I thought if you ever got out, we should just go and do it!"

"Why Australia?"

"Well, they have big ranches for one thing. I thought you might like a busman's holiday. Then I figured they have everything there that we might want to do. White water rafting, parasailing, scuba diving, bungee jumping."

"Bungee jumping? *Bungee jumping?*"

"I just threw that in to see if you were listening. What do you say, Steve?"

"Suppose we could rent a motorcycle down there?"

"I'm sure of it."

Steve walked back and forth in front of the fire, pretending to be deep in thought, all the while stroking his chin. "It would be a great place for a honeymoon all right."

"Honeymoon?"

"Honeymoon."

"You're talking marriage, right?"

"Right."

Now Tory took up the pace and walked back and forth running her hand through her hair. "Is that the only way I can get you to go?"

"You don't expect to travel for God knows how long, in a foreign country halfway around the world as you said, without making an honest man out of me, do you? People will talk, for heaven's sake."

Laughing, Tory caught Steve in an enormous bear hug and whispered, "Of course, I'll marry you, Steve Turner. God forbid that we give anybody reason to gossip."

"Does this mean we're engaged?"

"I suppose it does."

He wrapped his arms around her waist and kissed her nose. "I feel like a goddamn teenager. What am I supposed to do now, phone your daughter or son-in-law for permission?"

Before Tory could answer, the phone rang and all she heard was a female voice saying, "Mrs. Hardisty, the barn is on fire. You better come quick! The fire trucks are on their way." The sound of the fire truck speeding up the road was cause for both of them to run out to the front porch.

23

TORY DRESSED QUICKLY AND BY the time Steve had the car started and turned around, she was jumping into the passenger seat. More volunteer firefighters were hurrying up the road by the time they pulled out of her driveway. Steve's face was ashen and his knuckles holding the steering wheel were white.

"I hope to God they got the animals out."

"Maybe it's not so bad. Maybe it's just the garage. A shed maybe."

It wasn't long before they could see the smoke above the trees and Tory's heart sank. It was far worse than either had imagined. She hoped that Skip and his family were unharmed.

The activity was intense in the yard. Steve pulled to one side, barely beyond the gate near the road. He could see the firemen getting the pumper truck in position and he ran to check on the whereabouts of the livestock while shouting at Tory to stay near the car.

After several minutes of leaning against the car, feeling useless, Tory headed off in the direction of the barn. She could make out the shapes of several men heading the horses and cattle out, through the corral, and into the pastures behind. The firefighters had the pumpers going, trying not only to put out the fire in the barn but to keep it away from the trees nearby. The barn was far enough away from the house and there was enough snow cover on the ground that the immediate danger from that aspect was not great. The main concern was getting the animals to safety and keeping it from spreading into the woods behind.

In the commotion, she lost sight of Steve as she moved closer to the house. Everyone seemed to have a job and was executing it, so she thought she would see what she could do inside. She looked for Skip's sister whom she had not yet met, but couldn't find her. Looking for liquid refreshment that would not require pulling water from the well, Tory started going through the cupboards and down into the basement to see what she might find there. She knew the firefighters would be parched and thirsty from the smoke so she would feel slightly useful by finding something for them to drink. It was about a half hour later when she heard excited shouting rise outside and upon looking out the window, saw that the fire had caught in the trees. For the moment the house was still safe even though the burning trees would bring the fire a little closer. The trees closer to the house were quite tall but it would have to travel a couple of hundred feet to reach them. Surely, they would be able to keep it from moving in that direction.

Just in case, she climbed the stairs and went into Steve's bedroom. He kept a small box in one of his dresser drawers with a few personal items inside. One of these was the picture of him as a child. It was his only link to the past and she would hate for it to be destroyed. She felt like a trespasser going into his room and going through his dresser without him, but hoped he might appreciate what she was doing, and why. She noticed the picture of Steve and Aunt Lottie on the night table by his bed. Picking it up, she sat on the bed as she ran her finger over the glass. Smiling, she recalled how forlorn he had looked the Christmas before when he was overcome with the feeling of family for the first time in his life. So much had happened since then. God, was it only a year ago?

Tory pulled the picture to her chest and smiled. The two people in the picture were the two people responsible for her being here now. Had her aunt planned this? She wouldn't be surprised if her aunt hadn't plotted to have Steve and Tory find each other. That was silly. Her aunt hadn't planned on having a stroke. She shook her head, set the picture on the bed and opened the top drawer of Steve's old dresser. As was all the furniture in his house, the bedroom suite was pre-second world war she was sure, but all beautifully cared for. She saw the little tin that held his keepsakes and lifted it from the drawer. Taking it and the picture from the bed she started for the doorway. There was a loud crack that drowned out the crescendo of voices rising from the ground. Tory turned toward the window and felt the house move at the same time as the ceiling came down on her. The last she remembered was being knocked to the floor and lying on her side seeing sparks and sky above her, then feeling a rush of cold air.

"Holy old jumped up…!" Steve looked up when he heard all the shouting and saw that enough of a breeze had come up for the fire to jump the branches of the trees and move it closer to the house. The firemen maneuvered part of their equipment around to that area. By the time they were in position, the tallest tree had caught fire near the bottom where a burning branch from another tree had fallen. The firemen warned the others to stay well back and out of the way of any trees that might fall.

No sooner was this warning issued, than a crack like thunder split the air and one burning tree fell onto the tall tree. In its weakened condition from its own fire, it in turn broke and fell toward the house.

Steve quickly turned to make sure that Tory was well out of the way, staying near the car. When he couldn't see her, he called out to her and waited for a reply. When she didn't answer, he ran and pulled the car door open. He called to one of the men nearby and asked if he had seen Mrs. Hardisty.

"Not since she went into the house a while ago."

"*She went into the house?* Did she come out?"

"Can't say as I paid any attention, Steve."

He looked again in the direction of renewed shouts. The fire had gone up the tree and now the first tongues of flame were coming from the roof of the house.

"Damn you, Tory. You better not be inside there."

Calling her name, he ran up the front stairs into the house and checked the main floor. He ran back outside and looked all about the yard, all the time shouting her name. "She must be upstairs."

The fireman heard him as Steve ran by him and back into the house. "Don't go in. The upper floor is burning pretty good, it's not stable."

Steve paid no attention. Halfway up the stairs he was almost overcome by the heat and smoke. "Tory? Tory? Damn you woman. You up here?"

From the hallway, he caught sight of her shoe in his bedroom. Crawling on hands and knees, he tried to make his way into the room. The roof had collapsed under the weight of the fallen tree and he was unable to see beyond the branches blocking his way into the room. He heard someone behind him and realized a firefighter wearing a mask had followed him in.

"Her shoe is on the floor. She must be in there."

"I'll try to reach her. You get out of here before you pass out from the smoke."

"I ain't leaving, and we'll damned well do more than *try*. We *will* reach her."

He started to climb over the tree limbs and saw her lying still about three feet beyond his reach. Coughing and short of breath, he climbed over the top of the fallen tree and saw that her shoulder and arm were caught under the weight of a portion of the roof that had broken and fallen inside. It must have glanced off the side of her head and pinned her under it. He felt for a pulse and noticed her chest rising and falling ever so slightly.

"Thank Christ. Don't you even think of dying on me, woman. Do you hear? I won't have it."

Tory thought she could hear Steve mumbling something about damn stubborn, foolish women never doing as they're told, but he sounded so far away. Was he lying on her arm? He was so heavy and it was hurting.

"Move over," she moaned.

The firefighter had made his way in and was leaning over her. "She wants us to move it over."

"Unconscious and still giving orders. That's her! Damn, foolish... woman."

"I can't brea—"

"What did you say?"

Steve was near panic level trying to remove the tree from her all by himself.

When Tory didn't respond, he started tearing at the branches but found his own breathing was becoming more difficult. His chest burned with each breath he took. Two more firefighters joined them and one forced Steve out the door and dragged him fighting down the stairs. He collapsed near the front entry and resuscitation was started when he was laid on the front lawn. Within a few minutes he was coughing and felt like his throat and chest were being crushed. He tried to ask about Tory but found he couldn't get any words out. Soon a new round of shouting and hollering started and he thought he heard something about the roof collapsing. He was unable to make anything out of the din, and tried to stand. He had to get back inside and help Tory but when he stood up, the yard spun around him and he found himself on his hands and knees vomiting. Someone helped him onto a stretcher and two men carried him to an ambulance. "I can't go. Tory's inside." His hoarse whisper was not heard above the noise. When he glanced back at the house, he saw it was all aflame and then he passed out.

When Steve opened his eyes again, there was moonlight coming through the window of a room. It took a few minutes for him to realize he was in bed in a hospital room. "What the hell? What am— Oh my God... Tory... Tory?" He tried to lift himself up only to realize he had an intravenous port stuck in his arm. Noticing a nursing station call-button on his pillow, he pushed it and waited.

Seconds later a nurse bustled into the room. She immediately took his wrist to check his pulse and greeted him with a cheery, "Hi there, Mr. Turner."

"Where is Tory Hardisty? I have to find her."

"If you'll wait until I finish checking your vitals, I'll try and find out for you. Was she supposed to be admitted here? I don't believe she's on this floor but I'll check."

She frowned slightly when she took his blood pressure, which didn't go unnoticed by Steve. "If you think my blood pressure is high now, then find out about Mrs. Hardisty or it's liable to pop your little gadget there."

She smoothed his covers then turned on her heel and hurried from the room. About twenty minutes later, Liz walked in to Steve's room to find him standing with the closet door open, reaching for his clothes. The intravenous tubing, with syringe attached, was lying on the bed. "Where do you think you're going?"

"I'm going to find Tory if I have to search this hospital room by room."

Liz breathed deeply and hesitated before speaking, "Steve, Tory's not here."

24

"WHADDYA MEAN SHE'S NOT HERE?"

"They flew her to the burn center in Calgary a few hours ago."

Steve had to grab the door handle to steady himself. "The burn center? How bad is she?"

"I don't honestly know, Steve. She was not admitted here so there are no records. They brought her here only for transfer by air ambulance. That's all I know."

"I gotta get to her."

"You're not strong enough to drive home, let alone all the way to Calgary. Listen to you. You can hardly talk. You shouldn't even be out of bed. Those fluids were being given to you for a reason."

"I gotta get there, Liz. I can't lay here when I don't know whether she's... whether she's OK or not."

"I'm off duty in another hour. If you'll get back into that bed and let me redo your intravenous, I will try to find out something from Calgary Hospital. Then I'll take you to wherever you have a change of clothes, and then I'll drive you to Calgary myself."

"Why?"

"Why? Because I care about Tory, too. She's one hell of a lady and I feel I owe it to her... and to you. I'm sorry, Steve, for jumping to conclusions about you and I would like to make it up to you somehow. I can't take back the words, but I sure will try to eat them no matter how bitter they taste."

"Will you phone right away?"

"I'll go to my office as soon as you climb into bed and allow me to hook you back up to your IV."

Steve reluctantly slid between the sheets again. Realizing he would not find out about Tory unless he cooperated, he stuck his hand out for Liz to insert a fresh needle. Surprisingly, he dozed off after a few minutes and later felt guilty when he realized Liz was shaking his arm to wake him.

"She's resting comfortably, Steve, at least as comfortably as they can make her. She has burns to her legs, a broken upper arm and concussion, and she suffered lung damage from smoke inhalation. They are monitoring her closely. She is suffering from severe shock. She's not regained consciousness."

"Good God, Liz. I've got to get to her. I have to hold her and let her know I'm there."

"I'm all ready to go. Do you have a change of clothes?"

"I have a few things at Tory's house."

"Then let's go."

Liz tidied up Tory's kitchen and put the thawed turkey in the refrigerator while Steve showered and changed into clean jeans and shirt. He had only the jacket he had worn to the hospital and it stank badly from the smoke. They looked through the coats and jackets in Tory's front closet and found a parka that Steve had used the year before when he came to clean the snow in her yard. He quickly put it on, checked the thermostat, turned some lights on in the living room and entryway, and left one on near the back door. Within half an hour of arriving, they were turning away from Tory's driveway.

"Did you want to stop by your place while we're here and check out the damage? Although I don't know how much you would see at night?"

"The only damage I wanna know about is Tory's. Let's go."

The almost two-hour drive never seemed so long before. Steve couldn't will the car to go any faster. He was grateful to Liz for giving up her Christmas night to drive him. He had forgotten what day it was until he turned on the car radio and heard the Christmas music, the merry songs of sleigh bells and decking the halls. When a modern version of "I'll be home for Christmas" started, Steve shut it off and stared out the window so Liz wouldn't see his tears.

Tory had wanted him home for Christmas, had made it her personal mission to get him home for Christmas. Well, she had succeeded only to end up fighting for her own life all alone in a strange hospital on Christmas day. *Damn, it's not fair!* Steve slammed his gloved fist into his other open palm. He prayed that she would be alive and please, God, even awake when they got there. The farms along the highway were all decked out in their finest lights and decorations. It seemed almost a mockery to Steve. The people inside were probably enjoying their gifts they had received and laughing and hugging, full from their Christmas dinners, while poor Tory was lying unconscious. He remembered Christmas the year before with the children, the gifts, the laughter, and carols. Tory had been so happy, he had cried for the love of her. He never felt like he belonged before, never really belonged. Tory, his Tory, had changed all of that. When he had gone to prison he did everything he could to make her forget him. He never dreamed they would ever find the real killer, never hoped they would even try. He was a big time loser and as far as they were concerned, he was guilty.

Tory was the only one who had believed in him and she had convinced his lawyer to keep poking at it. Even when the killer's girlfriend turned the killer in, they never would have hurried the case

Fire in the Foothills | 187

along without Tory breathing down their necks. Tory. Where would he be without her? He couldn't lose her now. He just couldn't! He didn't realize he was openly weeping until he felt Liz's hand on his arm and heard his own sobbing. Embarrassed, he blew his nose.

"I'm sorry, Liz. I know this isn't how you intended spending your Christmas night off."

"I don't think it's how Tory intended to spend hers either. The least I can do is deliver you to her."

"Sorry for the sniveling. I don't normally carry on like a damn fool."

"That's OK, Steve. When I first learned she was in such a bad way, I cried too. As a matter of fact, I was so upset, I threw a coffee cup across the room. The cleaning staff had a mess to clean up. Ah, here we are. I'll drop you off and then park the car."

Steve took the hospital steps two at a time. After taking the elevator to the fifth floor, he was stopped at the desk and not allowed to go in because he was not next of kin.

"I'm sorry," said the buxom fifty-ish nurse at the reception desk, "but only the immediate family is allowed to see the patients in this ward. I understand Mrs. Hardisty's daughter is on her way from Ontario. Until she arrives we cannot allow anyone else in."

"Are those Becky Anderson's orders?" Steve couldn't believe that they might be.

"No, that's hospital policy."

"What's the problem, Steve?" Liz stepped off the elevator and moved toward the reception desk.

"It seems only immediate family can see her. If we were married now instead of next week, I could go in. Right now, I'm nothing to her according to the hospital."

"Does a common-law husband not have the same rights as a married husband?" Barb asked the nurse.

"I have no way of knowing what this man's relationship is to Mrs. Hardisty. I'm sorry. I will have to check with administration."

"Then get on with it." Steve barked.

"I'm Liz Coates, the head of nursing at Weston Memorial Hospital, and I can vouch for Mr. Turner, that he's engaged to Mrs. Hardisty." She hoped she had heard and understood Steve correctly. As she handed the nurse her identification card from her own hospital, she continued, "He was injured in the fire as well, and I personally have escorted him from our hospital so he can see Tory and be with her. In fact, it was his ranch that caught fire and his house that Tory received her injuries in."

The reception nurse took her card and studied it.

"Make a phone call and find out for yourself, but do it quickly. Mr. Turner has just had his IV removed and would like to sit down, I'm sure, preferably beside Mrs. Hardisty's bed." Then Liz added, "If Dr. Krelinsky is around he can vouch for who I am."

The nurse handed Liz her card and waved them both past her desk. She pressed a button on a speaker and announced that two persons with close connections to Mrs. Hardisty were coming into the burn unit.

They had to scrub and put hospital gowns over their clothing, then masks and caps over their faces and heads. When Steve walked through the second door into Tory's room, he couldn't believe it was the same strong woman who had fought so hard for his release. She looked still and helpless. He walked over to her bed and looked down at her. If the monitor hadn't said she was breathing, he never would have guessed it. The bedding was tented over her legs and feet, and her face was pale. He whispered her name over and over. He bent and kissed her cheek through his mask. "I love you, woman. You fought for me, now you have to fight for yourself."

Liz stood behind Steve and looked down at her friend. She had never met a woman as strong and of such fine character as Tory Hardisty. How could she have misjudged them so? She should have known that this woman would not have fallen so deeply in love with a man who wasn't as upright as she was. It just wasn't in her nature. She hoped she would have the opportunity to tell her how sorry she was and to beg Tory's forgiveness. She told Steve she was going to grab a nap in the visitor's lounge and he could find her there when he was ready.

He nodded without taking his eyes from his beloved Tory. A short while later, an intern came in and checked the monitors and Steve asked how she was doing. The intern motioned for Steve to follow him through the door into the little room between the hallway and Tory's room.

"I understand you and Mrs. Hardisty are engaged?"

"Yes. My name is Steve Turner." He removed his glove and offered a hand.

While they shook hands, the doctor told him he was an intern and that his name was Gerald Summers. "Well, Mr. Turner, this lady has been through quite a trauma. Her burns are bad enough, but the concussion and state of shock right now are our greatest areas of concern. We are trying to stabilize her blood pressure and ease the swelling inside the brain. Both are difficult in their own right, but together they're a real problem. However, she seems to be holding her own and we're hopeful she'll come out of her coma shortly. Sometimes we induce coma as it seems to help with healing but we're concerned about her concussion. We've set her broken bone and are assisting her breathing. We're anxious to get on with the treatment of her burns. She has a long haul in front of her but once her concussion is behind her, we'll feel more confident. For now, all we can do is keep her comfortable. Are you a man of prayer, Mr. Turner?"

"I am now."

"Good. A little prayer can go a long way sometimes. I'll check her again in about half an hour."

He left and Steve went back to the chair by the bed. He held Tory's hand in his re-gloved one and brought it to his mask. "Hang in there,

Tory. I didn't come this far to spend the holidays alone. I want you awake and hollering at me about something or other. I not only want it, I need it. Damn it, woman, I need you!"

He leaned with his elbows on the bed and held her hand and while he rubbed her cheek, he prayed. At some point he dozed off and awakened when he realized the young doctor had returned and was shining a penlight into Tory's eyes. "How's it looking, Doc?"

"There doesn't seem to be any change. She's remaining stable. Why don't you go and get some proper rest? I understand you were a patient in hospital yourself."

"I'm OK. I think you young guys see anyone over fifty and think you better put us to bed before we expire from old age."

Gerald laughed and took a good look at Steve. The old guy was pretty wiry and probably stronger than Gerald. There probably was some truth in his last statement. "I still think you should get some rest. Mrs. Hardisty is going to be here for a long time and you can't sit by her bed twenty-four hours a day. Her friend is sleeping in the visitor's lounge down the hall. Why don't you join her for a while?"

"Her friend worked all day while I slept. I'd rather stay with Tory in case she wakes up."

"Suit yourself."

The intern left and Steve once again took Tory's hand and held it to his cheek. He sat studying her face, trying to get his fill of it. As he sat and stared, he couldn't help but wonder again what in the world had drawn her to him. He was just a skinny, old guy—not even nice to look at. He knew he had a mean face and smiling had never come easy. His ornery disposition was what most strangers encountered, only those very close to him knew he cared, really cared. Only one or two knew he had a great sense of humor, but Tory seemed to take to him even before she had seen those sides of him. He shouldn't look a gift horse in the mouth, he knew, but he couldn't help but wonder. She sure had a great face—kindness and character were etched right into it. Her body was pretty good too, one that a woman twenty years her junior would be proud to have. She had an education and a lot of class. Dammit, he was lucky to have her, but why? Why did she want him? Him, Steve Turner, drifter, killer and ex-con. She cared enough even to marry him. That was the big surprise. He had been afraid to even hope she might say yes. He had blurted out a marriage proposal before he even thought it through. What if she'd said no? What then? Would it have changed what they had? Would it have been embarrassing for him, for her, to carry on with their friendship? Probably. He could have ruined everything with that one question. *Well hell, don't start second-guessing. Accept what you've got and treasure it. You're a lucky man.*

He kissed her hand and ran the fingers of his free hand over her forehead. "Wake up, Tory. I have to see your eyes. I have to know you're OK. Please wake up, darlin'."

The steady beeping of her monitors and the whooshing sound of the breathing apparatus were the only responses he received.

After another hour or so of sitting and staring, Steve heard the door open when Liz came in. "Want to take a break? I'd like to sit with her for a while. If you don't mind."

"I guess my legs could do with a stretch. Maybe I'll take a little walk. I won't be too long in case she wakes up."

Liz watched him reluctantly leave after kissing Tory on the cheek and promising to come right back. God, she never thought a year ago that she would be envying how lucky Tory was to have this man care for her. Boy, had she pegged him wrong. But then the whole town had. Almost every woman in Weston was frightened of him and he had never done anything to alleviate their fears. When he was charged with murdering Joanne Dimmery, everyone just knew he was guilty. He had that look about him, and then when his past murder conviction became public knowledge, there was absolutely no doubt in anyone's mind. Now here he was, fresh out of jail and Liz wishing she had someone like him to look after her. Go figure. It took Tory's cool dismissal of all the townspeople who had slighted Steve for not believing in him, before Liz realized they had formed a tight circle with no evidence and kept Steve on the outside. In doing so, they had also alienated Tory, Lottie MacArthur's niece. Both Lottie and Tory had done more for their little town than half the population had. Tory had settled right in and had become a part of the community while her aunt was still alive. She had sewn and knitted and baked, donating all her finished goods to the hospital gift store, church sales and the library auxiliary. She had given cash donations to the Boy Scouts and when her aunt died, she had been very generous indeed with some of her aunt's money. How had they treated her in return? Stared, pointed fingers, called her "that Steve Turner's woman."

Everyone felt she must have had a hand in it too. Why else would she protect him and downright flaunt their relationship in public for all to see? Even after he was charged, they were seen riding around on his motorcycle, laughing and acting as if nothing were even wrong.

Liz shook her head. "Tory, do I owe you a big apology. You have to pull out of this. You can't die on me and leave me with all this guilt. Even though it would serve me right."

She absent-mindedly checked Tory's monitors and made mental notes. She picked up Tory's chart which was fastened to one end of the bed and read all the notes. She realized her friend was very seriously injured. Sitting on the chair looking at her, Liz voiced her wishes, "Tory, show us your spunk. You are a strong woman, a real fighter. Do it now. Steve will fall apart without you. He needs you badly... And so do I."

Half an hour had not gone by when Steve returned.

"Well, that was a fast walk."

"I couldn't stay away. I kept thinking maybe she'll wake up and I won't be here." He looked down at the unconscious woman. "If I lose her, I don't know what I'll do."

"You're not going to lose her, Steve. Tory's too stubborn to give up without a struggle."

"I hope you're right, Liz." Steve interlaced his fingers, turned his hands palm side out and stretched his arms out in front of him. "That's why I'm not leaving again until she wakes up and gives me some of her sarcasm. Only then will I know she's OK."

Liz laughed at the attempt at humor and put an arm around Steve and whispered to him, "She's very lucky, Steve. I envy her."

Taken back, Steve searched for a reply but Liz let him off the hook by asking if she could make arrangements for him to have a room near the hospital. She knew a couple of places close by that gave inexpensive rates to family members of patients. He thanked her and was about to refuse when she almost pleaded, saying she wanted to do something for her friend and this was all she could think of. He relented, knowing that sooner or later he would need a shower and a change of clothes if he were going to stay here for as long as Tory needed him. Liz slipped out to see what she could find in the neighborhood and promised to come back as soon as the arrangements were made.

Liz found him a room within walking distance and paid for the first week. She purchased groceries and put them in the fridge and made him promise to eat. If he were going to keep a bedside vigil, he would need to keep up his own strength.

Steve sat with Tory through the night and well into the next day. Finally, the doctor told him to leave and not come back for several hours as they had to send her for an MRI and other tests.

The cold hit him like an Arctic blast when he stepped outside the front door of the hospital. He did up his parka and pulled the hood up over his head to protect his ears. The distance to the address that Liz had given him was short, so he walked. He had promised to call collect if any change occurred. The cold air hurt his damaged throat and lungs so he tried to keep his mouth shut and breathe through his nose. His room was very plain but spotless. He opened the little fridge and saw that Liz had bought coffee, cream and sugar as well as bread, margarine, sliced ham, juice and fruit. On the cupboard were canned beans and pork, a few different soups, a box of cereal flakes, peanut butter and canned dinners.

Well, he wouldn't starve. He also noticed an envelope propped against the lamp by the bed. In it were two hundred dollars in cash and a Visa card in Liz's name. This was all wrapped in a note saying,

> Steve,
>
> I know you would be too proud to accept money and a credit card, so consider them a loan. I'm sure you didn't have time to make any arrangements for cash.
>
> You will need some clothes, and will have other miscellaneous expenses, perhaps a car or truck rental.
>
> Please feel free to use as much as you need. The card has a high limit and no balance at present.
>
> Your friend,
> Liz

Steve was overwhelmed. He knew then that Liz was truly sincere in wanting to regain Tory's friendship. Last winter, there was no way she would have given him the time of day, let alone the carte blanche use of her credit card. Well, she was right, he had been released from prison with only travel expenses home and the few dollars he had earned in there. And he certainly did not have a credit card. When the fire broke out, that was the last thing on his mind. He didn't even know where Tory's personal things were. Did she have her purse with her? Was it sitting in her car in his yard? Would it still be there? Well, for now he would have to take advantage of Liz's generosity as he really did need clothing. He took a taxi to the closest shopping mall and bought a change of jeans and a couple of shirts and a sweater. Several changes of underwear and socks and a toque rounded out his wardrobe. He picked up some shaving and personal care supplies and headed back to the rooming house.

After showering and shaving, changing his clothes and eating a bowl of soup, he headed back to the hospital. It was after dark and even colder. He was glad the hospital was only a couple of blocks away, any further and he would have to buy some long underwear and warmer boots.

When he got up to Tory's room and had scrubbed and covered himself with a sterile robe, he let himself in only to find she had not been returned to her bed yet. He moved the chair closer to the window and watched the traffic in the street below. Everyone appeared to be hurrying somewhere; the red brake lights on the cars seemed appropriate for the season. The houses were brightly lit with all the colors of Christmas. There was a huge spruce tree near the entrance to the parking lot and the red and green lights flashed on and off like a giant neon sign. Watching it, he could almost hear them blinking in unison. *To-ry, To-ry, To-ry.*

After some time, he was becoming concerned. What kind of tests could possibly be taking so long? Had they run into a problem? Did they see more damage than they had originally? Had she given up while she was being put through all of this? Feeling the panic closing in, he was just about to go out and start asking questions when he heard voices in the antechamber of her room. Soon the door was pulled all the way open and a stretcher was brought in with a very gray-looking Tory lying, eyes closed, with a sheeted tent covering her from the waist down. He shrunk into the corner while the two female and one male nurse lifted her back onto her bed.

He asked how she was and the male nurse said that the doctor would be in shortly and would to answer his questions. One of the female nurses started fussing over her and re-attaching her monitors while the other two left with the stretcher. She looked at her watch, made notations on Tory's chart and started to leave.

"Can you not tell me anything?" Steve asked.

"I really don't know anything. I wasn't with Mrs. Hardisty while she was off the floor. I'm sorry. One thing I can say is that her vitals are relatively strong considering she's been through a very trying time." She offered Steve a comforting smile.

25

FOR THREE MORE DAYS THERE was no change. Steve would go to his room only long enough to freshen up and grab a bite to eat. He took power naps in the visitor's lounge so he would be available if Tory woke up. The doctor said the swelling from the concussion was starting to ease and her vital signs were improving. He was quite hopeful that she would make a full recovery. That only increased Steve's need to be with her. In the meantime, Becky had arrived and left her things at Steve's nearby rooming house. While they took turns going to sleep, both were almost constantly at Tory's bedside. They talked to her, begging her to wake up. Both repeated how much they loved her and needed her, hoping she could hear them and would respond.

Becky had spent the morning with her mother while Steve had gone to his room to shower and freshen up after sitting most of the night with Tory. She was watching him cross the parking lot on his way back into the hospital and couldn't help but marvel at how this man had captured her mother's heart. His devotion to her mother certainly was evident.

She had no doubt about his love. The difference between him and her own father was day and night. Is that what the attraction was for her mother? She knew her mother had not had an easy time during her marriage to her dad. He had never been around much for either of them. They must have been in love at one time, at least enough to get married, to want to spend the rest of their lives together. They just seemed to drift apart. They had similar backgrounds, knew the same people, had gone to the same schools. Certainly they had more in common than Tory and Steve had.

Her mother had told her that Steve had not had an easy life prior to meeting her great aunt Lottie. Even after that, he had been a loner and wasn't exactly a real friendly guy. He had a reputation for having a general disdain for women in particular. Yet here he was, obviously shattered by Tory's injuries and leaving her bedside only long enough to sleep when necessary and to shower, change, and eat. There was not a doubt: *this* woman he loved. She knew her mother definitely loved him. She had been living in purgatory all the time Steve was in prison, never giving up for one minute the idea that Steve would be home again soon. She had believed in her man enough to know he was innocent when everyone else thought him guilty. Surely, God would not separate them now. Surely, He would not bring Steve back only to lose the one woman who believed in him and loved him. Becky was confident they were meant to be together. Steve had told her that her mother had accepted his marriage proposal. She could sense that he was apprehensive about Becky's response to that. When she had thrown her arms around him and kissed his cheek wishing them happiness, he had clearly been overcome with relief. She had told him how delighted Josh would be to have him for a grandpa. He had tried to hide the tears that came to his eyes but she had seen the handkerchief come out. She could hear him now in the next room scrubbing up.

Becky leaned over her mother. "Mom, Steve's coming back in to sit with you. Don't you think it's about time you quit playing this game and opened your eyes? The poor man needs some proper rest. He's too old to be sitting around here waiting for you to take your sweet time to come back to the world of the living."

Becky was kissing her mother on the cheek as Steve came into the room. She answered the question in his eyes with a negative shake of her head. "I think I might go down to the cafeteria and grab a hot meal. I had only a bowl of cold cereal this morning and I'm ready for a bowl of soup to warm my tummy. Did you eat, Steve?"

"I had some of that canned stew." He looked down at Tory and took her hand. "I can hardly wait to have a piece of your mother's chocolate cake again."

Becky hugged him from behind and kissed the back of his shoulder. "Soon, Steve. It will be soon, I'm confident."

He nodded and sat in the chair that he was sure must by now have the outline of his rump molded into it. When Becky looked back from the doorway, Steve was holding her mother's hand in his with his head bowed in prayer. "Please God," she whispered to herself as she closed the door.

"I hope the new year brings a change in the Arctic high that seems to have such a grip on the entire province," Steve said to Tory. "I'll probably have to go buy a pair of long underwear it's so damn cold. It's hard to believe that in a few months I'll be hauling the old Harley out. Now there's a picture to warm me up, the old Harley with you sittin' on it in your purple leathers. 'Deep purple,' you called them. God, Tory, you looked magnificent in them with your silver hair and all."

He was sure he felt a slight pressure from her fingers on his hand. Was it his imagination? He watched her face for a minute then stared as her fingers definitely tightened around his. He brought them to his mouth and kissed them, silently begging her to open her eyes. He was sure her lids fluttered a few times and her mouth curved so slightly into a smile before her face became still again. He rang for a nurse.

When Becky came back upstairs, she found Steve in the scrub room crying and could hear voices inside her mother's room. She was terrified to ask.

Steve grabbed her and held her tightly. "She squeezed my hand, Becky. She squeezed my hand. The doctor's with her now."

They hugged each other, laughing, then crying for several minutes. The door opened and the doctor joined them in the little scrub room between the hallway and Tory's bedroom. He told them that Tory did in fact appear to be sleeping rather than in a comatose state. He warned them that she would be kept sedated for a while though because of the pain from the burns. If she awakened, she would be having a fair amount of discomfort. They would continue with the treatment of her burns, which would be a long, slow, painful process.

When Becky and Steve tiptoed back into the room, Tory had been propped on one side slightly and seemed to be sleeping peacefully. It wasn't until the evening that she stirred and opened her eyes momentarily. Both of them were sitting talking to each other about the hockey scores and didn't notice at first until Tory tried to lift her hand. The slight movement caught their attention and both started to talk at once. She was only able to keep her eyes open for a few seconds. The light seemed to bother her, but she waved her fingers weakly.

Steve let Becky kiss her mother's cheek while he took hold of her hand and brought it to his lips. Both had tears running openly down their cheeks.

Becky sobbed, "I love you, Mom." Then she stepped back and let Steve get in close.

He brushed a thumb across Tory's forehead while he kissed her eyelids. "I love you, too, darlin'. You go back to sleep now and next time you wake up, we'll talk."

Tory smiled and drifted off again. Becky rang for the nurse and then she collapsed against the wall and sobbed. When the nurse came into the room, the young intern, Gerald, followed her. He looked into Tory's eyes with his light and nodded to Steve and Becky. "She's sleeping. I would suggest at this point that the two of you go somewhere and do the same. In fact, the two of you should go out and enjoy a good meal. She won't be waking up for a while."

Becky looked at Steve and said, "Why don't we take a taxi and find a nice restaurant somewhere. Can you suggest one, Doctor?"

An hour later they were sitting in The Steakhouse, enjoying a glass of beer, while they waited for their dinners.

"I'm afraid for your mother, Becky. I wish there was some way she could get through the treatment ahead of her without the pain. Damn it, it should be me in there, not her. It was my house that burned."

"It wasn't your fault. I shudder to think how it might have ended had you not come home the night before. Nobody would have noticed she had even gone inside, let alone upstairs. I just can't figure out why she would go upstairs when there was a danger like that. She always uses more sense. It's just not like her to be so foolish."

"I guess we'll know soon enough." He lifted his glass of beer, "Here's to Tory's health," and took a long drink.

Their steaks arrived and Steve savored the aroma permeating the air. He had ordered extra mushrooms and onions with his. Becky remembered the appetite he always had and wondered how he had survived on prison fare. She didn't want to ruin the high their emotions were on at present so she didn't ask him. They ate in silence, each deep in their own thoughts.

"Steve, if Mom comes around pretty good over the next couple of days, I'll probably go home on Thursday."

"Do you have to rush back?"

"The kids are on holidays right now. If I know Mom is out of the woods, I would like to spend some time with them before they go back to school. They're worried about Grandma, too, and they'll know she's safe if I'm able to leave her and go home. I know she's in good hands with you so I can go guilt free. Besides, it will be downright sickening to watch the two of you mooning over each other the way you do." She winked at him and took a big bite of steak. Before he could answer, she went on. "I think she might need me more when she goes home. She'll require some help with her personal care and I will feel more useful then, helping her with her hair and things and doing some cooking for her and for you."

"Becky, you know I've enjoyed having your company and support the last few days. I think your mother knows you're here, too. If you want to go home to the kids, that's fine. But I promise not to seduce your mother in front of you if you want to stay."

"I'll come for the wedding, Steve, but I'll give you and Mom the time in between." Becky patted his hand and motioned for the waitress to bring more coffee. She smiled as Steve ordered a piece of strawberry cheesecake.

When they returned to Tory's room, the nurse was with her and assured them that she had been sleeping soundly all the time they were gone. They noticed that the respirator had been removed and she was breathing on her own with just oxygen to assist her. Steve motioned for Becky to take the chair facing Tory. He sat on the window ledge and watched the traffic leaving the parking lot and all the lights outside. "I never had a Christmas ever in my life like the one last year. I hope we'll be able to do it again one of these years. Do you think we might?"

"Why don't we plan on it? I would love for you and Mom to come and have Christmas at our place next year. The kids could take you to their favorite toboggan runs and you might catch one of Maggie's hockey games. We'll talk about it with Mom when she's up to it."

"Sounds good."

Tory lifted the hand on her good arm and lightly touched her broken arm. There was a noticeable flinch and then her hand fell back on the bed. Becky leaned forward and touched her mother's cheek, "Are you OK, Mom? Is your arm hurting?"

Steve came around to that side of the bed in time to see Tory open her eyes and look at Becky. She reached for her daughter's hand and brought it to her mouth. Becky smiled through her tears and motioned in Steve's direction. Tory lifted her eyes and saw Steve standing to one side of Becky. One tear fell on the pillow and another nestled in the hollow in the side of her nose before slowly trickling over the tip of it. It was as if no one wanted to speak and break the spell. For several seconds, Tory looked from one to the other then closed her eyes again with a smile on her face. A few minutes later, Steve blew his nose and Becky broke into full sobbing. She stood up and walked to the window then motioned for Steve to take the chair. He sat and took Tory's hand in both of his, drawing them up under his chin with his elbows planted on the bed. Tory attempted to roll over and opened her eyes again. "Do you want to lie on your back?" Steve asked.

She nodded.

The nurse came in seconds after Becky rang for her and took the pillow from behind Tory's back. "Now, Mrs. Hardisty, you let me move you. Don't try to do it on your own, OK? I have to move your legs first and that might cause some discomfort." She started to lift one of Tory's feet. They heard a gasp and the look on Tory's face told of the excruciating pain.

Steve told Tory to hold on to his hand tight and he kissed her forehead. The nurse moved as quickly as she could and once Tory was settled on her back, she went out to fetch something to ease her pain. By the time she came back, Tory was extremely pale and her knuckles were white from hanging on to Steve's hand so tightly. The nurse slid the needle into Tory's intravenous tube. Before long, Tory's grip eased and then her hand went limp once again.

It just about killed Steve to see Tory in such pain. "Why? Why did you go upstairs?" he asked an unhearing Tory.

All night Becky and Steve kept vigil, spelling each other off to catch a bit of sleep, but Tory didn't wake again until late the next morning. When Becky looked up from her magazine, she realized her mother was watching her. They smiled at each other at the same time and simultaneously said, "I love you." Becky's voice was strong and clear while in comparison, Tory's was raspy, hardly more than a whisper. "Oh, Mom, you had us so frightened."

Becky fell on her knees beside the bed and took her mother's hand in hers, kissing it long and hard. "Steve has hardly left your side. He makes me go to eat and sleep while he just sits and watches you and holds your hand."

"I know," that raspy whisper once again. "I felt him."

"He blames himself you know. He says it was his house that burned. He feels he should be the one in this bed not you."

Tory shook her head and couldn't help the tears.

"Mom, if I go and get him, will you be able to stay awake for a few more minutes do you think?"

Tory nodded.

"I'll see you later." She kissed her mother's cheek and started to leave.

"The box." Her mother whispered.

"What box? What are you talking about, Mom?"

Tory tried to speak again but her throat was too tight, too dry.

"It's OK," Becky assured her, "you can tell us later."

She stopped at the nursing station on her way to fetch Steve and told the nurse that her mother was awake and talking. She woke Steve with a shake and told him that her mother was waiting for him. He sat up and Becky asked, "Do you know what my mother means by 'the box'?"

Steve shrugged and said he couldn't think what it might be. He tried to remember if there had been a box on the ground around the ranch or a box in Tory's house that might have something she needed. As he headed down the hall to Tory's room, he said, "I'll try to find out what she's talking about."

The nurse was holding a glass of water with a straw and Tory was attempting to sip it. The nurse explained that Tory's throat was very dry and parched from the smoke and the heat and she probably would have a hard time speaking for a while. Tory took the nurse's hand and asked, "Where's the box?" then broke into a cough.

The nurse told Steve she had been asking about a box in her sleep the day before and did he know what she meant by it? He shook his head and noticed Tory's look of concern.

"Listen, darlin', you don't worry about it now. We'll find out later. Right now, you give that throat of yours a chance to heal. Just let me look at those big, beautiful eyes of yours before you feel the need to close them again."

The nurse smiled as she closed the door on her way out. Who would think that such an ornery looking old man would be so romantic? "Oh well, Mom always said that looks aren't everything."

Steve could tell Tory was distressed and tried to get her mind off that box by telling her all the hockey scores and how Becky wanted them to come to her place for Christmas next year. He told her about Liz's bringing him to Calgary and staking him for living expenses until he could get some of his money. She looked surprised at that last bit. "I think she's genuinely sorry for treating you and me the way she did. She told me she wants the chance to make it up to both of us and I believe she means it."

Tory smiled and nodded. She mouthed the words, "I love you" and kissed his hand. Then she motioned for him to come closer. When he leaned forward she puckered her lips inviting him to kiss her. He did, long and tenderly. She held his face in her one free hand and kissed his nose, his chin, his forehead and finally his mouth again. This was how Becky found them when she came in the door again.

"Oh, jeez! That's exactly why I'm going home!"

Her mother laughed, coughed, and mouthed "Don't make me laugh," then kissed Steve again.

Steve turned and winked at Becky, "I can't help it if I've got the kind of face women can't keep their lips away from."

"Give me a break! You're worse than a couple of teenagers."

Tory looked at Liz with concern. "You're going home?" She half mouthed, half whispered the question.

Liz told her that she knew her mother was out of danger now so she wanted to go home and spend the rest of the Christmas break with the kids. "I'll come back later when I can be more help to you, Mother."

Tory nodded her approval and reached for her daughter's hand.

"I'll stick around for another day or so, I want to see you talking and eating before I go. Besides, I have to keep Steve in line until you get some strength back. I told Steve I would come back for the wedding."

Tory smiled and looked at Steve.

"Yeah, I told her I caught you in a weak moment and you agreed to become Mrs. Turner."

"I'm so happy for both of you. I told Steve that Josh is gonna think it real cool to have him for a grandpa. Steve was already pretty high up there in Josh's estimation anyway, but when he found out Steve rides a Harley, well... He could hardly wait to get to school and tell everyone about Grandma's cool boyfriend. I'm sure he raised a few eyebrows in the staff room that day."

Becky stroked her mother and Steve on their cheeks. "I love you both and I want to see the two of you happy. I'm going back to our room now, Steve, and grab some shuteye. When I come back, Mom, I hope to see you drinking some juice—or tea, at least." She blew them both a kiss and went out the door.

"Am I lucky, or what?" Steve looked at Tory and the tears welled in his eyes once again. He kissed her hand and settled back in the chair.

Tory lay for a long time just looking at Steve. How had she ever thought him ugly, she wondered. His eyes were honest and his mouth kind. His moustache added to the cowboy look and even extended to a kind of rugged, sexy look. She knew now, that what she thought was such a menacing face when he found her in potentially dangerous predicaments, was just an anger and a fear that was genuine concern. She had done some foolish things, like driving at night in an old car that she was unfamiliar with. Then venturing out in a snowstorm without any regard for her own safety. No wonder he felt that women were such foolish, brainless creatures. Probably, the most foolish thing she had done was go upstairs in his house to fetch his personal treasures. That bit of foolishness had almost cost her her life and she still didn't have the box. She tried to remember what had happened. She knew she had it in her hand when she was knocked to the floor and she knew she still had hold of it when they lifted her from under the tree. She had been determined not to let go of that box for anything. But she didn't have it now. Where had it gone? Steve's only picture of himself as a child was in that box. Had the house burned? Was everything lost? She had lots of questions that needed answers and her throat hurt too much to ask. Her legs were hurting too. She felt like all the nerves were raw and when anything touched them she just wanted to scream with the pain. Right now her legs were hurting like the devil, but she didn't want to let on because they would give her something that made her sleep. She hadn't had her fill of Steve yet, she wanted to look at him a little while longer, then she would accept sleep.

❁ ❁ ❁

Steve noticed the sharpness in the focus of her eyes. He guessed she was in pain but wasn't saying anything. He took her hand again and tried to will some of it away. If only he could transfer it to himself. If only it were that easy, if only...

She tried to move her broken arm and flinched.

"Tory, are you uncomfortable, darlin'? Should I call the nurse to bring you something?"

She shook her head, but not convincingly. He stroked her forehead and promised to stay if she wanted to sleep. She smiled and pulled his hand down so she could kiss the inside of his palm. She continued to stare at him with her pain-filled eyes until he could stand it no longer. He reached for the buzzer and pressed it. "It's for your own good, Tory. I can't stand to see you suffering just because you want to stay awake. I'm going to be here for a long time and I need you healthy and rested. You go to sleep now and I'll do the same right down the hall. I'll put the buzzer in your hand and if you wake up before me, just press it and tell the nurse to come get me."

The nurse came in then with another needle that she slid into Tory's upper thigh. Steve waited until she was asleep once again then he wandered down the hall to the lounge. He found the paper with Liz's number on it and phoned her collect.

Becky left a couple of days later as planned, with promises to come back if and when needed. Tory was talking more easily and taking liquids and soft foods by mouth. With taxi waiting, Becky and Steve stood on the hospital steps hugging. Becky gave him a big kiss on both cheeks and told him they dare not sneak off and get married without her there to stand up for her mother. She started to go then turned back once more and wrapped her arms around him while she leaned against his chest.

"Steve, I know that I can leave her and you will take the best care of her. I'm grateful that you two found each other and I'll be so happy when you become a member of our family. I love you like a father already."

He hugged her tight and whispered that her love was important to him and that he felt she was as close to him as any natural daughter. He kissed her forehead and pulled her away from him. "You better get home and look after my grandkids."

Then he shoved her toward the taxi and wiped his eyes with his sleeve. She waved out the back window while the car traveled away. He turned to see Skip standing in the doorway watching him.

He raced up the stairs two at a time and grabbed the young man by both shoulders, then shook his hand hard as if he were pumping water. "Skip, I was wondering what became of you. The phone lines to the house were down of course, and I didn't know where else to find you. God, it's good to see you. I was hoping you were all right."

"Yeah, I'm OK. How's Mrs. Hardisty? I hear she got burned pretty bad."

"She's lucky the burns are only on her legs, but they're still bad. She suffered a concussion and a broken arm. I think she's got some other bruises and scratches but nothing else serious. She just came out of a coma a couple of days ago."

"Do you think I could see her?"

"Well, they were only letting family in, but let's see what they'll say. I'm sure she'd be happy to see you."

They took the elevator up and faced the buxom, stern-faced matron at the desk.

"He's almost family. He's like a son to her." Steve wished he had a face for flirting to soften her up with.

It was Skip whose charms won out in that department. A few words from him and he had the woman smiling and flirting right back. They finally convinced her to let Skip in for a one-time only visit.

In the antechamber, when Skip laid eyes on Tory, he whispered to Steve that he was almost sorry he had insisted on coming up as she was so small and frail. He wanted to remember her as strong and cheerful, cooking her big dinners and baking her cakes and pies, not as this wisp of an old woman lying sleeping.

"Darlin'?" Steve said. Tory opened her eyes and smiled at him. "I found a young fellow hanging around downstairs wanting to come up and see you."

Tory looked over his shoulder and her face lit up when she saw Skip, looking scared, hanging back by the door.

"Come on over here and give me a kiss, Skip Wronosky," she spoke in her raspy voice.

He approached, taking a wide sweep around the tent over her legs. She took his hand and pulled him closer until he was close enough to kiss her cheek. "You look great, Skip."

"Thanks, ma'am. You're looking pretty good yourself. I was worried when I heard they sent you here directly from the ranch. This is the first chance I had to come down. I had to get my sister Gail and Danny back to the airport today so I was hoping they'd let me see you while I was here."

"Where are you staying, Skip?" Steve asked.

"We've been staying at the inn in Weston up to last night, then we came into the city. I have to talk to you, Steve, about what you want to do out at the ranch."

"You two will have lots to talk about and I'm getting a little sleepy. Go have some beers and a steak with Skip and talk ranch business."

"We can go have something to eat and talk, but I'll be back right after."

"Steve, you don't even know what shape your place is in. I think you should get a ride to Weston with Skip and get your affairs settled. I'm in good hands here, and I could do with some rest anyway." She winked at Skip. "He hangs around morning, noon and night—a lady can't have any time to herself at all. Do me a favor and get him out of here."

"She's probably right, Steve. You have to talk about something with the insurance company. And there's some salvage you should take a look at, too. Why don't you and me go out there? You could come back in a day or two."

"Both of you could stay at my place, and you'd be doing me a favor. I've been worried about it being left unattended. Skip, you take one of the rooms and make yourself at home, stay as long as you like. I don't think I'll be getting out of here for a couple of weeks and I sure would appreciate having someone taking care of my house."

"I hate to impose, Mrs. H, but I sure would appreciate a free bed for a few nights."

"You stay until I get home, then we'll talk about it. Now. Both of you get out of here. My throat's sore from talking."

"Hey, I haven't said I'm going yet." Steve gave Tory a belligerent look.

"I'd love for somebody to bring me some of my own stuff." Tory looked pleadingly at the two men.

"We'll go have supper and talk about it."

"Great. In the meantime, I'll make up a list of what I'd like."

"Damn, stubborn woman," Steve mumbled as he started out the door.

When the nurse came in a little later, Tory asked if they had anything personal of hers that they may have put away when she was admitted. "I'll take a look in your file, Mrs. Hardisty, and let you know."

Steve and Skip were back about an hour later with the news that they would both be going back to Weston. Skip agreed to stay in Tory's house for two or three weeks and then he might head south until the end of February. Steve was going to assess the damage and get some financial matters tended to and then he would be back. Tory gave him a list of personal items she wanted and told him to have the lawyer draw up the papers for her to turn his ranch back over to him. He promised to be back in two or three days and gave her hand an extra squeeze and kiss before he went out the door.

While he was gone, Tory had the first surgery on her legs.

26

SHE HAD KNOWN IT WAS coming and that she would not find it pleasant, but she was not prepared for the extent of the excruciating pain. When Steve returned three days later, he was not happy to find out that she had tricked him into being away while she had this surgery. She was too sedated and too tired to argue much in her own defense.

"I knew you'd find it hard to sit and wait while I was in the operating room so I took advantage of an opportunity that presented itself." She tried to calm him. "I didn't plan it. It just worked out that way."

"Holy smoking… Cripes, woman, what kind of a man do you take me for? Here you are, going through all of this and me none the wiser. If I had really set my mind to it, I probably could have been back here yesterday."

"To do what? Storm the hallways? Holler at the nurses because things weren't happening fast enough? Get in a snit because I'm in pain and nobody's doing anything? Steve Turner, I rested easier last night knowing you weren't here stewing."

"Tory, if you ever pull anything like this again, I swear, woman, I'll... I'll..."

"You'll what, Steve? Never bring me back to this fun place?"

He dropped into the chair by her bed and took her hand. "I just feel so helpless watching you laying here in pain. You didn't have to go through that all alone. Even Becky would have stayed."

"That's precisely why I didn't tell either of you. Why would I want to put you through the agony of the waiting room and watching the clock go round? I was very well cared for and I didn't feel obliged to stay awake and wear a smile for company." Her hand was heavy in his and her eyelids were droopy.

"You don't have to stay awake, Tory. You sleep now and get some rest. I'll just sit here and throw you dirty looks while your eyes are closed and maybe, by the time you wake up, I'll be over my mad."

She smiled sleepily and squeezed his hand.

A few days later, she was sitting in an armchair when Steve came into the room. She was grinning from ear to ear and held out her hand to him. "It's surprising how much I feel like a human being again just being allowed to sit up and look at the world from an upright position."

He bent and kissed her soundly on the mouth just as the nurse came through the doorway. "Are you two lovebirds at it again?"

"I'm trying to talk her into running away with me," Steve replied.

"Oh, Steve, I wish I could. As fond as I am of these nurses, I'm starting to suffer from cabin fever. Hopefully, the doctor will let me out soon, even for a short while. I'd like to go home and spend a few nights in my own bed. I want to sit in front of the fireplace and watch a hockey game and make popcorn."

"It won't be long, darlin'. Have patience."

"Oh, by the way, Mrs. Hardisty, I have your personal belongings that you were asking about. She handed her a large manila envelope that was bulging at the seams. "The paramedics from the helicopter gave us the box that's inside. Apparently, they practically had to use a crowbar to pry it out of your hands."

"What the hell were you hanging on to so tightly? Couldn't be your false teeth, you don't have any," Steve teased.

Tory took the envelope and couldn't believe it had arrived safely with her. She thought surely it had been lost in the fire after she'd been knocked unconscious. She handed it to Steve. "This is yours."

He looked questioningly at her and took the envelope. "Didn't the nurse say these were your personal things?"

"Just open it and please don't be angry with me."

Steve ripped the big envelope open and peered at the contents. He sat open mouthed as he held the gaping pouch in his hands. "What the hell...? Tory Hardisty, is this what you were doing upstairs?"

"Don't be upset. I wouldn't normally go into your private drawers without your permission, but I was afraid if the fire came to the house you would lose your only connection with your childhood."

He lifted his eyes from the envelope to her. "You risked your life to get this for me."

"I wasn't risking my life at the time. When I went upstairs, I didn't know the fire was that close to the house. I only wanted to get them. In case."

Steve opened the box and took out the picture of himself as a child. As he studied it, tears welled. "I don't have a picture of my son but he looked exactly like this. Somehow, I like to think of this as a picture of him."

Tory shed the tears for Steve. She tried to imagine what it would be like if she had lost Becky as an infant—not to have watched her take those first teetering steps, her first day of school, her first lost tooth, her first phone call from a boy, her first date, her graduation, and finally her own first child—Tory's first grandchild. She took Steve's hand and brought it to her cheek. "I could not let you lose that picture, and whatever other treasures you have in that box."

"The treasure I value most is you, Tory. If you had died up in that bedroom, I would have gone clean out of my mind."

She took the picture of her aunt and Steve from his hand and stared at it. "How do you suppose she knew?"

"Knew what?"

"That you and I would be right for each other. She never, ever mentioned you by name. Just that she had this very kind neighbor who took good care of her. She told me once that if I had a man like him to take care of me, she would quit worrying about me being alone. I always thought she just said those things so I wouldn't worry about *her*."

"Then how come she never introduced us when you came to visit?"

"She only talked about it in the last few years. Somehow, I always thought of her as a very independent woman and able to fend for herself. The last couple of visits we had were in Peterborough. She used to think of them as her vacation even though she loved the mountains more than the hills of Ontario."

"What makes you think she knew we would find each other?"

"I just feel it. My aunt had a way of maneuvering things to go her way. If I didn't know better, I would say she was strong and stubborn and fought that stroke just long enough to bring me out here to spend sufficient time to get to know you. Her heart must have been bursting with happiness to see us together at her bedside when she died."

A few days later Tory was allowed out of quarantine. Steve was able to take her in a wheelchair up and down the hall. Before long, she was dressing in her own housecoat and slippers and walking on her own. The doctor finally felt she was ready for her second skin grafting. This time, Steve would not leave her side and slept in the chair by the bed during her first night following the surgery. She was in extreme pain and welcomed the hand to squeeze when she woke up in the middle of the night. She dreamed of old Alfred and pictured him sitting in his chair in his living room smiling at her and Steve. Then he seemed to be agitated about something and before he could tell them what it was, he faded away and Tory woke up short of breath and perspiring.

It seemed to take longer to recuperate after the second surgery. Her arm had healed well but her legs were an endless source of pain. There were no aftereffects from her concussion and she hoped that as soon as her legs healed, she would be allowed to go home. She longed for the sofa and fireplace in her farmhouse. She yearned to stretch out in her own bed with Steve at her side. She wanted desperately to stand in front of her big kitchen range and make a fresh pot of soup and open the oven to retrieve her freshly baked bread. She wanted her life to return to normal. Steve talked continually about their marriage, being very impatient to make her his wife. He never talked about the loss of the ranch. Tory wasn't sure whether he didn't want to open any psychological wounds for her or whether he was too broken up to even think of losing the only real home he'd ever known. All she knew was that she had been in the hospital far too long and wanted to go home.

Finally, it was late February, and the doctor came in and told her she could plan on going home within a couple of days. Steve phoned Skip and told him to make sure the house was ready. "The boss is coming home."

It was a warm, sunny day with the snow melting and puddles on the side of the road when they turned off the divided highway and headed up the road toward Weston. Tory thought she had never seen a day so grand. The sky was as blue as the sweater Steve was wearing and there was not a cloud in sight; it must have been well above freezing and the air had that fresh promise-of-spring fragrance. Liz's vehicle was parked near the back deck when they pulled into the yard. Steve quickly came around the car to help Tory out and when he opened her door, she could hear the water running down the drainpipes from the snow melting on the roof. Once on her feet, she took a few deep breaths of the fresh mountain air and started to cry.

27

TORY SMILED THROUGH HER TEARS and reached for Steve's hand. He put his arm around her shoulders and whispered that he understood. They remained side-by-side, Tory leaning on him, breathing in and appreciating the beauty of the foothills, the azure sky, the melting ice.

Creaking hinges startled them and they looked over to see Liz with the kitchen door open waiting for them to come up the steps and inside. The faint aroma of beef stew wafted out to them, and upon coming closer, Tory could smell fresh baked bread.

"Tory Hardisty, I always thought it was your own special talent to make bread better than everybody else, but your secret is out. It's this kitchen stove. Even me, the worst cook in the world, can make the most delicious rolls in this baby." With an oven mitt, she patted the stove and pretended to kiss it.

"Oh, Liz, everything smells so good. I've been drooling for home-baked bread. How did you possibly know?"

"A lucky guess." She smiled at Steve. "Now look, I know you must be tired and you've got Steve here to baby you, so I'm going to hit the road. I just wanted to make sure you had a nice warm lunch waiting for you when you got home. And I also wanted to welcome you home personally." With this she gave Tory a light hug.

"I won't shatter when squeezed, Liz. Thank you for being so thoughtful. I'll enjoy that stew and those rolls. Please come by again soon. You're right. I am tired. I guess I'm not as strong as I thought I was. The ride home actually did me in."

"I'll make sure she gets into her housecoat and lays down for a while. Thanks, Liz, I appreciate all you've done for Tory. And for me." Steve helped her with her jacket and held the door for her.

Skip had been hanging back but now came forward to give Tory a kiss on the cheek and a hug. "I've got my things over at the hotel so I'll be on my way, too. It's great to see you back home, Miss Tory."

"Why are you rushing off, Skip?"

"When Steve called to tell me you were coming home I went to get some fresh groceries. That's where I ran into Liz. Anyway, I had made some tentative arrangements a month or so ago and I've been accepted into a college in Wyoming. I found one that has a program on animal husbandry and if I get down there within the next couple of weeks, I can register for the spring semester. I thought that would just give me enough time to visit my sister for a week or so and then head to school. Thank you for getting me started in that direction, Miss Tory. I wouldn't have done it without your encouragement and help."

Tory felt the pride of a mother when her son goes off to college. "Oh, Skip, that is the best news yet. I just know you're going to be at the head of your class. Do you really have to go so soon? Couldn't you stay a night or two?"

He looked over at Steve. "I think it's time for you and Steve to have some time together. I'd love to be best man at the wedding but if I don't take this course now, I'm afraid I won't do it. Hope you understand."

"Of course, we do. Don't we, Steve." It was a statement rather than a question and Steve just nodded agreement.

Tory held Skip in her arms and wiped her teary eyes as she gave him a kiss and asked if he needed any money. He thanked her but declined and headed for the door, his eyes damp as well. Steve followed him out and stood by the young man's truck, talking for quite a while, then slapped the fender and waved as Skip turned the truck around and drove out of the yard. He stood on the driveway watching the road for quite some time. Tory couldn't help but think that Skip was the closest thing to a son Steve had.

"Skip really appreciates all the help you've given him, Tory. He never woulda given college half a thought if you hadn't encouraged him. Someday he hopes to own a place of his own and figures he'll need all the education he can get. It's not simple like it used to be, everything's scientific now. From feeding right through to slaughtering. Maybe my place burning down was a message from up above telling me it's time to get out of the business."

"What would you do, Steve? I can't imagine you sitting on the porch in a rocking chair."

"I don't know, darlin', but the thought of starting over is just too much for me right now. What I'm gonna do first is make sure you're back on your feet again. The next thing will be our wedding, just as soon as you can decide who's doing the job. Then we're going to relax for a month or so. Maybe I can get some of your rooms upstairs painted. After that, we're gonna take a nice long holiday, maybe go see the grandkids for a bit. What do you say?"

"I say yes, yes, yes! It seems like forever since I've seen them. They'll be so happy to see you again, too. They were ecstatic to find out you were here on Christmas morning. The only thing that bothered them was that they had sent your gifts to the prison. I had a hard time reassuring them that they would be forwarded here. Which, by the way, I forgot to ask Skip about."

"Skip said there's lots of mail and some parcels upstairs in your bedroom. When you've rested, you can go through all that. Right now, though, old girl, I'm getting you some of that stew Liz made and then I'm taking you upstairs to lie down for a couple of hours."

After Tory had eaten and rested, she tackled the stack of mail sitting on the corner of her dresser. Sure enough, there were a couple of packages for Steve that had been rerouted through the post office from the penitentiary to his house, and then to her house. There was something to be said for small town post offices and employees who knew everyone's business. She opened her mail and sorted it alphabetically—a matter of habit—then pulled the bills for payment. The junk mail went into the wastebasket and the rest she took downstairs to read.

Steve was clearing snow from the roofs of some of her outbuildings, so she put the kettle on for tea. After standing at the window watching him work for a short while, she picked up the phone and dialed her minister's number.

Before Steve came in for his tea break, she had all the arrangements made for three days later. All they had to do was go into town and apply for a marriage license. Then she had pulled an apple pie from the freezer and warmed it in the microwave. The fact that it was still there was some kind of a miracle after Skip had been staying there for so long.

Steve hadn't needed to be called twice. When he came in and hung his jacket up, he went to the sink to wash his hands. Tory slid her arms around his waist and kissed the back of his head.

"What's that for, Miss Tory?"

"Just because."

Steve turned around and saw that her eyes were damp. Looking concerned, he slid his arm around her waist as if to steady her. "What's the matter, girl, did you overdo it your first day at home?"

"No. I just cry sometimes when I'm so happy my heart could burst."

"Maybe you should keep little flash cards in your pocket and hold them up for me to know the difference—happy or sad, happy or sad. What's making you so happy, darlin'?"

"Oh, everything. I never thought I'd ever be looking out my kitchen window watching my own wonderful man working around the yard. It seems like this past year and a half has been such a rollercoaster ride. It was difficult for a while to believe I could ever be happy again." She moved closer to him and lifted her arms around his neck. Feeling a warmth course through her body, she leaned into him and startled him with a very passionate kiss.

"Easy, girl. You're gonna have me blushing in a minute."

"Steve, you make me feel like a young woman again." She whispered, "Let's lock the back door and head upstairs for a bit."

"Tory, what would Miss Lottie be saying if she knew her niece was inviting cowboys up to her room?"

"She'd probably say, 'You go girl.'"

"Are you sure you're up to this?"

"Steve, if we're gonna be married on Thursday, I better make sure all your parts are working before it's too late. It's been awhile you know."

"My parts are working just... what do you mean getting married on Thursday?"

"I phoned the minister while you were outside and he will marry us as soon as we have the license. Which means Thursday."

"Ahh, Tory." Now it was Steve's turn for damp eyes. He drew her in closer and wrapped his arms around her. "I've been so afraid you would change your mind. I know I'm not the easiest guy in the world to live with and I'm not exactly a pillar of the community either. Most women would be embarrassed to be seen with me. I know I'm just about the luckiest old fart around and I'm going to spend the rest of our days letting you know how much I appreciate you."

"Well, Steve, right now you have a decision to make."

"What decision?"

"Tea and apple pie—or me?"

He put his hands out in front of him as if weighing the choices. "Let me see. Warm apple pie or sex. Oh, boy. What a decision. Can I think about it for a minute?"

Tory cuffed him on his arm and turned to the piece of pie she had already cut, shoving the plate into his hands she said, "Here. Just cause you're so pathetic, I'll let you have both. I'll be upstairs waiting for you when you're through, Steve Turner."

Grinning, he warned her not to start without him and slipped a large bite of pie into his mouth.

28

THEY DROVE UP TO THE front of the town clerk's office just before closing to fill out the registration form for their marriage license.

Three days later, Steve and Tory parked their vehicle in the gravel parking lot of the same church in which Miss Lottie's funeral had been held. Today, there was no crowd spilling outside the doors and down the steps. Theirs was the only vehicle in the parking lot. They went inside to wait for Liz to arrive and take her place beside Tory. It was quiet in the church. The wedding couple sat in the first pew and held hands, shyly smiling at each other like young lovers.

In the quiet moments that followed, Tory reminisced about how she and Steve had started on such rocky footing. She smiled to herself now when she thought about how terrified she had been of him in the beginning. Tory knew most people in town were still frightened of him and thought she was right out of her mind for allowing him into her home. If only they knew him the way she did. If only they had known each other in their younger days. If only Aunt Lottie hadn't taken so long to make them become acquainted. If only she could stop wishing she could change the past and just start to enjoy the future! They weren't that old. They still had many good years ahead of them. They were financially comfortable and could probably travel anywhere they chose. Whatever they did, or wherever they went, she would devote her life to making up for all the love he hadn't had over the years. She would love him so much he would forget he'd been without it most of his life. She would smother him—

The door of the church was pushed open with such force it swung around and banged against the wall. Startled right out of her reverie—and her seat, Tory jumped up to see who was in such a hurry to get inside.

"Hi, Grandma. Hope we're not too late to see you and Steve get married."

There was Josh, big as life, with Maggie just a few steps behind. Next came Becky and Ian, with Liz trying to hide behind them.

It was Steve who spoke first. "Hey, little fella, glad you could make it to see your grandma and me tie the knot."

"I thought you and Grandma were getting married. What kind of knot are you tying? Is it to keep the cows in the yard? Why are you doing it inside a church? Where's the rope?"

Everyone laughed and Josh couldn't figure out why they were all looking at him and Steve wasn't answering.

"Tying the knot is another way of saying we're getting hitched, Josh. Your grandma and me are getting hitched for life, for better or for worse. Although, I'm not so sure I'm doing the right thing marrying a crazy woman."

Tory turned on Steve and glared at him eye to eye. "What do you mean a crazy woman, Steve Turner?"

"Well, Tory, there is no other explanation for it. I've got no money, no home, I'm uglier than sin, and you've told me often enough how mean-mouthed I am. So who but a crazy woman would want to spend the rest of her life with me?"

"Craziness must run in the family then, because if I wasn't already married, I would consider myself lucky to tie the knot with you." Becky closed the few steps separating them and hugged Steve in a tight embrace. It was only when the minister cleared his throat that she let him go and kissed her mother on her wet cheek.

"We seem to be attracting quite a crowd." The minister looked at everyone standing teary-eyed at the front of the church.

"Yes, Becky. What are you doing here and how did you know we were doing this today? Liz, did you let the cat of the bag?"

"Did you get a cat, Grandma?" Again everyone laughed at Josh's expense.

"No, honey. That means Liz told a secret."

"I did not. My lips were sealed."

"Then, who? Ohhh, Steve. I should have known you couldn't keep this to yourself. Now you made these kids disrupt their lives and hightail it halfway across the country."

"And thank goodness he did. Mother, how could you even think of getting married without us?"

"Darlin', all I did was phone Ian and ask, if he didn't have plans for today, whether he'd mind being best man at my wedding. Now what's wrong with that?" Steve was sliding his arm around Tory's waist as he continued. "Besides, is it too much to ask to have my family be at my wedding? You wouldn't deny me that one little thing now would you?"

By this time his mouth was just inches from Tory's ear and turning she saw the eyes, brimful of tears, just inches from her own. "No, Steve. I won't deny you that, or anything else that will make you happy. It was selfish of me to want you all to myself."

Again the minister coughed. "If we don't soon get started with this wedding, you'll both be too old to cut the cake. And I say that with only the utmost respect." He winked at them and moved into position, a book open in his hands. "Besides, at the rate the tears are flowing around here, we'll pretty soon have a flood from which even Noah couldn't save us."

After the ceremony, the wedding party went to the Steer and Beer Cafe which was the only place that had a full menu, a liquor license, a dance floor, and served children. They were surprised to learn that Liz had made reservations when she found out Tory's family was coming, and had arranged for a tablecloth and a floral centerpiece. As everyone was enjoying the wedding cake, which Liz had ordered as well, the three-piece band that usually played only on the weekends, started setting up.

"Liz, you've been busy since Monday, haven't you?"

"Tory, Steve, I have so much making up to do to both of you that the least I can do is give you something that resembles a wedding reception. I was delighted to learn that your family was coming and that I could do something nice for all of you. I can't tell you how happy I am that you found each other in spite of me and all the people in this town. I want your wedding to be perfect just like the life I wish for both of you." She had to stop because her voice was breaking and her eyes were filling.

"You listen, girl," said Steve. "You've done more for us than most friends do in a lifetime. I don't want to hear any more talk about the past. Tonight's a celebration of the future and I'm taking my bride out on the dance floor now so we can enjoy some of that great music you paid for."

Steve, in his gray suit that he'd purchased after the fire, and Tory in a beautiful rose-colored two-piece crepe dress, walked out to the center of the dance floor. He left her there while he went and talked to the guitar player. He came back and slid his arm around her waist as he winked at her. The pianist started, then the drummer and guitarist picked up the melody. After a few bars, the guitarist nodded and smiled at the two dancers, then in true Sinatra style, started belting out the words to "The Best is Yet to Come." Steve smoothly guided Tory around the small space in the middle of the room. She didn't see the other people in the restaurant watching. Her eyes were closed and her cheek tucked closely into the side of Steve's neck.

It wasn't long before he realized his shirt collar was damp. He released Tory slightly to see the tears rolling down her cheeks. "Dammit, woman. I told you to get some flash cards. What is it this time? Happy or sad?"

"A little of both. I'm deliriously happy that you are all mine for the rest of my life, but sad that it took me so damn long to find you, Steve Turner."

"Well, Mrs. Turner, we've got each other now and nothing but time to enjoy each other." With that he swung her out and twirled her under his arm as the music slowed to a close.

They danced with each of the grandchildren and then Steve danced with Becky, and Tory with her son-in-law. Steve taught Liz how to polka—the right way, he insisted. After Josh's third yawn, Becky decided it was time to call it a night. It had been an exhausting day starting with a long plane ride. As she scouted under the table for Josh's shoes, she called to Ian to gather Maggie's things together. Ian didn't hear her because he was out near the dance floor waving to Steve who was doing a two-step with Tory.

Ian gave Tory an affectionate kiss and wished her happiness. Tory hurried off to say goodnight to her grandchildren. Ian then slapped Steve on the back, engulfed him in a hug and took the older man's hand in a death-grip of a handshake. He looked Steve directly in the eye and asked in an unsteady voice, "Since you and Tory are married now, would it be all right for me to call you Dad?

This knocked the breath out of Steve. When Tory and Becky finished wiping off the children's faces and looked around for Ian, they both stared with open mouths. The two men were standing beside the dance floor, with arms wrapped around each other. As Liz walked the children toward the door, the men turned and joined their wives, still holding arms around each other's shoulders, like old buddies.

While Steve danced again with Liz, Tory chatted with people at another table. Word had spread rather quickly about the wedding celebrations at the cafe and it didn't take long for the restaurant to fill. When it came time for the newlyweds to leave, they were pleasantly surprised when the whole room full of people shouted good wishes and saw them out the door. Several men shook Steve's hand and offered help to get his ranch up and running again. By the time they were able to close the car doors and enjoy a moment of quiet, Steve was well aware that the people of Weston were quite ready and willing to make amends. He was overcome and again felt in his heart that it was the goodness of Tory that had encouraged everyone to accept him. She was the one who had turned his life around this time and he still could not believe that she had actually become his wife.

    He had pretty well given up the hope of ever having a wife and family, let alone one like Tory and her family, now his family. When Ian had asked permission to call him Dad, it was all he could do to keep from crying right out there in the middle of the dance floor. Having lost his own son, he never thought he would ever hear anyone call him Dad. Ian had confided that he had never known his own father. His mother had been deserted weeks before Ian was born so he had grown up without a father figure. His mother had lost her trust in men and had never remarried. She never dated and had no brothers, so Ian had to rely on teachers and basketball coaches to give him any insight into the male viewpoint. His mother had encouraged him to become involved in athletics as she realized the importance of male influences, but he had no one he could really confide in. When he met Steve that first Christmas at Miss Lottie's house, he had felt a kinship that he couldn't quite explain. When the relationship between Tory and Steve grew, he was happy. He believed he had finally met a man he could respect and love enough to consider a surrogate father. Steve, in turn, had liked Ian instantly. In fact, it was Tory's young family that had stirred feelings in him that had been dormant for too many years.

    When he and Ian were taking the kids out in the bush on the snowmobiles and on the snowshoes, cutting firewood together and discussing ranching and hunting, it had created a need for a bond with the young man and his children. Steve had gone home and imagined what it might have been like had his own son been alive. He liked to think he might have had a family and grandchildren similar to Tory's. He had been so afraid of that gut-wrenching hurt again, of losing another family, that it had frightened the daylights out of him. He had thought it better to remain distant and keep pain at arm's length, than to go through the heartbreak once more.

Now, he couldn't take his eyes away from this beautiful woman sitting beside him, this woman who had just taken his name and who had promised to love and honor him, in sickness and in health, for better or for worse. He just could not grasp that it had actually happened. Steve not only had the most incredible woman in the world, but he had a family, too. He had a son who was proud to call him Dad. With these thoughts going through his mind, he couldn't help himself. He burst into tears as he pulled Tory to him and held her so close she must have thought her ribs were being crushed. Sobbing unashamedly, he whispered over and over, "Thank you, thank you, oh God, thank you."

Tory was not sure if it was she or God being thanked, but she did realize that Steve was overcome with emotion. Managing to squeeze her arms up and around his back, she moved her mouth to his and kissed him. It wasn't long before her tears were mixed with his.

"Look at us, Steve Turner. You'd think we just came from a funeral instead of our wedding."

"I don't think I've ever felt this much emotion at anybody's funeral. I can't believe God has given me all this. I keep thinking I'm going to wake up and find out it's all been a dream. You, the kids, my freedom. It seems like whenever anything good happened to me, it didn't take long for it to get turned around and there I'd be, back in hell again. I'm not going to let that happen. Tory, I'm not going to let anything bad happen ever again."

"We both have a lot to be thankful for. I still think my aunt must be sitting up there on her cloud laughing, enjoying the way her interfering turned out. She had this all planned, Steve, and nobody is going to tell me any different. She was one smart old lady, and if she thought we were meant for each other then, by God, we were. Now, I don't know about you, but I figure it's about time we started our honeymoon. What do you say?"

Without a word, Steve put the car in gear and headed out the highway. Tory didn't question where they were going. She had been told to have her bags packed and loaded in the trunk of the car. When they headed south on the highway, Tory knew they were going to Calgary. Just as she'd guessed, Steve pulled up in front of the hotel in which they had stayed the night of their first hockey game. He had even managed to reserve the same room in which she had slept. The only addition was a chilled bottle of wine and a large bouquet of roses on the bureau.

When Tory opened her suitcase, she found a small gift-wrapped parcel lying on top of her nightie. She looked at Steve who motioned for her to open it. Inside she found a silver brooch. It was a motorcycle. Several amethyst stones were inlaid to look like a woman dressed in purple astride the bike.

"Deep purple. I heard your voice, Steve. You were talking about how magnificent I looked. I wanted to wrap my arms around your waist and just ride forever."

"We'll ride, Tory. We'll have the best damn ride that two married people ever had."

"I didn't get a gift for you, Steve."

"Yes, you did. You gave me a wife, children and grandchildren all wrapped up in one package. No man could ask for more."

"So you're happy then? Contented?"

"Couldn't be more so."

A troubled look crept across Tory's face.

"What's the matter?

"I'm wondering if this might be the best time to tell you that I backed into the corner of the fence when I was putting the car away before we left for the church..."

"What?" Steve stomped into the bathroom, muttering, "Of all the damn fool women..."

"Remember how magnificent I look in my leathers and my silver hair."

He peeked around the doorway. "It's a damned good thing I'm the only one who drives the Harley. With the damage you do on four wheels, I shudder to think about you on two." He closed the bathroom door, but it didn't drown out the muttering.

"Are you coming to bed soon, Steve?"

The muttering stopped, but the door remained closed. "You figure you can make me forget about you banging up the car by offering me sex?"

"I'm wearing a deep purple negligee."

"I'll be right there, darlin'."

Acknowledgements

My talented grandson Brandon who orchestrated the cover art; Anish Parmar who was instrumental in producing the cover; CAA–NCR Centrepointe Writing Circle members who critiqued my first chapter and sent me in the right direction; my editor, Sherrill Wark of Crowe Creations, whose keen eye and velvet scissors shaped my story into the book I always knew it could be; my friends who read the early drafts and cheered me on; and Louise Rachlis, in Ottawa, who offered me support and opportunity.

Phyllis Bohonis was born in Saskatchewan, lived most of her life in Thunder Bay, Ontario, then moved to Ottawa where she lives in semi-retirement with her husband Ray. Her education and career path were in accounting but her passion has always been to work with words, not numbers.

Phyllis has traveled extensively in Canada so some of her favorite places are the inspiration for settings in her novels. She's had several memoirs and short stories published. *Fire in the Foothills* is her first novel.

Coming soon!
The Wilderness
by Phyllis Bohonis

Made in the USA
Charleston, SC
15 August 2013